BEST FRIENDS

REBECCA DE WINTER

Storm
PUBLISHING

Ebook ISBN: 978-1-80508-063-3
Paperback ISBN: 978-1-80508-065-7

Cover design: Henry Steadman
Cover images: Henry Steadman

Published by Storm Publishing.
For further information, visit:
www.stormpublishing.co

For Ceri, Gethin, and Iestyn. Without whom, this book would not exist.
Diolch cariads.

PROLOGUE

THEN

When she fell, she landed on the roof of the art block. One arm hanging over the side, face pressed to the skylight. I can only imagine the screams of the class in there at the time. Terrified and crying for their mothers. No one does mass hysteria better than a bunch of teenage girls.

They set up a shrine to her – teddies, candles, flowers, chocolates. Every lunch break, girls gathered in huddles, sobbing. Perhaps if they'd cared more about her before she died, it wouldn't have come to this. They also would have spotted the vulnerability, instead of just us seeing it.

We didn't plan for it to happen. But sometimes opportunities reveal themselves. *In the end* – as Alice whispered in my ear – *I had no other option*. There could only be one.

Rumours spread fast about how she died, what killed her. Did she jump or was she pushed? Was it the height of the fall? The internal bleeding? The broken neck?

But a photograph and a broken heart killed her.

Alice and I killed her.

But that day changed my life too.

And one day, I'll change it back.

PART 1

TWENTY YEARS LATER

ONE

NOW

The air is rich with expensive perfume and, distantly, bleach. Hordes of women in business casual – tight black skirts, loose silky blouses, leather loafers and burnished brogues – throng the counters and cubicles. A queue snakes out the door.

Around me, inane chatter, voices high pitched with excitement. Someone passes a tampon under a door. Another offers lip balm to her friend. There is the crisp spray and scent of deodorant.

"Love your shoes!"

"Um... thanks."

I don't know her, but it doesn't matter – this is what we do, we women, we talk to each other in bathrooms.

It always baffles men – why would you talk somewhere that, really, isn't that nice? What men don't realise is that it's the perfect place for us, precisely *because* there are no men in there.

Here we can drop the facades. We can outright judge each other, eyeball to eyeball through the mirror. We can offer support, share secrets, mop up the tears, plan the take-down, adjust our crowns. It's a microcosm of female relationships, away from the spotlight. If men bond in sports bars and strip clubs, we bond in bathrooms, secret and segregated.

I've always struggled with it though, to open my mouth – and my heart – to a stranger. I think it's from school really. When you had to be invited to accompany the clique and the queen bee to the bathroom, it wasn't a free for all. Always on the outside, looking in. And now, it's no different, despite all the years.

The woman next to me wants to talk, but I can't make the words come out. Her face falls briefly, so she turns to her right and lights up as the woman there responds, then smiles and touches her arm. They dry their hands together and walk out of the bathroom in unison.

I want to know their secret. How do they know what to say? How do they move *en masse* from the classroom, the corridor, the lecture theatre, the bar, the meeting room – and share their most intimate details with, in some cases, a complete stranger?

I sigh. I'm hardly in the most friendly frame of mind. I hate work conferences – does anyone really like them? All the hard sell, the networking, talking to strangers, trying not to make it too obvious that you're working out if they'll make you money, constantly looking over their shoulder. But they're a necessary evil in my industry. I sometimes think entire businesses would collapse without this backslapping and palm greasing.

Mind you, I only have myself to blame because I did actually ask to come to this one. Rupert nearly passed out when I mentioned it, but he's the one always talking about bonuses and KPIs and how calibration season is nearly upon us. It's all such crap though because, despite the fact I am consistently bringing in clients, it's never reflected in my bonus. Freddie also reports into Rupert, and I am constantly bailing him out of trouble, but mysteriously, he is the one splashing out on new cars or a fancy watch, or being rewarded with a trip to Bali for bringing in the highest client by revenue ever. Except by my calculations, I did that three years ago.

Rupert wasn't thrilled about me attending, doesn't understand the need for these female-focused events – *what's next, pink laptops?* He's the type of guy who thought *Mad Men* was a documentary and doesn't understand why we don't all still work like that. I baffle him though because I'm not sexy – not to him, anyway – but am good at my job. I'm reliable and consistent, and when Freddie, or one of his other lackeys – lets him down, I'm there to pick up the pieces so we don't lose face with clients.

Women control eighty-five per cent of spending decisions, I told him. *There is money here. We don't want to lose out, do we?*

He gave me a thin-lipped smile. I could tell he thought I was making something out of nothing, so I tried a different tactic.

Look, it'll please HR and we'll look good, working with female-owned businesses, etc, narrow the gender pay gap. Not that Rupert would know much about that last one.

Fine, he said, *if this is what we need to do to sell to the wokerati, the snowflake crowd.*

So, I'm here in some upscale chain hotel outside the city, in a conference room that looks like it hasn't been updated since the nineties, with hideously patterned carpets and orange wood seating. The food is terrible too – all gluten-free and vegan friendly, but also taste-free. I'd kill for a muffin or a cookie – or better, a full-fat macchiato. I try to focus on the positive – it'll make it easier to stick to the fertility diet I've been on for what feels like forever: no processed sugars, fats, caffeine, alcohol, red meat. Ollie calls it "no fun".

I'm saved from my thoughts by the announcement that the speaker sessions are due to commence in five minutes. I'm walking through crowds of women who mostly look like me – white, blonde, well-spoken. We are all polished and glossy, but I wonder if they too are fretting about if they left their straight-

eners on or booked a grocery delivery slot for Friday or paid the
cleaner... or, or, or, the list is endless.

Do they also wonder what happened to the person they
were? The person who didn't constantly worry about conse-
quences or the future, only lived for the now. Not that I ever
managed that very successfully – until I met Ollie, of course.

As we move as one, someone catches my eye. Despite my
general jumpiness, it takes a lot to properly unnerve me, yet
here I am, suddenly pushing past people to catch a glimpse of
pale hair, the curve of her hip. The way she holds herself is so
familiar. The way she looks around, as if it's exactly *you* she's
looking for.

But no, I calm myself, this has happened before – and after
all, don't they say that everyone has a doppelgänger?

Before I can get any closer, I lose her as she disappears
behind a closing door.

It's not Alice. It can't be.

Because what would she be doing here?

I hurry into my afternoon breakout session and sit in the
closest available seat – near the front, which is no bad thing. If
you can make eye contact with the speakers, they remember you
later at the networking after one too many glasses of chardonnay. The organisers are already dimming the lights, welcoming
the compere on stage as I flick through the conference brochure,
to check who the speakers are for these sessions. *It can't be her,
it can't be.* Well, logically it could be. I don't know where she
works, I don't know what she does now, I don't even know if
she's dead or alive. My imagination starts to spiral and I try to
rein myself back in.

I reassure myself that I can't find her name in the glossy
pages on my lap. It was a trick of the light, someone with similar
bone structure. Around me people are applauding and the
speaker on stage has stood up to welcome her guest.

My phone is beeping so I miss the guest walking on. When

I do look up the first thing I notice are her heels. Nude, patent court shoes, polished, uber-corporate. Then legs – no hose, just waxed, lightly tanned, gleaming. A Diane von Furstenburg wrap dress, falling just past her knees.

I'm uber conscious of my greasy roots, my grown-out highlights – I've been trying to avoid bleach on this endless conception rollercoaster. The IVF hormones make me bloated, I've gained weight – my jeans are a bit tight and this floaty blouse makes it look worse.

Then I see her face.

It is Alice.

Why is she here? How? I don't get it. My brain is too overwhelmed to process anything.

She doesn't look any different. Apart from the changes you'd expect after nearly twenty years.

The last time I saw her we were sixteen – all feathered Rachel from *Friends* haircuts and skinny eyebrows. But she's still a natural blonde, in a way that always felt unattainable to me, perfect, princess-like.

She's got a massive rock on her left hand, matching wedding band, eternity ring on her right. Leather tote too at her feet.

Her skin is immaculate. Not a wrinkle or dry patch.

Saliva fills my mouth, I have to push past people sitting down as I dash out, feverish sweat prickling across my back and chest.

I only just get to the bathrooms – luckily no queue this time.

When I lift my head from the porcelain bowl, too nauseous to worry about being face first with who-knows-what, bile burns my mouth and lips. *How has she done it?* Leopards don't change their spots... do they?

When I go back out the session is over, and the networking has started. I gulp down a glass of tepid chardonnay, all thoughts of my diet gone from my mind, and look around. The women from the bathroom earlier have commandeered a table in the corner and I see them making notes on who to approach first. I can't face talking to anyone, not now.

Any confidence I had is gone. I'm right back where I was, all those years ago, to that last morning, being driven away, no time for proper goodbyes, just waving at Alice out of the back of our family car, watching her get smaller and smaller until she faded into the distance.

I try to focus, turn my mind to Rupert and his dubious attitude to this conference, the urge to prove him wrong is strong. I force myself to speak to a few people, hand out some cards, but my heart isn't in it. It's trapped somewhere else, long ago, wondering if the person who helped break it is suddenly back in my life.

TWO

It's a monthly thing – "brunch with the girls", as Ollie calls it. Though we're hardly girls, just the wives-and-girlfriends of Ollie's friends. I've known the core group – Nina, Veronica, Dakota – almost as long as we've lived in Boston, but others have come and gone without a word of goodbye. They've always been welcoming to me but, for some reason, I've never really clicked with any of them on a deeper level.

Maybe my expectations are too high – I yearn for a different kind of friendship. The kind built on illicit drinks when you're teenagers, holding each other's hair back when you're sick, or rescuing you from the attentions of some loser in a club by kissing you and telling him you're lesbians. The people who don't care what your hair looks like or where you're meeting or what you're wearing or what diet you're following. Perhaps adult friendships are inherently different, and maybe it's me? I truly want to like them. I want to connect with them.

It doesn't help that it's only been days since the conference and I'm exhausted, but I show up on time, determined to engage, summoning up some energy from somewhere.

We sit outside, keeping warm under the parasol with the outdoor heating, enjoying the early spring sunshine, surrounded by the civilised clink of silverware on fine china, the low buzz of polite chatter, the occasional pop of a cork released from a bottle. Everyone is tanned from late-winter trips to Vail and Aspen – except me, of course. I'm praised for my English rose skin, but then in the same breath they tell me I look pale and tired – do I want the number of a dermatologist? They know a great one, they always do. I'm sure they don't realise how they sound. I think they mean well.

We order a variety of off-menu or customised items, so much so I'm amazed the wait staff even retain the original menu. I'm the only one going for Eggs Royale, though I've specified wholemeal muffins, only the egg whites and vegan béarnaise sauce. Still, I noted Nina's eyebrow raise when the waitress confirmed I wanted smoked salmon.

"Really, Evie? I thought... well, never mind, babe, it's your body."

"Leave her alone, let a girl have what a girl wants," Dakota interjects.

It's hard not to feel judged by Nina for my food choices. The subtext that if I really wanted a baby as much as I say I do, I wouldn't be having the smoked salmon, I'd make sacrifices.

"Just looking out for you, hon. I want those newborn cuddles!"

Sometimes I'm too quick to jump to the negative, Ollie tells me. Americans are different. He forgets that my mother was a Texan. But maybe she'd assimilated too much, became more British than American. I try to remind myself that these women are kind, they sent care packages after my last miscarriage, after the last round of IVF failed, baskets of organic muffins and daily fresh juice deliveries.

"Well, you won't be waiting long – Ronnie, you look ready to pop!" Dakota trills.

I thought it was never good to comment on a pregnant woman's size, just in case, but Veronica rubs her bump, smiles beatifically. I feel bad for not saying anything now. She does have a glow and her bump is round and beautiful. It hurts to look directly at her sometimes. I want to be pregnant so much.

"How are you doing?" I ask.

I really do want to know, I do care. I hate all the pretence around pregnancy, that growing a person isn't tiring, gruelling work. But despite these women's claims to be their authentic selves, I know they feel the pressure too. I just want Ronnie to know she can be honest with me about how she's feeling. I won't judge her if she's not loving it. Even though part of me would hate her for it.

"I'm glowing and my hair is AMAZING and honestly, I cannot do enough yoga. I have this great masseuse—" but under the table I see her hiding the swollen ankles, the ginger tea drinking, her nose wrinkle at the smell of my smoked salmon.

Dakota chimes in with how she was the same when she was pregnant. And how she couldn't get enough of her husband.

"Oh my God, ladies, I'm not kidding, I was so sensitive everywhere – I mean *everywhere*. Ed just had to touch me and I'd be dragging him off to the bedroom."

I really don't want to know any of this. When will it be my turn to laugh about rampant hormones and heartburn? I know they can't help it, they're so excited for Ronnie, but I wonder if i can keep seeing them if this is how it's going to be.

"Ed's a lucky guy for sure."

"I mean, it worked for me and I'm sure that's why he put a little extra into my push present."

We all duly admire the diamond and platinum band adoring her right hand. I'm not sure about push presents. Don't get me wrong, I love jewellery as much as the next person but really, a reward for giving birth? It all just seems a little... archaic.

I don't voice this though, I'm the odd one out with these thoughts, as far as I know. Everyone else is quite happy to join in the mutual admiration society – and if there's an algorithm for the perfect life, these ladies are living it. With their Insta stories and podcasts, they've turned your average basic momma lifestyle into an art form. You can't really blame them for it, what else are they supposed to do? I only wish I could be more like them... God knows, everything would be easier.

"How are you doing, Evie? What's new with you?"

The three of them turn to look at me, expectant.

"Well, we're going to give IVF one final shot."

Their eyes go wide and Nina reaches to clasp my hand in hers, wooden bangles sliding down her slim brown arms. I want to pull back at the intensity of her emotion, her touch.

"You should have said before."

"Yeah, we would have supported you."

"I've not gone for implantation yet. I'm not sure when it'll be."

It unnerves me a little, the way they like to be involved in every life decision we make. It feels so voyeuristic. I worry about them messaging each other after this lunch, pitying me. They all, obviously, have two kids apiece and Ronnie is pregnant with her third. Nina naturally had twins without any help. They all breastfed, co-slept, baby-wore and religiously followed various Attachment Parenting influencers. I'm the failure of the group, not outstanding at anything – work, life, parenting.

"Well, let us know, hon. We'll look after you, make sure you've got everything you need."

"I just can't stop thinking about the previous round though."

"You can't let yourself go there. Positive mindset, babe, positive thinking. You need to do affirmations – are you doing affirmations? I can give you some."

"Oh, and are you doing acupuncture? My friend has this guy she swears got her knocked-up with a single needle!"

They want to help so much. They go around the table recommending various supplements and diets, health food stores and influencers to follow. They absolutely believe that because I'm not, you know, polishing my chakras with rose quartz, I'm not pregnant yet. Although to be honest, I'd do anything right now.

The table has gone quiet and they're all looking at me. *Shit, did I say any of that out loud?*

"Evie, I'm sorry. That was really insensitive of me."

Ronnie is looking at me like a puppy expecting to be kicked. Then I realise they've been talking about her baby shower.

"It's okay. Honestly. Don't worry about it."

And they immediately carry on with the planning and I knot my linen napkin in my lap. I'm tired of going for brunch and dinner, watching them place their hands over their wine glasses, claim ear infection, throat infection, detox. And then the smug smile, the announcement and later on the hand on the bump, the invite to feel the kicks. The opened doors, the offered seats. For something that so easy to do. For everyone but me.

I've done baby showers, push presents, christenings, naming ceremonies, first birthdays, second birthdays, third birthdays. They just keep coming. Balloons and cupcakes, donuts and discos, piñatas and playgrounds. I have all the invites in a box in my wardrobe. Keep count of the cost of my outfit, travel, gift, everything I'm owed, everything I want when it's my turn.

I remind myself to be kind though, even if I don't always feel it. Whatever happens with the IVF, I'm going to need friends, support, care. And they've provided that before. I'm lucky to have them really, I am. It's me, not them. Always awkward, always the odd one out. I mean, it would be way worse if I didn't have anyone. I've been there before. It wasn't good.

· · ·

As we leave the restaurant, Ronnie hangs back.

"Seriously, are you okay?" She walks beside me, puts an arm around my waist, pulling me into her side. She's the only one who knows the gory details. We see the same specialist, and I really needed someone to confide in, who understood what I was going through.

"Sure, all good. Promise. How about you?"

She looks at me, like she knows I'm lying. If anyone could get the truth out of me, it'd be her. But I can't deal with her bland platitudes right now, her perfect conviction that it'll be my turn soon. I might scream – or cry – or worse.

"Well, if you need me, I'm here, if you want to talk about anything." She looks at me intently, as if trying to read my mind, to understand what's bothering me, even though she knows.

"Thanks, I appreciate that." And I lean over to hug her, breathing in the scent of Coco Mademoiselle, hoping she'll take this as a sign that I don't want to talk anymore.

"Is it... do you have any more... frozen?" Her voice trails away at my expression.

"Yes."

She puts her hand on my arm, baby blues wide as she looks up at me.

"You can do it, I know you can."

As if I have anything to do with it. As if I can instruct my body to keep that tiny piece of person, made in a lab, by men in white coats, keep it safe inside me, without machines and wires and test tubes and petri dishes. I think that's one of the hardest parts. The lack of control – that so much seems up to chance and even with all the science, we still don't know why it sometimes doesn't work.

"It's not worked before, why would it work now?"

"You can't think like that."

Suddenly, I'm tired of pretending to be okay. "I don't know

how to think otherwise." I pull away from her, fold my arms. Try to regulate my breathing, it's not her I'm mad at.

Her eyes flit about, looking to see if Nina's watching, but she's gone ahead, clambering into her hybrid, ready to trek off to barre or SoulCycle or whatever the latest class is. I catch myself, I'm so bitter about everything. How have I let things get this bad? I really need to sort myself out.

To my surprise, Ronnie takes my hand.

"Look, I know how you feel. Really, I do."

"You do?"

"Yes."

My hopes lift. For a moment I think, maybe someone, after all this time, understands me at last.

"When Noah didn't get into the nursery we wanted him to go to, I was so devastated. But you can't blame yourself. It's one of those things. And sometimes it works out all for the best. The new nursery he's in offers so much more – Mandarin, Yoga, Ballet and a vegan kitchen!"

She kisses me goodbye, hops into her minivan and peels out of the car park in a spray of white gravel and a waved hand, eyes hidden behind massive sunglasses, leaving me adrift behind her. I'm genuinely winded, breathless by her casual cruelty. I know she doesn't mean it, but her words sting even so. My struggles are nothing like hers.

I am in no fit state to go home now. Ollie is out anyway, playing golf I think he said. I decide to take a walk down the street, to the little parade of upmarket boutiques in this area of town, to try to get my head straight.

As soon as I see the baby store, I know I'll go in. It's probably one of my biggest vices since we started trying for a baby. Ollie doesn't know about this bad habit. But in my wardrobe, at the top, there is a shelf filled with shoe boxes, only they don't contain shoes, but baby clothes and accessories. I can't help it. I need the comfort that buying a tiny onesie, little socks, or a knitted cap brings me. I don't do it often. But I'm weak right now, vulnerable. And I pay for things on a credit card that comes out of my account. What Ollie doesn't know won't hurt him.

Inside the store, the light is clear and mellow, delicate piano music plays, although I recognise the cover of a popular grunge song from the nineties. I walk around the store, stroking the soft blankets, picking up the stuffed toys and plushies, looking at the sterling silver rattles and teethers.

"Is it your first?"

I freeze, but the shop assistant misinterprets the look on my face.

"Oh, honey – me and my big mouth, are you not telling people yet? Well don't worry, your secret is safe with me. Early days, is it? I remember those all too well, the nausea and oh my goodness, the exhaustion."

Her hair bobs with the enthusiasm of her words, her excitement for me and my assumed baby.

I can only nod and allow her to guide me around the store again, showing me where they keep things for moms also, soft nursing tops and bras, comfortable pyjamas and lounge sets *for those days when we just need to be wrapped in softness*, blankets and bath oils and foot massage lotions. I would follow this woman anywhere, I want to stay here with her forever, being fed herbal tea and trying out the latest biscuits they've been sent that are supposed to help with milk production. She nestles me on a chair, puts my feet on the matching footstool.

The rocking function is great, try it.

Between the whale song playlist she's now put on and the warmth of the store, I know if I don't leave now, I'll fall asleep.

"I'm sorry, I can't do this. I'm so sorry."

I burst out of the chair, discard the blanket on the floor in my haste to leave, push the mug of tea into her waiting hands, and hurry back to the car. In the lowering light I see that despite everything, she still waves and mouths to me to look after myself.

THREE

Our house always seems suspended in time – too quiet, too still. Ollie doesn't agree with me, but I think it feels empty without children to fill it with shrieks and chaos and mess. Today the silence is louder than ever, so the first thing I do when I get home is pour myself a glass of wine and put some music on, something to suit my mood. I want to forget everything about today and listen to Lana del Rey wail about bad boyfriends and broken hearts in a blurry haze. When we moved in, we initially had plans to decorate it, pictured ourselves christening every room with rollers in paint tubs behind us, rolling around giggling in drop cloths. But it took us three months to paint one room, and we soon realised that DIY was not our forte, so Ollie hired an interior designer who came highly recommended. The end result is a house that is not a home.

Oh, it has the right colour grey on the walls, the right white gloss units in the kitchen, the rainfall shower and glass bricks in the bathroom. It's got graffiti art in thick black frames on the walls and silver framed wedding photos in the living room. There's shaggy sheepskin rugs and the carpets are thick and plush. But if I switched out the photos of us, took away the odd ornament or framed band poster, the house could belong to any couple in their late thirties – childless, childfree – with half eaten containers of takeout in the fridge, unopened bottle of grey goose in the freezer.

Sometimes it makes me feel like our whole life together is equally as transient and fragile, a house of cards, ready to come tumbling down with a slight breath of wind. I really need this IVF to work. I need that white picket fence life that the others have, the happiness and fulfilment. It keeps eluding me, a balloon floating out of my grasp.

I'm so absorbed in my thoughts, my misery, that I don't notice Ollie bursting in.

He looks quizzically at me and the glass of wine. "You're back late, darling." He walks past where I am, curled up on the loveseat by the window, blanket over my legs, and snaps the Bluetooth speakers off.

"Babe... Hey! What did you do that for?" I pause the playlist from my phone, shuffle my feet into my slippers as he reaches down to kiss my cheek, but not before I see his frown of concern.

Out of the window behind him, the lights in the houses opposite flicker on, the sky is a dusky blue, the sun not long burnt out, a cigarette butt disappearing over the horizon. I keep mouthing Lana's lyrics along to myself. Dusk is falling already. I've lost time sitting here.

"What's going on, Evie? What are you doing?"

"I'm drinking wine, what does it look like?"

"Well, I can see that. I thought you – we – were giving up, no?"

"Oh, that. Can't I have a glass of wine after a day of dragging my failed uterus out for lunch and shopping?" Irritation courses through me. I walk through our open-plan living area to the black granite topped island that borders the kitchen space, put my wine glass down loudly. Ollie winces at the clinking noise, the glasses are crystal, part of a wedding present set we received from his family.

"But normally it's you telling me not to drink? Because of..." And he gestures in the direction of my stomach.

"Oh okay, I'm sorry if it's such a struggle for you, restricting yourself."

He rolls his eyes. "Right. I'm not talking to you when you're like this. You're your own worst enemy."

And he takes a chilled bottle of aloe water from the double wide freezer, meant to hold enough food for a family of six, stalks into the den, closes the door. I sigh. I'm not even pregnant yet and it's forcing us apart.

The house falls silent again. He may as well not even be home. I think about going upstairs for a rest, but the hallway is already so dim and dark, I can't face it. I think about dinner instead, but I know neither of us have done the shopping. I know I should go and apologise to Ollie, but I don't want to. There is something comforting about stewing in my own frustration, I don't want to see his side or admit I'm wrong.

The den is his territory, like the bathroom is mine. It's so cliché – all black leather recliners and massive flatscreen TV, surround sound, a wet bar, mini fridge, fully soundproofed. I don't go in there if I can help it. Too many memories of another, similar place – the scent of whisky and cigars. The noise of an analogue radio, crackly and battered, the sound filtering through the ether. I wonder if Alice remembers those sounds and smells also.

I want a bath, but I'm too far gone tonight already. I've fallen asleep in the bath too many times, water up to my chin, hair floating. Instead, I walk back over to the sofa, I switch the music over to one of those random Spotify radio channels, turn the side table lamps on and pull my iPad to me. As the light finally dims and darkens outside, I click on the familiar blue and white app.

Social media is the work of the devil – and we're all at the mercy of the temptation to find anyone you've ever met and mine their page for insignificant and deeply personal information. Given how that tech conference finished seventy-two hours ago, it's amazing I've resisted searching for Alice until now. Especially as her firm has since contacted me to discuss some work for them. Despite my melodramatic reaction to seeing her, I managed to stick it out and network enough with her colleagues to exchange details. I didn't spot her in the crowd.

I'm not sure what's driving me this time. It's not anger or hatred, or curiosity, even. I think it's simpler than that – despite everything, I miss her.

Seeing her at the conference reminded me of what I'd lost. There's been times before when I've felt alone, but now, I feel lonely. After what she did, I know she has no right to anything from me, any emotional energy or wasted time yearning for her. But right now, between Ollie and work, and everything else, seeing her has reminded me of the person I thought I'd long forgotten I was, a person that perhaps I was too quick to leave behind.

When everything happened the way it did, I was forced to leave everything and take a route I hadn't planned on. And everything has snowballed since then, bringing me to where I am now. But what if things had been different?

It's not that I haven't thought about her over the years – I have, a lot. But I tried to persuade myself that living well is the best revenge. That I didn't need to validate my life by comparing myself to her, I convinced myself I was – *am* – better than that. And whenever I tried searching for her, I could never find her. Now I know where she works though, so I try again, this time including the name of the company she works for in the search bar.

Bingo – I find her immediately. She's hidden in plain sight –

using her first name and middle name only. It's a tiny thumbnail photo, but I'd know her anywhere. I click through and she goes from tiny to full size. A face, screen-sized, that I never thought I'd see up close again. Alice McDonald, my Alice. My best friend, my worst enemy. The closest thing I ever had to a sister and then the furthest from it. I touch the screen with a fingertip. Right now, I miss the idea of her so deeply that it makes the very marrow of my bones ache. I ignore a text from Ollie, asking if I'm going to order any food for dinner. He can sort himself out. This is more important.

When I click through to her full profile, I realise that – unlike most people – she's not set it to private. I can't scroll through her photos fast enough, watching her face change in a time lapse on my screen from wife to mother to working woman and back again. And that same sunny smiley face beaming out, those grey eyes just as I remember, her blonde hair in a neat ponytail or bun or side-swept, clipped up, falling loose over toned and tanned shoulders, waves rippling down a bare back. I twist and lie back on the sofa, rest the iPad on my knees so I can linger over each picture, drink her in.

I go further and further back, to pictures from almost a decade ago, watch her children shrink from preteen to school age to preschooler to toddler to infant. I browse down, click through holidays, wedding albums, mini-breaks, work trips, ski trips, surfing, climbing, everything. I soak up the pictures of her life, her house that is a home, full of noise and fun and happiness.

Ollie messages again *I'm getting pizza, want some*, so I must be forgiven. And I do, want some that is. I need some comfort food, dirty and disgusting, even though I'll regret it after.

Yes, ham and mushroom on mine pls, I tap out, and he sends the thumbs up emoji back. I wonder if all couples communicate best virtually. I know once it arrives he'll come back out and we'll curl up on the sofa and even probably take a picture of our feet entwined and share it on Instagram, caption it Sunday Nights Done Right and add a #blessed.

I flick back to Alice's Facebook page. There are no pictures from before 2008. Nothing from her childhood or her teens. Not even a photo of a photo, freshly removed from a frame or peeled from an album, not like the only one I have of us, curling cornered and sun faded.

I pause on the wedding photos. She had a vintage theme. All antique teacup centrepieces and blousy roses in shades of peach and pink and violet. Her dress is long and slinky, a lovely cream silk, cut low to show the small of her back, with fine skeins of lace trimming the edges. She is every inch the blushing bride, especially with a full-length veil over her mid-length bob.

But it isn't Alice that catches my eye, despite her beauty and youth – she must have gotten married very young. It's her husband. Just in profile. But I recognise him straight away. I'd know the tilt of his head, the hunch of his shoulders, even now, all these years later. It can't be him. Can it? I click on the photo. It is him.

I have to put the iPad down. Go out to the kitchen, pour myself another glass of Chenin Blanc, take a quick swig, then another. The glass is shaking in my hands. The ache inside me doubles, trebles.

I go back to the sofa, message Ollie, *when's the pizza coming?* I close the wedding pictures, Alice's husband is a puzzle to unpick another day.

I keep scrolling, Ollie tells me 10 mins until pizza time, so I've not got long. Alice is tagged in girls' nights out, mums' nights out, baby group days out, birthdays, work achievements, fun runs. All with hundreds of likes, comments, that blue thumbs up emoji on everything, winky faces, kissy faces, face palms, cry laughing.

She has 1,528 friends. She has one husband, three children. She is female, married, she belongs to 53 groups. A whole life documented, but what's the reality here, who is the real Alice? Which life is hers? Which life is mine? There are so many variants. In hindsight, Alice always was good at being everything to everyone. And we all thought we were getting the real Alice. These days I'm not sure if any of them were really her.

I pull the throw over me, snuggle down under the thick lambswool and flick back to the start, to her profile picture. Do I really want to pick this scab, this scar? It's never healed properly and I'm not sure I'm ready for this. I linger over her carefully neutral face. She used to be able to cry on demand. She even taught me. But she never smiled when she was truly happy. No, happiness for Alice was usually expressed in other ways. In absorption and concentration. Still as a pool of water, her real thoughts – unreadable. I wonder if any of her friends now, any of those fifteen hundred people, her husband, her children even, see that part of her. Especially her husband, given their – *our* – history.

I don't believe people truly change. Not really. Inside of her somewhere is that tightly coiled snake, that inner kernel of Alice, that made me do what she wanted and take the blame for her.

It's not fair. If someone like Alice can have everything, can have that perfect life, why can't I? So in the end, I click to send her a friend request. And just like that, I'm course-correcting after almost twenty years.

By the time I go to bed, bloated and queasy from too much pizza, my brain is spinning, memories floating up, stirred up sediment in my mind after my Facebook antics. When I go through my night-time face-care ritual in our immaculate bathroom – cleansing balm, serum, moisturiser, in the mirror my eye is continually drawn to the fine white line that tracks across the top of my left forearm. I hold it up in front of the mirror, imagine my arm without it, undoing history. But it's not possible.

Maybe it should have been a warning, that first time we met, when I broke my arm falling out of the apple tree that bordered our garden but sat squarely in hers. But like any sensible six-year-old, I was fascinated by the little girl next door, who had a swimming pool in her back garden, blonde plaits long enough to sit on, and a daddy that carried her about like a princess on a throne. Maybe it should have been a warning against her daddy too – that not all men are princes, no matter how much they seem it.

It's not like I had any reason not to be curious. Mama prided herself on her hands-off approach to parenting – or at least that's what she told me later. I never thought to question the fact that Mama let me run around unsupervised at such a young age, until I was a lot older. It didn't occur to me that she could play with me, or take me to the park or on playdates. My mama didn't do that sort of thing.

I toss and turn next to Ollie, but I can't sleep so I slip out of bed as quietly as I can and wander into the kitchen, the ceramic tiles cool against my feet, pull out a mug, a peppermint tea bag and go over to the sofa, flick on *Peaky Blinders*, but even Tommy Shelby's tortured heartbreak isn't enough to distract me – the memories of the past flooding into my brain. I lie down on the sofa, pull the blanket over, close my eyes and give in to them.

The summer I turned ten was endless. There was a heatwave too and by late August, the grass was a dirty yellow, the earth riven with cracks. I remember constant runs to the corner store for ice or drinks, and the chime of the ice-cream van.

I remember Mama being so fed up with me that she'd count down to our weekly Sunday lunches next door – after my fall from the apple tree solidified her friendship with Alice's parents. Saturday nights were for prepping, for brushing out our hair in the mirror one hundred times, for massaging Guerlain body cream into our arms and legs, the richly cloying smell hanging over me for days.

She used to say to me, *it's never too soon to start looking after yourself* and keeping young and beautiful were her watchwords, I should heed her advice so that I could *have the pick of the guys* when I was older. And not make the mistakes that she made. She never told me what those mistakes were, but she'd prod and pull at the tiny fold of skin on her belly, measure her waist, lift her breasts in her hands and shake her head – and then look at me. She'd weigh us both at the same time each week, fully naked. Note down the figures in a little notebook.

She told me it was for our own good, it was important to stay healthy, and how did I think she'd walked the catwalk when she was younger, been on the cover of *Vogue* that one time? Sometimes she'd take me over to her dressing table, hold my face in one hand, examine the line of my jaw, my cheekbones, puff her fluffy brush of powder over my skin, making me sneeze.

That summer she was still really into aerobics. Every other night she'd put her Jane Fonda video into the VCR and start doing grapevines up and down the sitting room, marching on the spot, using little pink hand weights. *Join in, sweetie, it's fun! Look at us, spending quality time together.* She'd make poached chicken and cabbage soup and whatever faddish health foods were in. And if I dared to ask for cake or a cookie, she'd look at me, her eyes narrowed, and say *do you really think you should.*

I wonder what she'd think of me now – stuffing myself with pizza before bed. She used to have a quote ripped out of a magazine and pinned to the fridge – *you can never be too rich or too thin.* I bet she'd still narrow her eyes when she looked at me, surreptitiously pinch my waist when she put her arm around me. She'd love Ollie though. He'd charm the pants off her. I've yet to find a woman that doesn't fall for his posh-boy charisma.

The day I'm remembering though was when everything started. Because of what Alice and I did. And I think Mama never really forgave me for that, she blamed me for taking away her time off, when she could be safely herself and not worry about me.

I remember the day as snapshots of colour in my mind's eye – blinding white sunshine, neon blue sky, Alice's red sunglasses and the peeling pink skin on the back of her shoulders, the copper scatters of freckles running rampant across my cheeks.

It was after lunch. We were given ice lollies and had wandered down to the back of the garden, by the pool. The pile of empty bottles the adults had left under the table was huge, no one was watching us. Everyone was stuffed to the gills – Uncle John's barbeque was about the size of a spaceship, Alice nagging *Daddy, Daddy*, to use the tongs, fascinated by the glowing coals, the occasional splutter of sparks. We could do what we wanted.

Uncle John made some joke about sausages that he thought we wouldn't understand but we ignored him and Mama said *I love a good banger* and Auntie Meredith *shhhhh-ed* at Uncle John. I could see them all looking at each other and my skin prickled up into goosebumps that spelt out a word and that word was, *opportunity*.

Alice tore off her sundress, flung her jelly sandals away from her. *Hurry up slow coach*.

I distinctly remember her bathing suit because for the first time, she had a two piece, a red spotted Minnie Mouse bikini. After that day, she took to stuffing the top with tissue paper until that one time when she jumped in the pool and left a trail of disintegrating paper in the water.

Never mind, that's what the pool boy is for, but I knew she minded really.

The pool boy was tan all year round, with big brown eyes

and a fine gold chain around his neck. When she didn't think I
could see, Alice watched him. And when he didn't think I could
see, he watched my mother.

Mama had long blonde hair that she twirled around her
fingers whenever Uncle John or the pool boy or any man was
around. Even then, I saw how men looked at her – their eyes
flicking from her red mouth to her red nails, to her pointy
breasts and back again. She had the tiniest waist that she
emphasised with belts, pulling her in and out in a perfect hour-
glass curve. And of course she had blue eyes, blue like the
pacific ocean, she told me.

Alice had gotten in the pool, she was lying on a hot pink lilo
and she'd painted her nails red, trailing them through the water.
Alice was always very... well, she liked to look nice, even when
we were small.

I was in a floral playsuit. I remember because it was getting
small – tight around my chest. Under it I also had a two-piece
suit, but mine had proper cups on the top half. Alice didn't like
that.

Alice always paid a lot of attention to how I looked. We
used to score ourselves. We'd compare every inch of skin, every
mole and freckle, our hair, our eye colour, giving ourselves
marks out of ten, adding up what we thought we were worth.
But that summer, we'd started to lose our similarities. For the
first time, I had something Alice didn't and something she
couldn't buy. I was changing and developing, and there was
nothing she could do about it. I felt different. And people
noticed. Uncle John had begun to treat me just like Alice, called
me his princess, hugged me tight and tickled me.

I would tell him *I'm not a baby anymore, I'm going to
secondary school next year* and then he'd say I was getting to be
such a big girl and that I'd better not forget my uncle John. He'd
kiss my cheek and his moustache tickled and scratched.

When he did this, Aunty Meredith smiled and said *he*

always wanted another daughter and my mother pretended to tell him off, calling him a ladies' man – he'd just wink at her and she'd giggle and pat his leg.

In the pool, Alice and I liked to play a game to see which of us could hold our breath the longest. I have no idea how we got away with this – sometimes it felt like our parents gave up that summer. Predictably, that afternoon like all the others, the adults beat a swift retreat from the heat, leaving us alone, with only the distant sound of Stevie Nicks' banshee wails for company. Thinking about it now, I can still smell roses and cut grass.

I got in the water, fought against it so that I could push my way to the bottom. Over my head the world became a shivery blur of blue light until I was just about sitting on the tiled floor of the pool.

I didn't last down in the pool for long. Once she saw where I was, Alice dragged me out, complaining that I couldn't play without her. The music still played on, louder now. My mother loved Stevie Nicks. She dressed like her, did smudgy cat flicks with her eyeliner, when she sang in her bedroom, she even sounded like her. Some nights she shut herself away with the tape player and wine, told me to sort my own supper. The morning after those nights the house smelt smokey and sweet – Mama told me once it was the scent of regret.

Alice told me she wanted to play *the game* together but not yet, and she waved a bottle at me that she'd stolen from the patio. I climbed out of the pool and lay in the sun to dry off, the heat melting and warming my limbs. Alice passed me the bottle, the wine inside warm and sweet and sharp. We drank the dregs of every bottle we could find after that, laying giggly in the grass. Still, no one came out and the sun began to dip down behind the trees.

Are you ready? Alice held out her hand to me, nails shiny red and bitten down.

Always.

It felt like flying, running back down to the pool, I wanted to lift off like jet planes, leave everyone behind. She climbed in carefully but I jumped, splashing water everywhere.

We bobbed about together, holding hands, and then dipped under the water, bubbles our breadcrumbs home.

On the floor of the pool, Alice let go of one hand to hold on to the pool filter, anchoring us. I closed my eyes, opened them again, she stared at me. This time was harder than last time. I was good at holding my breath – I could go over a minute, but so could Alice. The last few times we played I had only just beat her.

The bubbles had stopped by now and it seemed like there were rose petals floating down around us in the water, dark red like the marks Mama sometimes left on me, holding me too tight. Calmness washed over me, the way I felt when Uncle John put on music for me and Alice, relaxing on a blanket in the shed, listening to "Purple Rain".

I closed my eyes and drifted into a velvet blackness that came down around me.

When I woke up, I was back in my own bed, cold and dark and damp. Somewhere downstairs came Mama's laugh, but when I tried my bedroom door, it was locked.

Afterwards I found out that an ambulance was called, the neighbours had seen us, questions were asked.

We weren't allowed to play in the pool unsupervised again after that.

FOUR

When the IVF clinic calls the next day, to follow up on our decision about next steps, I take it as a sign.

Ollie is at work. He's asked me not to call him there but I do anyway, to update him.

"They've recommended doing the embryo transfer the week after next, if we're ready." No one is ever ready to put themselves through the injections and hormones. But it's worth it, it will be, it has to be.

"Sure, just let Audrina know when and she'll block out my diary, darling."

Why is it not important enough for him to do it himself?

"Please can you do it? I need to know you'll be there this time."

I've always been praised for my perseverance – "laser-focused" a previous line manager said of me.

There's silence.

"Are you doing it?"

"Yes, darling..." There's a clattering noise and muffled voices, a clink of glass, the fizz of a can opening. "Okay, right I'm scheduling it right now."

"Promise you'll be there – there won't be any random client issues or urgent last-minute meetings?"

He covers the phone with his hand briefly, more muffled voices, laughter.

"I promise." His voice comes back on the line.

"Pinky promise."

"What?" He's laughing now though.

"Do it." But I'm smiling.

"I'm holding my pinky up to the phone."

I switch to video.

"Me too."

And then there his face is. And his little finger. Love and something else, something darker, all bound up so tight. My future in his hands and my body.

"Hate you, baby."

"Hate you more."

That same old crooked smile that I tripped over all those years ago. Maybe we're not broken, not yet.

When he comes home that night, I've made dinner – his favourite, beef wellington. Well, I say made, but in fact I bought it ready-made, kept it warm in the oven. With my cooking skills, it's for the best, really. The table is laid with our wedding-list linen and silver, his favourite Malbec open – breathing, apparently. I have lit candles around the room. It's as close and intimate as we get.

"Wow, sweetheart, this looks amazing, you're amazing!" He pulls me close, kisses me, runs his hands over my hips, down my bottom.

I bat his hands away. "Go and wash up, it's time to eat!"

But after supper, I lay down the ground rules.

"Until the appointment there will be no sex, no booze, no

drugs, no cigarettes. No processed meat, no processed sugars, no takeaway, no MSG."

He rolls his eyes. "No fun more like."

"I mean it."

"You're crazy, you know."

"It's why you love me."

"Who says I love you?"

But he comes up close. Puts his arms around me. Presses those lips to mine, leans me up against the kitchen counter. Reminding me of our first time. I want to – it's a good sign, right, that I still fancy my husband after all these years?

"Babe..." I pull away, squeeze out from between him and the counter.

He pouts and does puppy eyes.

"Nope, down boy!"

"I'm not even the one who gets pregnant. Why do I have to miss out?"

"Because I have to, cheeky!" I swipe at him with the dishcloth.

"Oh, it's like that is it?"

And then we end up chasing each other through the house and for the first time in a while we are laughing together, so hard I can't breathe. Maybe, I think, this is a good place to bring a baby into.

I wasn't sure he'd agree to this. After the last time, when it didn't work – and the time before, when he came home to a puddle of blood and wife and tears – he said never again, it hurts too much, he couldn't face it, couldn't put us both through it.

Slipping out of the kitchen, I talk to myself in the bathroom mirror, persuade myself this is it, it's going to work. We can do this. I know I need to be the one leading us through the woods, bringing us safely into the light on the other side. And besides, if

Alice has that life, then surely if there's any justice in the world, I should too?

Later, we are coiled in our bed, watching *Drag Race*.

"What makes you so sure, this time?" he whispers.

"I don't know. I just am."

He kisses my forehead and I snuggle closer into the nest of his arms, letting his body heat warm me down to my toes.

We look picture perfect, if only we can make it a reality...

It wasn't easy persuading him to try again, but his friends are so competitive – toxic masculinity and the pressure to prove their fertility seems to have its upsides. There's too much of the alpha male in them all. Ollie has said it himself, he sometimes feels like the only way he can prove he's a man is to get me pregnant, even if it's via a test tube and a lab.

The next day I call work and tell them that I need some time off before the procedure. The short notice doesn't go down well but, as I mutter to myself "if you call me a baby-making machine for long enough, there's a chance I'm going to become one."

Rupert complains about the previous time off I've taken – only a handful of days, one time when I was miscarrying. I point out that I worked through it all, unbeknownst to him I even took client calls with a speculum inside me. And I even dare to wonder why my body wouldn't hold on to our babies for long enough. When I couldn't even love them enough to switch off from work for a few hours?

I finally pull out the big guns with Rupert and reference talking to HR.

He's silent. While he thinks about his next move, I check my shopping list for foods with antioxidant properties on Google Keep: blueberries, broccoli, kale, spinach, pomegranate, jack fruit.

"Fine," he says. "But don't turn your phone off."

"Hey, I'm taking leave, not going crazy."

And he laughs before disconnecting us.

By the following Monday morning, the day of our embryo transfer, I'm both anxious and bored out of my skull. I'm not cut out for days of lying on the sofa. My idea of relaxation is miles away from meditation or yoga or practising mindfulness. Self-care is so much more work and so much more boring than Instagram makes it look.

I'm tired of affirmations but I've persisted with the ones the girls gave me. The rational part of me doesn't believe any of this for a minute, but as Nina texts me about not creating negative vibes, about trusting my body, I wonder if sheer belief is the most important part, more than anything else. So the part of me that reads my horoscope and won't walk under ladders and avoids black cats, insists on doing this every morning too. After all, what's the worst that could happen?

Though I've been using the guest bathroom to do them, Ollie overheard me the first time and nearly gave himself a heart attack laughing. Also, no one tells you when exactly to say them. Before you shower, with bedhead and sleep creases and morning breath? Or after, when the mirror is steamed up and you look like a drowned rat?

Nina tells me I should try three to five affirmations a day and say each one ten times – unless I have a lucky number. "And some people say up to fifteen each day."

"Do these people not have jobs?" I asked her.

She looked at me like I was crazy. But, these people wanting to manifest their dream lives must have another source of income, because there is no way anyone with full-time paid employment has the time to repeat 150 lines before breakfast.

One. My body was made to nurture a baby.

When I started these, only a week ago, I muttered them, a curse, a spell, ashamed.

Two. My mind is open to new life.

But everyone's always telling me to loosen up, to be less inhibited.

Three. My womb is ready to bear fruit.

So now I say them clearly, enunciating every word – I've even taken to lighting a candle, these last couple of days. Just to get away from the faintly *Handmaid's Tale* vibes to the whole thing – before I become fully OfOli.

This morning the bathroom is scented with jasmine and chamomile, steam and smoke mixing, leaving me feeling faintly mystical. I don't believe in manifesting a life, I believe in hard work. But I do believe that sometimes, you also get lucky. And right now, we could use a bit of luck.

Ollie is meeting me at the clinic today. I'm not happy about it, I wanted him here, holding my hand, for us to have breakfast and travel there together. Not break the spell that bound us all weekend. I had booked us massages at home on Saturday and on Sunday we went for a nice lunch and a gentle hike in the countryside. Held hands and looked at each other like the gooey-eyed newlyweds we used to be.

I wanted us to be relaxed and together right up until I was in stirrups but apparently Ollie couldn't get out of his morning meeting – a crucial new project. Aren't they always, I wanted to say? Is our baby not a crucial new project? Maybe I should have created a PowerPoint, outlined the problem statement, objectives, KPIs.

The Uber that picks me up to take me to the clinic is warm and smells of synthetic coconut and hot plastic. But I take the fact that Stevie Nicks is playing in the car as a sign that things will turn out okay, that I will be a mother. There wasn't a day from my childhood that my mother didn't play her music.

. . .

In the end, Ollie arrives when I am already legs akimbo, in stirrups and has to stay in the waiting room during the entire process. It's a silent journey home as I rest my hands on my lower body, as if to feel for a bump that didn't yet exist.

"Why were you late?"

"I told you, I had a meeting."

"I called your office, they said it was cancelled."

"Well, they were wrong."

"If you say so."

"Do you think I'm lying?"

"Did I say that?"

We continue to bicker a little in the car on the way home. I'm so disappointed with him. As soon as he unlocks our front door, I brush past him without saying a word and waddle upstairs; cocooning myself in the duvet on our bed as if I am a Faberge egg or Lalique crystal vase. I feel as old as Ming dynasty porcelain though, fragile, prone to shattering everywhere, bruised and crampy. They told me to take some painkillers. If men went through this, I have no doubt they'd be fully sedated and hooked up to the good stuff.

I'm so tired, the last thing I need is an argument.

"Look, darling, I said I was sorry. I know how important this is to you."

"To us, you mean."

"Yes, to us." He picks up his phone, opening it and tapping away even as he talks to me.

"So why didn't you leave the meeting?"

"It was tricky. I wanted to be with you, I swear."

"It was already in your diary – how did another meeting get put in?"

"I don't know, okay, I'm sorry."

"It's fine. I get it, leaving early to watch your wife have your potential babies inserted into her failure of a body isn't a priority for you."

"Hey – you're not a failure. Don't be like this, please. I'll make it up to you, I promise."

And he tries, bless him, over the next two weeks as I take it as easy as possible, ostensibly resting in bed, but mostly working on client packs and dodging calls from the office.

He brings home plants and flowers and fruit and candles and jewellery. When he's not on his phone or at the office, he curates playlists and watchlists and takes messages and updates our friends. I even caught him scrubbing the grout in the bathroom once. On his hands and knees.

"The cleaner didn't get it clean enough. I want to get these spots out."

"Okay then, Lady Macbeth, but can I have a pee first?"

I know I should worry about him – about us – the constant attachment to his phone, the whispered calls when he thinks I can't hear. But I'm distracted, my head too full of the other possibilities happening inside of me. Cells dividing and multiplying, tiny brain stems growing, miniscule spinal cords, no bigger than a comma. It's as if I am implanting this embryo, growing this baby by sheer willpower. It feels as though, if I don't think about it at all times, it'll feel unloved, won't stick around. And also, this thing with Ollie – some intern or assistant getting attached – it happens every so often. It never lasts.

FIVE

I let myself get distracted by other women, in cities far away from me, on pregnancy forums online. The posts are a mix of acronyms, overthinking and in some cases, tragedy. If you're trying to stay calm, they are the worst possible thing.

I become addicted to the minutiae of these other women's lives, confessed at the darkest hours of the night or on the sunniest of days. It makes me feel less alone but also, shamefully, better than them. People aren't afraid to share intimate details online.

What is the best position to conceive in?

I'm cramping and nauseous – is this it?

His semen was watery – does that mean more or less wrigglers?

Which ovulation sticks are best?

If he hit me, can it cause a miscarriage?

Of course the real tragedies never get as many responses, much like real life there's a social hierarchy. But I'm protected, lurking quietly, undetected, hoovering up the posts and comments.

The morning that we're due to go for blood tests – at the

end of the two-week wait to see if my HCG levels are at "growing a baby or three" levels as the obstetrician called it – I read that two people I've been following have got BFPs on the forum. Big Fat Positives on a home test.

The IVF clinic warned me against testing at home, and if I did, not to do it too early. That blood tests are more accurate than home tests, that it's still early days. But I knew from the beginning that I was never going to manage that; they're lucky I even lasted the two weeks.

The forums are full of people testing sooner and achieving ghostly lines that require complex iPhone photo manipulation skills to see. After what I've read, I want to share my hopefully happy news with strangers on the internet as soon as I can. And a terrible part of me wants to make sure that other women will be jealous of me this time.

I wait until Ollie has gone for his morning run, I need to do this alone. I'm convinced it's going to be positive – I'm nauseous and tearful, my jeans already tight and if anyone touches my boobs I'm homicidal; but even as I try to remember that there's no guarantees, I am imagining first cuddles, first birthdays, first words, first steps – a life full of possibilities.

I have a secret stash of pregnancy tests that I bought ages ago, pre-IVF. I know they probably won't work. I'll get a false negative or a void. But testing is addictive, the dopamine rush as lines appear on the stick.

I sit on the toilet and pee. I'm well hydrated. Drinking at least two litres a day, a good diet, sleeping eight hours a night. And morning urine is the best to test with, the highest concentration of HCG hormones apparently. I saturate the correct end of the stick. Leave it on the side. Set a timer for two minutes on my phone.

I sit on the floor, back against the door. It's a beautiful day. I'm so calm, it's like I'm in the eye of a storm. Everything is still, I am serene. I know the test will be positive.

When I turn my head, the control line – which always appears first – is visible from clear across the room. And before even 30 seconds are up, a shadow line emerges in parallel. It is the shape of hope – and my hope is strong again, no matter what's happened before. Rapidly the line is no longer a shadow. It's strong and clear alongside its control sibling. No void and no negative.

I cup my belly, the slight bloating a sign. "Hello, little ones," I whisper.

I'm pregnant. Again.

The blood tests at the clinic don't tell us anything I didn't already know, but it's nice to be "officially" pregnant and I'm surprised all over again, delighted and tearful. I take the home test to show them and all the staff are overjoyed too, feigned or real, I don't care. Ollie is more reserved. After all, as he reminds me, *we've been here before, darling.* I understand, but I wish he could share my joy.

I know, this time it's going to happen for us. It has to. Third time lucky. There are so many times when we didn't get this far. Months and months of trying. The drugs, the chemical pregnancies. And then the first round of IVF, that ended so badly. But Nina for all her bullshit is right, *Don't look back, babe, you can't change the past, only the future.*

I think only of now, this moment – and all the possible future moments we will have now.

Back in the car Ollie tries to hold my hand but I just cup my belly, look at him with glistening eyes. I know it's the hormones, but I can't stop tearing up.

"Two babies," he says.

We laugh together at the shock, the surprise. It's always a possibility with IVF.

Two embryos were inserted and from the levels of HCG it seems like they both implanted.

"Well, there always was the chance, the doctors did say."

He smiles and reaches over to squeeze my hand.

"Can we get some froyo? The babies need it!"

I have such a craving right now for the synthetic fruity sweetness, melting on my tongue. It takes me back to my child-hood, to a sunny day in a green garden, a blue sky, heat on my skin, lightness in my feet – and to Alice. But Ollie doesn't know about her.

"Your wish is my command."

Both of us take the rest of the day off. We drive with the roof down for once, and I make a note to start researching bigger cars, the best for big families. We make a pit stop at a diner for lunch and despite the froyo. I eat a burger, cheese fries, a milk-shake – it can't hurt, not just this once. Ollie has the same, checking his phone whilst he orders, he can't put it down for a minute, it seems.

We take a walk, hand in hand, breeze running through my hair. Talk about names, changes we'd need to make to the house.

"How much space can two babies need?" Behind his Ray-Bans, Ollie's forehead crinkles.

"More than you'd think. Maybe we need to move," I say.

"Are you serious?"

We have a split-level ranch with three bedrooms. Ollie converted the garage so he could work in it. We have a decent sized garden and a great view. I'm not sure about schools and day care though. Will I need to cut back on travel? I know already that I won't be a stay-at-home mommy, I'm not cut out for that. And besides, I've made too many sacrifices for work to give up now.

"Well, I'm just saying. We might need more space. Your stuff is everywhere as it is."

"What? No, it isn't."

"That's because I'm always picking up after you. Putting things back in the garage."

"Oh yes, tidying." He makes speech marks with his fingers. "And I can never find anything."

"Well, if you put it away, I wouldn't need to tidy, would I?" Though, in my head I remind myself to tread carefully.

Before he can reply I pull out my phone, fling my arm around him, snap a cute selfie of us, the light golden behind us, post it to my stories, hashtag it #GorgeousHubby and then plant a smacker of a kiss on his lips.

"Shall we head back now? It's getting chilly."

We've been out nearly all afternoon and now all I can see is the setting sun, heavy and rich as treacle, the road unfurling beneath us, taking me closer to my dream, closer to what Alice has.

It doesn't last though, it never does.

I make it a week before the spotting starts. Dark ugly stains on my underwear. Ollie finds me crying in the bathroom when he gets home from work.

"Don't say it. Don't say I told you so."

"I wasn't going to, sweetheart."

I'm on the floor next to the toilet. He crouches down next to me. Puts his arms around me.

"When did it start?"

"Not sure. I was in a meeting all morning. There was nothing at lunchtime. But when I got home and went to take a shower..."

"It does happen – it doesn't have to mean anything. Have you called the clinic?"

"Not yet."

"I'll do it now."

True to his word, he does. My hero. At least one of us is capable of doing something. Unlike my stupid useless body.

"...can we come in for a scan? Yes – Evie Robinson. Yes, like the film." He rolls his eyes at me. "Tomorrow morning? That's fine. We'll see you then." He ends the call.

"All sorted. Now what can I get you? You can't stay in the bathroom all night."

I don't know if it's because we've been here before, or because he's in work mode but he seems a little too upbeat to me. I, on the other hand, can't stop crying – again.

"You can get me a promise that I'm not losing our babies. How about that?"

He shakes his head at me. "You can't think like that. You don't know what's happening. We just need to sit tight until tomorrow morning."

"Oh, that's all we need to do. Sit tight. Shall I cross my legs too, put a cork up there? Stop them falling out?"

I know none of this is his fault, but I'm angry – with myself really – I was stupid to think we could actually get this lucky. And it's true what they say, we always take it out on those closest to us.

"Don't be like that. You know that's not what I meant."

"What did you mean then? Because you seem fairly chirpy. Don't you care?"

"I... what? Of course I care! I don't know what else I can do but I do know you sitting here like some drunk teenager, clutching the toilet isn't the answer. You need to rest and eat and let me take care of you."

"Are you saying this is my fault now? That I'm not taking care of myself?"

"Evie. Stop putting words in my mouth. I'm not the enemy here."

He's so calm. As if he's not about to go sext some twenty-year-old with a septum piercing once he's tucked me into bed.

I put my head in my hands. I can't let myself go down this route. I need to stay calm for the babies, if not for myself.

"Just message her already."

"Message who?"

"You know. Don't pretend. You're on your phone all the goddamn time."

He throws his hands up. "I can't do this when you're like this."

"So don't. I didn't ask for your help."

He turns around and opens the door, walks out.

"Yeah, leave, why don't you. You can sleep in the spare room too!"

I hang my head and pat my belly, whisper to them, *I'm trying, babies, trying to keep you safe. Please stay with me, I love you.*

When I enter the kitchen, Ollie is ordering Thai from my favourite noodle place, specifying long-stem broccoli and bok choy in the sauce I like. Tofu and noodles. He's not that mad at me. How many other marriages are like ours? Hating and loving in the same space, but still both of you against the world. Is it our shared history keeping us together?

"Hey." His face softens when he sees me. "What are you doing in here?" And he banishes me to our bedroom under strict instructions to rest up, he'll bring in supper when it arrives.

I lie on our bed obediently and wait for him, watch *Married at First Sight* and wonder if they have had the right idea all along.

We eat – well, Ollie eats.

"You need to keep your strength up."

"Not hungry."

I've got no appetite, worry about the babies squeezes me tight from the inside. My body doesn't have time for digestion. It barely has time for breathing, or keeping my heart beating, only to keep the babies alive.

Ollie clears away the cartons after dinner, carefully placing my uneaten plate in the fridge under a towel. He brings me chamomile tea, but I reject that too.

"It's got caffeine in it."

"It's a miniscule amount. And besides you had coffee yesterday."

"That was before."

"I thought it might help you relax, you need some sleep."

"Nothing short of prescription drugs is going to relax me, Ollie." Still, he puts the cup down on my bedside table, he's remembered to use my favourite one.

We watch some other programme on Netflix, about tech-startups and corruption, but I can't follow it and instead flick through social media on my phone. I regret it though, too many pictures of babies and bumps. I've muted Nina and Ronnie, obviously, but right now the entire world seems fertile. Damn algorithms – always listening. I fling my phone across the room as Ollie heaves the blanket over him and passes me the remote.

I spend the night flicking from reality show to reality show. Anything to distract me from my own reality. Around 3am I get up and go to the bathroom. When I wipe the spotting is fainter, just a dark shadow. Maybe it's going to be okay? I want to believe it. I was so sure. Hope is still there, in the back of my mind.

I manage a restless doze until the alarm goes off. When I look in the mirror to do my affirmations, nothing short of a miracle would make me look less haggard right now. Pale grey bags ring my eyes, those ageing brackets around my mouth that

I should get filled seem like crevasses rather than crevices. Nevertheless, I chant to myself about being open and ripe and fertile and keeping my babies safe.

"Are you ready or are you still casting spells?"

I shoot him a look as I emerge, the cloud of steam not helping my case. He is firmly in the court of anything remotely spiritual – including yoga – being nonsense.

"I'm here now, thank you."

"Sorry, just trying to make you laugh. Probably not one of my best ideas."

"No."

He leaves first, but when he sees my hands are shaking too much to lock the door, he comes back, gently removes my keys and does it for me. He picks up my bag and puts an arm around me as we walk to the car together. I don't want to go. Right now the babies exist. Someone might take that news away soon.

Ollie backs us out of the drive, one arm across the back of the seats.

"How was it... are you... this morning?"

It's easier to describe the state of my underwear when he's not looking at me. Once upon a time this would be dirty talk.

"It's... it's better. I might have panicked."

"Was the blood dark or light? Remember what the nurse told us. Dark blood is old blood."

"I don't want to talk about it."

I am silent in the car, on the freeway, watching as everyone else's life rushes past, whilst ours is on pause. He squeezes my hand, my knuckles white under his fingers as I cling to the rollercoaster that is our life.

I flick on one of Ollie's playlists, some sort of awful electronic club mix. "Been reliving your glory days, have you?"

He shakes his head and squeezes my hand again, but doesn't take his eyes off the road, his expression unreadable.

I chew my lips, twist my fingers in my lap, ignore the

churning in my stomach. It's not a long drive. I try to do some calming yoga breathing, counting in for four and out for four, but to no avail. There is nothing to calm a woman who is afraid for her children. It's primaeval, it's how humans have survived this long, until the biggest risk to us is ourselves.

In the clinic, we're swiftly ushered into a treatment room but not before I glimpse myself in the mirror. For a moment, the picture I see has a glitch and I see Alice instead, diamonds glinting at throat and wrist, a bump swelling my tunic top. We always did get mistaken for sisters.

I remove my leggings and underwear, array myself in the stirrups and cover myself with a blanket. I have no shame any longer, I don't think I've ever taken my clothes off this fast for a man – even Ollie.

When the technician arrives with the ultrasound, Ollie makes a quip, but I shush him. I need this over with. I need to know what's going on.

"Right, where are we?"

There is the cold gloopy feel of lube and then an invasive pressure inside me.

Ollie reaches for my hand as the sonographer fiddles around, getting the probe practically by my left ovary – or so it feels.

"I can see from your notes that you had two embryos transferred?"

"Yes, that's right."

"Okay." She turns the screen round to face us and presses a button. A sudden thudding like a galloping horse fills the room.

"Here's your baby!"

She points to a white flickering dot, beating in time with the horse's hooves. "Really good heartbeat too – quite fast, so that could mean a boy!"

I don't know what to say. *A baby. Our baby. But...*

Ollie beats me to it. "Where's the other one? Our other baby?"

The sonographer is silent as she manipulates the probe again, I'm a puppet on her string, trying not to wince, feeling like I am about to fall from a great height.

She points to a much smaller mass on the screen; the room fills with silence.

"Unfortunately, it looks like the other embryo failed to successfully implant."

I hold on to Ollie's hand. "So... is that what caused the spotting?"

"Most likely, yes. It's common for your body to reject the faulty embryo, thinking it's just the usual menstrual product."

Ollie looks at me as my lip wobbles, I can practically hear him thinking *focus on the positive.*

"But the first embryo – is it okay?"

"Yes! Looks great, measuring slightly ahead as well."

The probe moves and the wild horse is running through the room again, and inside my heart is an echo.

"Hey, baby!" Ollie waves at the screen and pats my belly. He kisses my forehead as we watch hope in human form flickering on screen.

"Would you like some prints?"

"That would be great, thank you!"

She turns and presses some buttons and a machine whirs to life on the opposite side of the room, spitting out rectangular black and white images, surprisingly polaroid-like.

"I'm going to take the probe out now, but we're happy to scan you weekly, given your history, to give you that peace of mind. And if you have any more spotting, feel free to just come by, we can always fit in an emergency scan too. It comes as part of your package."

She removes the probe, rolls off its condom-like sheath and

hooks it neatly on the machine. Flicking the camera off, she passes me some paper towels to clean myself up.

"I'll see you outside in reception and we can get you booked in for the next few scans."

"Thank you... so much." The words stick in my throat, I swallow hard to get them out, giving her a watery smile.

She says kindly, "It's okay, I understand – it's what we're here for."

Ollie waits and watches as I get dressed. "Are you okay?"

"I mean... yes, I guess so. I... one baby, though. We lost one. I lost one."

"Sweetie—"

I know what he's going to say. That it wasn't meant to be, that it wasn't ready to grow and form. That we should be grateful – we have this baby. And I want to feel like that, I really do.

"I just need a minute, okay? It's a lot... a lot to take in."

"Sure, honey. I'll be right outside."

I sit on the edge of the bed.

Maybe he was right. Maybe we shouldn't have done this again. I'm only going to be on edge now for weeks and weeks. Possibly the rest of my life. There are so many hurdles to clear. Each scan, each Doppler. For our baby to be alive and healthy.

And yet when I think about those photos of Alice, with her brood, her tribe – I want to lose my mind. After everything she did and now she has the perfect family – the perfect life.

All I want is a child. Is that so much to ask of the universe?

I cup my belly again.

"It's you and me baby. We're in this together."

Ollie drops me home after the scan. Because of the spotting the clinic has advised against working for the next couple of days. Telling me to rest and put my feet up.

Fat chance of Rupert letting me do that though – so I tuck myself into bed with my laptop and log on. When my phone pings I'm halfway through prepping a deck for a client presentation.

Alice McDonald has accepted your friend request

For a moment I'm confused.

But then it comes back to me. That night a few weeks ago, on Facebook.

I set aside my laptop. It's time for a quick break anyhow. I've already set the scan picture as my background. It's not long to go until twelve weeks.

"Hi, baby bean." I stroke the little white spot in the picture before unlocking my phone.

Alice has changed her profile picture. It's a snap of her aged about six, in her bedroom at home.

All it takes is a glimpse of the wallpaper behind her for me to tumble back in time. Pink rosebuds, green leaves, tiny clusters of them sprinkled on a white background like pox on a toddler. If I close my eyes, they repeat over and over again. I see them so clearly, it's like being back there.

We used to draw spider webs in the petals, the gossamer fine threads binding us together. Our fingers becoming tickly spiders up each other's arms as we giggled together, as only six-year-olds can.

I wonder what happened to that house? To her parents? I wonder if the apple tree still bears fruit that is mouth pucker-ingly sharp and delicious.

When I first met Alice, she was sitting in that tree, lying in its branches like a lazy cat, diamonds of sunshine dappling her limbs as she offered me a bite of one of those apples. Mama had warned me about playing with little boys. But she never thought to warn me about little girls.

I remember Alice's hands reaching out for mine.

You're almost there, Evie, one more step. Here – grab my arm.

I never did make it to the top of that tree. Had to settle for seeing the sky from the ground, one arm under me, the sharp snap of bone, pain searing and white hot. Above me the world turned to black, with Alice at the centre, touching heaven.

After that, we were never apart. She was the only person I allowed to sign my cast and she drew leaves and flowers and apples all over it, with our names entwined in the centre. We spent every waking moment together as kids. Until we didn't.

And now I'm here, half a world and half a lifetime away from her.

The little dot next to her name is green. She's online.

And then the messenger box pops up.

Hello stranger... it's been a while.

Immediately I am back there again, in the house and the heat, the scent of roses and chlorine heavy in my head. The feel of a leather sofa beneath my sun-scorched legs and the taste of cherry cola and Mr Whippy. And then after that the smell of impulse and Lynx Africa deodorant, the vomit-inducing synthetic peach of schnapps and lemonade, and the way snakes of excitement and fear entwined inside me. The sound of a man's voice and a boy's voice. Behind them, Mama, high and breathy and southern. And then further back, something darker, twisted bitter and sharp.

Hi...

There's a pause, the grey dots move hypnotically. *Alice is typing.* I'm too afraid to look away, in case I break the spell and they stop.

I don't even know what to say.

I don't either LOL

What made you message me?

There's the Evie I remember, straight to the point.
I can't help but smile.
I like to think I've changed a little bit, I type.

Not too much I hope

We've all changed since childhood – no?

Haha, yes, a bit.

It feels weird to ask this but how are you?

She pauses, and then types again.

I'm not sure we can catch up on 20 years in one line but yeah,
things are pretty good. You?

Yeah… I mean, compared to back then, things are good.

I don't even know how to begin to tell her anything. I don't
know what to say. She's a stranger and she's not.
This is really weird, isn't it? I type.

Cool though. I thought I'd never see you again.

Me neither

I wonder if she remembers that last day, hands waving

through the windscreen, shrinking in the distance. Sky the
colour of the inside of a shell, pearlescent with promise. Thom
Yorke singing from the car radio about fading out. Like I was.

I'm not sure I can do this right now. She starts typing.

Tell me how your day went then?

Slowly.

Oh yeah? What's up?

It's strange how, despite everything – then and now – the
years are peeling away and we could still be those same two
girls, on the twin beds in her room, braiding our hair, watching
Clueless, mimicking Cher and Tai.

Nothing really, work. The usual – too much to do, too little
time. You?

I don't want to tell her about the pregnancy now. It's too
much, too soon. I can't rip the bandage off yet.

Same here, plus added kids' chaos.

I can't hear about her children, her husband. Without thinking, I write:

I can't do this. I'm sorry.

The grey dots dance endlessly. I put my phone down, carry
on with my presentation.

When I turn it over ten minutes later, there's a message icon
waiting.

Evie, I know a lot happened back then. I wasn't the nicest person. All the stuff with Rosie and the school. But it wasn't all bad, was it?

Remember the beach trip to Brighton?

Do you still have your tattoo?

Give me another chance.

I've missed you.

SIX

THEN

It was one of those perfect days. As if the world was created for us alone. The train shuddered and rumbled, the world outside the windows passing in a technicolour – fluffy white clouds, golden sunbeams, the sky a rich, endless blue.

Alice walked ahead of me through the train carriage and opened a random compartment. Peering over her shoulder, I saw a man. Fancy suit, shiny shoes. Briefcase, massive newspaper. In a flash, she pulled out a lighter, flicked it over the edge of his paper and ran off. His florid face stared back at me, jowls shaking, as he tried to pat out the flames. Instead, I followed Alice's blazing sun, blindly, laughing, ready to be consumed.

I smelt the sea before I saw it but when I did, I remembered why I loved Brighton so much, with its view of the sea and the great beyond, straight from the station exit, the sky split open with promise.

"Where do you want to go first?"

And then we both said *the aquarium* at the same time.

Love and hate are two sides of the same coin. Alice and I were two halves of the same person.

The aquarium was quiet, that mid-morning dead time. We

had the place mostly to ourselves, wandering past windows onto another world, the watery light stroked our faces and hair, leaving us glowing and luminous. The two of us were always so special together, even if we were better apart.

"Did you know jellyfish are older than anything else on earth?"

We watched their tentacles drift past us, their candy-floss bodies shimmering and pulsing until I felt it in my blood and my heart and my bones. The world rippled through us, facing each other, shadows and reflections crawling across and between us.

"I need to talk to you. But you can't laugh," she said.

She walked away from me, down to a deeper and darker part of the aquarium. I followed, as expected. Everyone always ended up in Alice's orbit.

"I won't. I promise." I catch up with her, pull her round to face me. "Tell me."

"It's stupid. I thought he loved me... I thought she was my friend."

The tanks around us were empty but shadows lurked in the reefs. Slowly, I got the story out of her. She'd seen her boyfriend Richard with someone else at a party.

"But, Alice, didn't you break up with him last month?"

"That doesn't matter. Why did he lie? Why did he tell me he loved me?"

I couldn't tell if it was the light or if she had tears in her eyes.

The shadows in the tanks grew more substantial, over Alice's shoulder, I saw them form familiar shapes.

"He's an asshole," I said.

"And her too."

"Yeah. She's a slut."

She smiled at that. The shadows swarmed – rendered themselves solid – it was feeding time.

"It must be great being a shark. All powerful. Nature's greatest predator. Cruising, in control." Alice's voice was tinged with envy.

"What do you want to do about Richard? Short of growing a fin, I mean." I smiled, but knew she had sharp teeth already, I'd felt them.

She told me.

And I gave her my word there and then.

"You're the only one I trust." She squeezed my hand.

It was nice to be needed. To be special without having to give anything up.

When I looked up, the sharks had gone. But their shadows were still there, flickering around the edge of the tanks, just out of my eyeline.

After that we mucked around, ran down the pier, played the games, won the toys, watched the Punch & Judy shows. Wound in and out of the lanes, with its sweet smell of incense and frying onions and cutting through it, a darker, herby scent of oblivion.

I didn't want to go home. Back to everyone in my life telling me what to do, to behave, to be careful, to be quieter, small, take up less space. Alice never told me what to do.

You're so fun, Alice. All my other friends, they're no fun.

She smiled and held my hand, pulling me after her.

We had chips and ice cream, smoked her Marlboro Lights. Nothing ever tasted so good.

The tattooist's bench was peeling, smelling of fear and pain. Things I was used to.

I said I'd go first. The merry-go-round ground to a halt as a stranger wrote our history on my thigh, forever an apple-tree girl.

That's what we are, Evie, apple-tree girls. You and me.

. . .

It was dark when we got home. Walking up the hill, the lights from a police car flashed neon across the night, our houses lit up like beacons.

"Where the hell have you been?"

Aunty Meredith appeared first, then behind her, Mama, and last, Uncle John. I was trapped again, despair setting concrete hard inside me with the realisation that nothing had changed. It was just one day of freedom.

Alice dropped my hand like it was burning her, ran to Aunty Meredith and flung herself into her arms. I can hear her force out uneven breaths, the way she does when she wants to make herself cry.

"Evie made me skip, I didn't want to."

Her words stung.

"That's not true! You made *me* go with you!"

But Alice only sobbed harder, arms tight around her mother, pushing her back into the house. Uncle John watched me, his gaze unblinking.

"You shouldn't lie, Evie, you're better than that."

And he shook his head at me.

When I turned around, Mama was behind me, watching and waiting. For a moment I wished I had a mother to cry on, to embrace me, like Alice did. Instead, I buttoned up these feelings, the rage, the injustice. Saved them for later, found other ways to release them. There was no point hoping for something that would never happen.

"What have you got to say for yourself?" Mama frowned. A sign she was really mad. She hated frowning, hated the wrinkles it gave her.

"Nothing."

"Don't you care? We've been out of our minds with worry. And you dragged Alice into your... your shenanigans."

A burly policeman emerged from Alice's house and appeared next to Mama, tugging his hat more firmly down on his head.

"You've given your mother a fright and wasted police resources. You're lucky we're letting you off without a formal warning."

Mama eyed him and his broad chest, looking up at him from under her eyelashes, unable to help herself.

"Thank you, Constable Halstead, you've been very helpful indeed." In the dark, he flushed red, and rubbed the back of his neck. He waved goodbye and folded himself into his car, leaving us with a miasma of petrol fumes.

Mama and I walked next door to our house and she steered me inside, anchoring her arm through mine, so hard the next day I found purpling bruises. I looked behind me, Alice was still closing her front door. When she saw me, she winked.

I still have that tattoo. It's the only one remaining. I got a few more at university, but had them removed. The usual ridiculous Celtic knot on my shoulder, a dolphin arcing over my hip, a feather on my foot. When we moved to Boston, I felt they didn't fit who I was anymore. They'd only ever been part of a mask I wore then.

But the first tattoo, that was never pretend. A tiny outline of an apple, delicately drawn leaves and flowers, on a branch. The lines have blurred with age and weight gain. But I'd never remove it. No matter what. Because I'll always be an apple-tree girl.

SEVEN

NOW

I've not been in the office much the last couple of months, so the first time I see Freddie, I know he's going to notice I look different. I wonder if he's smart enough to guess why.

"Hey, stranger!"

I hug him, try not to wince as he squeezes me, my sore boobs are killing me at the moment. Freddie and I have an odd little relationship. I speak to him more than my own husband and my friends. I see him every day – either in person or on a call – and yet I don't like him. It's hard to know how to explain it.

He's one of those upper-middle class white men who are always floating to the top in any big corporation. He's English, like me, but with a cut-glass accent, a signet ring and deck shoes. Even since moving to the hipster neighbourhood of Allston he's not succumbed to a man bun or a sleeve tattoo... yet. Even before he told me he went to Oxford – and let's face it, anyone who goes has to let you know about it – I could have guessed. And from his surname, Fotherington-Smythe, and stories about growing up in Surrey, telling me where he "wintered", I guessed he'd probably also been to Eton. Though, of course, he confirmed that too.

Unfortunately for Freddie though, despite everything he's still always trying to prove himself. He's a second son, his older brother being the one to inherit the family home. And even if he weren't the spare, he's the black sheep of the family for a glaringly obvious reason – well, to me at least. It's also why he's not brought a nice girl home to meet the parents.

"Good to see you, Freddie. Coffee later?"

"You bet." He winks at me and does a cringey little finger gun gesture. "We need to catch up on the new project Rupes has us on. That London law firm? I've already set up a call with the key stakeholders."

Oh no, he's not doing this to me again. This is why our relationship is so tricky. We've worked together a long time now, a good five years. We know where the bodies are buried, where the shortcuts were taken, where the crap is spread thickest. We've been there for each other through apocalyptic hangovers (his and mine), divorces (him) and tricky HR cases (both of us).

And early on, I had his back in a very tricky meeting. Let's just say it involved an ill-judged Grindr hook-up with a new client and Rupert turning out to be a closet homophobe.

But Freddie hates knowing that he can trust me. That I can keep his secrets. He thinks he's above relying on me.

So, in front of Rupert, Freddie does everything he can to one-up me, and then in private, the mask drops and we work beautifully together. It's exhausting, it really is. I've asked him how long he thinks he can continue with the charade, because it's doing neither of us any favours.

Needless to say, Rupert thinks the sun shines out of Freddie's behind and is oblivious to the fact that I'm the brains behind it all.

. . .

After a couple of early meetings where, thankfully, I don't have to dash out to be sick, I'm at my favourite coffee stand, psyching myself up to ask for a decaf latte, when my phone vibrates.

Where R U?

It's Rupert. He's far too old to be using text speak but seems to think it makes him relatable to the new grads so persists with it.

I'm in the office, where are you?

I like to annoy him by responding in full, correctly punctuated sentences. Let's say I'm sufficiently bored by him to do this. I imagine his head swivelling from his vantage point in the office, looking for me. I'll tell him I needed to work in a breakout area on another floor.

In my office. We need to talk.

I'll be right there.

I mime my order at the barista.

Rupert is so old-school. He's been asking – less and less tactfully – about my plans for procreation ever since I got promoted to senior manager a couple of years ago. If I could entirely avoid telling him I'm pregnant – even once I've given birth – I would. He seems to think they throw away a woman's brain along with the placenta. Well, he would if he even knew what a placenta was. I hope Freddie hasn't guessed and opened his big mouth to him. You never know with Freddie, but I'd like to think even he would be above such a low move.

When I get back, I nip to Rupert's office and – surprise,

surprise – Freddie is already there. Sometimes I think he's wedged so far up Rupert's backside a dentist could retrieve him.

"There you are."

Rupert beckons me over as if I've arrived late for a pre-arranged meeting, rather than a last-minute informal summons. Although I wouldn't put it past Freddie to say he'll set up a meeting for the three of us and then "forget" to invite me – he's definitely done it before.

"Morning, Rupert, I'm fine thanks, how are you?"

"What?" He's distracted, tapping on his phone.

"Just making polite conversation, inquiring as to my colleague's well-being."

"Right. Yes..."

He fiddles around on his laptop some more and Freddie and I sit down and sip our coffees.

"So, that ladies with computers conference you went to—"

I roll my eyes. "Women in Tech?"

"Yes! That's the one. Anyway, amazingly your visit has borne fruit and one of the clients you spoke to have retained our services on some restructuring consultancy work."

I nod. I already know this because I was the one who arranged it all.

"Anyway, Evie, they need someone to go on six-month secondment to their London office and I thought you'd be perfect!"

Oh. A secondment. The timing isn't great. Not that they realise.

"That's great news – well done, Britters!" Freddie calls me this, not in reference to where we're both from but because a client once thought I looked like Britney Spears and persisted in peppering phone calls with random lyrics. Freddie thought it was hilarious and never lets me forget it.

"It is great news. And more excitingly, I'm thrilled to announce that this total champ here..." and at this point Rupert comes out from behind his deck and yes, actually starts massaging Freddie's shoulders as if prepping his prize fighter for a match. "This champ here has been promoted to director! So, he won't have time to handhold you any more, Evie, this little client will be all yours. Time to take the stabilisers off!"

Unsurprisingly, I'm speechless. Rupert has pulled off a masterpiece of terrible management by both giving me something – the UK client, Alice's company – but then in the next breath undermining me by promoting my direct peer for no actual reason relating to his work performance that I can see.

The worst thing is that Rupert – and Freddie – will know that I'm raging, but unlike the men in the office, who are allowed to shout and throw things, I have to hold it all in, lest I be accused of being that worst of all things, an over-emotional woman.

"Freddie will pass across all the details from the new engagements team and then it's over to you. Don't mess this up."

What the hell? I can see from Freddie semaphoring with his eyebrows that even he thinks Rupert has gone too far.

I sip my coffee and try to find a way to depart the room before I lose it, but also maintain my dignity. The pregnancy hormones aren't helping – luckily making me mildly homicidal, rather than a blubbering wreck – but that could change at any moment.

"Evie, let's catch up now, yes? And then you can reach out if you need anything else later. We'll leave you peace, mate." Freddie stands up, pick up both our coffee cups and ushers me out of the room in one swift move.

Before the door is even closed behind us, I chuck my laptop at him and disappear to the bathroom.

. . .

The rest of the day flies past in a haze of pregnancy exhaustion and the temptation to think about things that have stayed long buried. Despite it all, I am nothing if not organised. I begin preparatory reading, flicking through the files on my desk about Alice's firm and their ambitions.

Alice and I were always pitted against each other at school and at home. I don't know if Uncle John and Mama did it on purpose or not. Probably yes. And Alice always won – well, most of the time. It's going to be weird being the one in control now, the high-powered consultant pulling the strings.

Once I get home, I strip off my suit, my bra, my tights and climb into my most worn out pyjama bottoms and Ollie's softest T-shirt.

How are things going?

It's like Alice is a mind reader. Since our first chat, we've been messaging off and on. We keep it to top-level stuff about being busy and work, and we don't touch the past, not since her message, apologising, asking for another chance.

The time difference means that if I message at dinnertime she's usually online – she always was a night owl, it must be close to midnight where she is. I think about her lying in their bed, him next to her. I still haven't told her I'm pregnant.

It's still a friendship – a strange one, but then our relationship never did fit in a box. I begin to type.

Might manage a trip UK-side this year.

Oh nice! How come?

Work – I'm being seconded to a client for a bit. It's a funny story, actually. It's a law firm.

Which one?

That's the funny part – I think it's where you work? At least, I think that's you on the website...

No way! That's so random. What are you doing with us?

I'm not sure yet, but I've got a briefing call next week.

I'm not supposed to tell her any of this really, but I can't see the harm. She reels off a list of people I might meet, various HR Directors and Partners. I don't know any of them.

When will you be over?

Probably early August.

How long are you staying for – assume you'll be London based?

I'm not sure yet, maybe six months? Depends on the project tbh. And yeah, I'm not sure, they have an office near Gatwick and one in London. Knowing my luck, I'll be stuck out in some crappy serviced apartment out in the sticks

Well... we're not far from Gatwick airport. Maybe 15 mins away.

Cool. Defo up for drinks when I come!

Sounds good.

And I want to see that gorgeous house you're always posting on Insta! God, it'll be so weird to see you with kids – and a husband.

The three grey dots show she's typing a reply, but they go on for a while and nothing comes my way. Eventually they stop and she goes offline. I go to bed, but even when I wake the next morning she still hasn't replied. I wonder what happened. I tell myself that maybe she dozed off or one of the kids woke or... something. But I know what it really was.

She always liked to be the first to say goodbye, to hang up the phone. *Always leave them wanting more, Evie.*

If I wasn't sure about going back, unpicking it all, maybe this was a sign... that I should.

EIGHT

It's normal, when we have new projects at work, for me and Ollie not to see much of each other. We've never been that type of couple who live in each other's pockets. Although at the start we did the whole leaving-notes-in-each-others' suitcases, order surprises to hotels, dirty-weekend thing, that died out a while ago.

Ollie is proud of it, boasting to his mates about how laid-back his wife is. It's true, our relationship was never like everyone else's.

I'm no good, he told me, the first time we kissed, *but I bet you're no good too.*

He'd tilted my head up so I'd look in his eyes – ridiculously long lashed, like a girl's. And even though I'm tall, he was taller. He always crushed the air out of the space we were in, filling everywhere with his presence.

I thought things might be different now that I'm pregnant again. And things did change, briefly. But now they're pretty much back to normal – he's out most nights, away every couple of weeks, leaving me to deal with everything else. Not like the last time when he was home before me every night – cooking, making sure I got all my nutrients, rest, anything I needed.

I think about how fast the novelty has worn off, how I can already feel him pulling away. *I won't let him abandon us*, I say to my stomach.

When I message him, I'm left unread. When I call, he doesn't pick up. When he does get home, he says he's been out with Ben – the other producer on the project. Ben is bad news for sure. The only friend of his who's not married and has a different girlfriend every time we meet for dinner. And that girlfriend is never over the age of twenty-five.

I don't understand why you always have to be such a bitch about him, Evie. What did he ever do to you?

Ollie is relentlessly loyal to Ben. I don't know why, but it won't be for any deep reason. They were mates at university – and from school originally, that whole private-school bonding thing. Ben dropped out in the end and then Ollie hooked back up with him when we moved to Boston.

The reason I want Ollie home tonight is that it's the twelve-week scan tomorrow. It shouldn't be a big deal, we've been scanned every week regularly now. But it feels it – following my friends on social media and seeing their announcements, it's my turn tomorrow. We've never made it this far before. I wonder what it would be like if I was back in the UK? If Mama was still alive. I wonder if Aunty Meredith went with Alice to all her scans, held her hand alongside her husband?

I message Ollie.

Where are you? I'm ordering Lebanese, want some?

The little ticks under the message turn grey and then blue after an hour but no reply.

Babe?

I give in and order when it gets past ten o'clock. I'm so hungry anyway and eating is the only thing that gets rid of the nausea. Which seems ironic really.

When the doorbell goes, I think maybe it's dinner, but then remember they send a message first. Maybe Ollie has lost his keys?

I fling open the door. "Babe, what the—"

It's not Ollie.

"Evie, baby! Sweetheart."

It's Ben.

"Hi?"

"Where's that handsome husband of yours?" He peers past me into the house.

"Out with you allegedly."

My tone must register as he fumbles to reply, rubbing his nose. "Oh... yes! Yes, we must be meeting near the studio. My bad, my bad, this stupid head of mine." He points at his shaved skull, which doesn't suit him at all. Turning, he jogs back to his Uber.

"Bye, Ben."

"Bye!" He's already talking on his phone. Glad Ollie will answer to someone even if it's not his own wife.

Ollie comes home an hour later, stinking of beer, sweaty and dishevelled.

"Sweetheart!" He reaches for me, smiling, but I back away.

"Where were you? I called you loads!" I don't mean for my voice to crack.

"Woah..." He holds his hands up in front of him. "I told you. Out with Ben."

"Hmmm, that's interesting, because he was here not long ago looking for you."

"Hah. Well, that's weird. Are you sure?"

"Yes, I'm bloody sure!"

"Calm down, darling. I'm just saying those pregnancy hormones, you know, they mess with your head. You've not been yourself. Sit down, I'll get you a drink."

"I don't want a drink."

He clatters around in the kitchen despite my protests, I follow behind, wary.

"Sweetheart, you need to look after yourself. You should be asleep, it's a big day tomorrow, remember?"

"It's not me that needs reminding."

But I allow myself to be escorted to a chair as he pours me a glass of iced water.

"What's that supposed to mean?"

"I wasn't the one out late with God knows who, leaving my pregnant wife at home."

"I was out with Ben, he forgot I told him to come to the studio. You know what he's like. Shit for brains, too much coke."

I want to believe him, I do. I mean, who cares who he was hanging out with tonight, he still came home to me. *I'm his wife, she's just some nobody. Let it go, Evie.*

But then he looks at his phone, smiles, typing and swiping.

"Who is she? I know you're messaging someone. You can't keep telling me I'm imagining it. You're always sneaking off for a call or smirking at your phone."

For a second I see I have him. His face aglow as he reads or sees what she's sent him. And then the mask slips down again.

"Who is... what? I don't know what you're talking about."

"Give me your phone."

"Darling—"

"Give it to me."

I reach for it and the glass of water he's passing me spills and goes everywhere.

"My phone!" His face is ugly with anger.

"Thanks a lot, Evie, I need that for work!"

After faffing around for a Tupperware container and some rice, he flounces out of the room. It's almost midnight. The scan is at nine.

I should be asleep, Baby. I cup my hand over my belly again. *What kind of family are you being born into, where Mummy and Daddy are already fighting in front of you?*

Ollie is in the den with his iPad in one hand and the TV remote in the other.

"Sorted it?"

"Yes. No thanks to you. I can pick up a new phone tomorrow."

He's not been this bad with his flings before. Normally his enthusiasm ebbs after a week or so. He's not in control this time, acting like a teenager with a crush. It's not okay. I need his commitment if we're going to do this. I'm not raising this child alone, I saw what happened to Mama.

We've got history together, surely that counts for something, buys me some loyalty?

"Ollie, I want us to start marriage counselling."

"What?"

"You heard me."

"Why?"

"Why? Because we're having a baby and we can't keep fighting like this. I love you and I thought you loved me."

"You're the one having a go at me for being out all the time but you're still working late every night, high stress. It's not good for the baby or for you."

I bite my tongue. The unfairness of the comment stings. I have to work twice as hard to be considered even half as good, or so it seems.

"Look, I'm not saying there's anything wrong, I just thought it might help us like it helped Nina and Rob—"

"Did it?"

"Yes."

Ollie puts aside the iPad, puts his head in his hands and then looks up at me. I can tell he's sorry, this time.

"It's okay, you're right. Let's try it. Let's see the counsellor."

And he reaches out an arm and pulls me into his lap. He smells musky and smoky.

"Babe—"

He kisses my neck, bites my ear. "I love it when you sigh like that."

I can feel him hardening against me. I want to resist, but I can't. I need this, need to know in the most basic of ways that he's still mine.

He runs his hands over my breasts, so much bigger already.

"These are gorgeous."

"Gentle."

And he kisses them slowly, peeling my cotton maternity bra off me and flicking his tongue across my nipples.

He lies me down on the sofa, crouches over me, bearing his weight on his arms.

"Why would I want anyone else when I can have this?"

He kisses his way down my belly, whispering as he goes. I don't want to know what he's saying, I don't want him to stop.

We've never been one of those couples who only fought and sulked. The chemistry was there from the start. The first time we had sex was in the photocopy room at university, next to the office of the professor I was sleeping with in secret.

Does he do it like this? he'd said as he put his fingers between us, stroking me into oblivion in seconds. For weeks after, I'd smell hot paper and ink when I came.

"Are you sure..." – he says now as he helps me wriggle out of my leggings – "...that the counsellor can improve on this?"

He spreads my legs and places his hot, wet mouth over me.

And then I can't say anything at all.

. . .

The scan goes fine.

"Your baby is growing well. Tracking nicely week on week." The sonographer congratulates me like I did something specific to contribute to this. The guilt I feel for having sex dissipates and I bask in the glow that comes from even the smallest praise, the sign that I'm doing this right.

They sign us off and back to the obstetrician for all future treatment. I want to dance out of the clinic, but settle for flinging my arms around Ollie instead.

"We did it! We made it to twelve weeks!" I am giddy with joy.

The sonographer emails us the scans for us to treasure and share. By the time I get home that night, Ollie has put one in a frame on my bedside table. When I lean down to kiss him, it feels like it means something this time. And he whispers, "Hey baby, it's Daddy," to my belly.

"We have an appointment with the counsellor Nina and Rob used on Saturday morning."

"So soon?"

"Well – why wait? She had a cancellation."

"Sure. Sounds good."

And I think maybe it's okay, we're on an upward curve again. We have sex again, every night that week. It's like the scan switched something back on in us both. I can't get enough of him, I want to drag him inside of me closer and closer.

"Harder," I tell him, breathless.

"What about the baby?"

But I only urge him on, faster. When we're together, it blots out the voices in my head, the worries, the noise – all my fears.

All I want to hear is him whispering my name over and over again when he's inside me. *No one else can give him this, only me.*

Mama once told me that was the way to do it, to keep a man – not that she ever succeeded. That it wasn't through his heart or his head, or even in bed. But something darker and deeper is needed to bind you so closely, until you're not sure whose heart is beating and whose lungs are breathing and whose skin you're wearing.

NINE

THEN

At home, Mama was endlessly frustrated with my inability to be beautiful and popular, like she'd been as a teenager. *I don't understand you, why would you want to look like this, wear these clothes?* She felt it was more important that I knew how to apply eyeliner correctly, than to explain basic biology to me, meaning that when I got my first period, at school no less, I thought I was dying.

The humiliation of having to leave the classroom with blood running down my legs took months to fade. Teenagers are so unforgiving, so relentless in their need to be cruel to others. My locker even now still had the odd sanitary towel stuck on it, or tampons were thrown at me.

She'd try to take me shopping, get me to try on tiny, pleated miniskirts and tight sweaters, knee-high boots. She'd take me to the beauty counter for makeovers. But when we got home, I'd scrub my face until it was pink and painful, pull on my baggy jeans and my black band hoodies. *You're no daughter of mine, all I do is try to help you and look at you – it's like you want to be awkward, ugly.* She'd scream it at me, and I'd silently head up to the privacy of my room, blast out Shirley Manson, Courtney Love, Dolores O'Riordan.

The women I saw everywhere – and the men who wanted them – were all like Mama, and Uncle John. And no matter how hard I tried at school, the good grades I achieved, the teachers' praise, none of that seemed to matter to them, only how I looked. Beauty was the only currency Mama cared about. And my baseline value, according to her, was low. If you're told something often enough, you believe it. I felt broken, faulty, weird. Eventually I only wanted to be around other people who were broken, hurting. People like me. It's much easier to have a relationship with someone like yourself – not fun, granted, but easy.

But Jake was my complete opposite. He never thought I was broken, he told me that the cracks were so the light could get in. I can't remember not knowing him. When you live on the same street, there's never a beginning. His brother was the golden boy, sporty, on a scholarship to the local grammar. Always mowing someone's lawn, washing the car, out front where his mother could revel in the praise. Jake was the opposite. Skulking down the road to the bus stop, skateboarding home from school, headphones on, avoiding eye contact. Something changed though, the year I turned sixteen. And suddenly, all I wanted was him. He made me hope for better. That anything was possible, with him.

Back then, the light from his room down the street was a lighthouse in the night, pulling me into his safe harbour. He used to play his guitar, when he thought no one could hear. But I heard. He'd leave his window open, and I'd listen to him, understanding that he was also trapped and bored, waiting for life to begin.

It didn't take long for watching each other to become talking to each other, to become kissing each other. To become everything to each other. Soon we were everywhere, all the time as much as we could, always secretly. Snatched seconds, minutes, hours. Even though we were in different classes at school, we managed heated looks in the corridors, snatched kisses behind the lockers. It was never enough. How could it be?

People write off first love in a very patronising way. As if feelings when you're fifteen mean less than feelings when you're forty-five. I know what they say about teenagers, but it wasn't just about lust. It was the look on his face when he sang for me, or when he saw the scars Mama had given me. He winced the first time, pressed a finger to the small red twists running up my side, normally hidden by my school uniform.

It was ages ago, I said, *it was an accident*. But I could tell from his face, as much as he tried to disguise the pity, that his mother would never fall asleep in bed with a cigarette. These days social services would be involved, and Mama would be watched, supported. But back then, it was easy to cover things up, for her to say I'd been playing with matches, even though she'd put them on a high shelf.

Jake was the only person who could see through me, see how I needed help. When he closed his eyes, the trapped wail of his singing set me free. It was difficult though, our love. I wasn't used to it, to be able to trust someone that much. It made me vulnerable. It scared me. He was my every breath, in each heartbeat, each fingerprint and skin cell and hair I shed, ingrained in my every thought. I didn't know where he ended and I began.

We planned out our lives together, despite our age. We agreed to stick out school then go to university together and then... *then we'll be free*. To live without Alice, without Uncle John and Mama and the whole nest of vipers. He changed his school schedule so we both took IT and Art. But the day I knew for sure he was the one, was the day Uncle John's shed burned down. What Jake had done – this symbol of his loyalty – was clear, despite a box of matches being found in my room and the parental accusations that followed. Nothing was ever proven though, not least because I had nothing to do with it.

Jake, Alice and I watched the shed burn from Alice's room – the sides collapsing in, the dark, oily smoke, hazing the night sky, staining the navy blue into black, obscuring the moon.

Alice was playing her usual games with Jake, flicking and twirling her hair, trying to sit on his lap. He caught my eye and mouthed *help me* over her head, nudged her hand off his leg. I hadn't told her we were together. But she could sense tension between us, like a shark scenting blood. She didn't really want him, she just didn't want me to have him.

Alice whined that she wanted to smoke. Jake patted his pockets, shook his head then resumed flicking through his magazine. He often looked at me though, the glint of his eyes darting my way when he thought I wasn't looking. Every time I met his gaze, I lit up like the shed. He would swallow and his sallow skin would flush.

'Let's go, guys. I need a smoke. Now.'

We snuck out amid the chaos. The park was empty.

'I'm going for a pee,' I said.

Eventually, Jake did the same. Alice was oblivious. She got what she'd come for, drifting away in a cloud of smoke.

Jake found me waiting for him in a clearing. In the darkness, there was no moon, all I saw was a boy-shaped shadow, the hunch of his shoulders, the awkward way he wanted me.

The night before, out the window at 3am, he had sung "Creep" to me.

I pinned him up against a tree. I sang "Creep" back to him, told him I was his weirdo, felt his mouth quirk in a smile as I pressed my lips to his. I kissed each of his fingers, inhaled the reek of kerosene rising off them. He told me then he'd die for me, he'd do anything for me.

"You already have."

"Guys... where are you? You've been ages..."

I sent Jake in Alice's direction and then I appeared on the other side of the clearing.

She'd cosied up to him and coerced his jacket from him.

"Brrrrrrr it's so cold!" She stumbled against him and sleepily batted her lashes.

He bit his lip, looked at me but I nodded and smiled. *This isn't real. If she had any idea of what we're really doing, she'd try to take him in a flash. This way, if we pretend he's into it, she'll be less interested and won't ever suspect the truth.*

Even so, I clenched my jaw, bunched my hands into fists as she entwined his fingers with hers. *Not now*, I tell myself.

It's another late night, after work. Ollie is out somewhere again, I don't know where. I know I should do something about it. I don't want to pull that thread though, not tonight.

Instead, I'm back on everyone's favourite social media stalking site. With all these memories resurfacing since I've been messaging Alice... something in me just needs to know, to see. I guess you could call it closure.

I can't believe they're married. I can't believe he's hers. After all our history, she's the one person I'd never guess Jake would go for. But maybe she really has changed – or maybe he has? Even all these years later, it hurts to see them together. I guess, for me, he was the one that got away. My first love. I have tried to stay away from these pictures for my own sanity, but my curiosity has got the better of me at last.

He's the type to hate social media. He never liked having his photo taken, even back then. My private introvert. He doesn't even have a Facebook profile I discover, but when I search for him on Instagram, I find a thumbnail of a tattoo alongside his initials and his date of birth. His account is locked. Of course it is. He's got a handful of followers and isn't following anyone.

I don't think twice about requesting to follow him. He'll remember me, I hope.

I remember us talking about tattoos – he wanted a full sleeve, but his mother wouldn't allow it. I wonder if that tattoo is his? It must be. Did he get that sleeve? I bet it looks incredible. Ollie doesn't have any tattoos, what with his needle-phobia. He'd look awful with one anyway. He once said he'd get a tribal mandala on his calf. I can't think of anything more basic.

I bet Jake's is different, I bet he had his done as soon as he left home. When I knew him, he got a nose ring and his mum hit the roof. His family were constantly buying the fanciest car or stereo or TV or bit of tech that was fashionable. His mum was covered in designer labels and they bragged constantly. Behind closed doors it was another story, though. I wasn't the only one trying to escape. I hope he did. I hope he's happy now, even with her.

I wonder when they got together – how. She only ever wanted him because he was mine. I can't see the attraction for her once I was out of the picture. And I can't imagine it started before then. I go back to Facebook and trace back the pictures of the two of them, but they only go back ten years or so. I've ended up with more questions than I started with. And now I have a new notification.

Jake McDonald has requested to follow you.

As I press accept, Ollie's key scrapes in the lock.
"Sweetheart?"
I hide my iPad under a pillow and walk out into the hallway. I'll leave my trip down memory lane for another day.

TEN

NOW

"What's this?"

It's like he wanted me to see the message – Ollie can't be that stupid. He comes out of the bathroom in a fragrant cloud of Aramis, with a mint green towel wrapped around his waist.

"What's what?"

He's over by the drawers, picking out boxers and socks. The counsellor is due in an hour and he needs time to select the right "I love my wife" outfit, but his expression is cheerful. It's bred into him, that confidence, the ability to know the exact right thing to wear and say, to hold a room in the palm of his hand – whether it's one person or one hundred people.

"This!"

"Evie, I have no idea what you're talking about."

I throw the phone at him and it lands with a thump at his feet.

"Hey! What was that for?"

"Why don't you ask 'C'?"

It's only a brief message – he seems to have sent her photos and she's replied with a smiley face. I hope he's not stupid enough to have sent her any nudes.

"Evie... it's not what you think."

He follows me into the bathroom, pulling his T-shirt on. He's started wearing fitted tops recently, all the best to show off his not-so dad bod.

"It's only a friend from the climbing wall. Cassie."

I want to see the picture he sent but I'm not going to stoop that low.

"Fine. If you say so."

He shakes his head at me and snatches his phone up, grabs his jeans and heads downstairs.

I know exactly who Cassie is. One time I picked him up from the wall and saw them chatting afterwards, all sweaty and smiley. She's tagged herself in some of his and Ben's pics too.

He should be embarrassed, being so obvious. She's a brunette, petite, slim – mid-twenties at a guess. What she sees in my husband and Ben is anyone's guess.

"Nothing's going to hurt you, boo." I pat my tiny bump as I step into the shower. The nausea is unrelenting again – I thought it was supposed to get better around now? I can't eat until after midday and even then it's just popsicles and saltines. I would kill for a Calippo or some Ribena.

I comfort myself with thoughts of the counselling session and the knowledge that my baby is safe and growing well. *Cassie is no one, I'm his wife, that's all that matters.*

"Why is she doing a house visit?"

"It's her 'thing' according to Nina. She sees quite a few celebrities and I guess they don't want to get caught going to her office."

"But we could go in."

"Her assistant said she was in the area and could she come to us?"

"I think it's weird."

"Not as weird as sending photos to women who aren't your wife."

"It wasn't like that."

"Wasn't it?"

"No. She wanted to know how the climbing session went, that's all."

"If you say so."

"I don't like how you're fixated on me being the bad guy here. You have guy friends, I have girl friends."

"Who are my guy friends?"

"Um... Ben?"

"He's not my friend, he's yours."

"Freddie?"

"He's my colleague and he's gay." At that the door chime rings out. "Saved by the bell."

Ollie rolls his eyes at me as he goes to welcome our guest.

Dr Lucinda – as she asks us to call her – is not what I expected. I'd looked her up online and read all the reviews and testimonials I could find, but in the flesh she's so intense.

She has a cut-glass Boston accent, proper WASP, all sleek chignon and pastel cashmere.

She greets us both warmly, clasping our hands in both of hers as she shakes them, telling us what a pleasure it is to meet us and how beautiful our home is.

Her voice is quiet and, despite the refinement, husky, intimate – making you lean in close to hear her better.

Her eyes come as a shock though – steel grey and not a hint of warmth, even as her lips smile – just like Alice.

Nina's words come back to me. *Nothing gets past her, trust me.*

We settle in the sitting room on the low sofas, where I've prepped the table with fresh glasses and chilled bottles of water. There's lemon and ice in tubs with tongs as well.

"If you want something else – tea, coffee... something stronger?" Ollie asks.

"Babe, she's not here for—"

"Water is fine for me, thank you."

She's taken the wingback chair in front of the window, which casts her in a slight shadow, her legs crossed to the left. She removes a slim notebook and a Montblanc pen from her bag.

When I look over at Ollie, he raises his eyebrows at me and then puts his hand on my thigh – ostensibly to offer up a public display of affection to the goddess of marriage counselling lest she judge us harshly – but also to still its trembling.

It's very annoying that even now I tap my leg in moments of stress, I really hoped I'd grow out of it. In the office it's easily hidden under a table or by walking around a room – but here, I feel open to scrutiny and I'm not so sure I'll pass muster.

Dr Lucinda takes a sip of water and carefully places her glass back on the coaster in front of her on the table.

"So – Evie, Ollie – would you like to tell me a little bit more about why we're here today?"

Ollie and I look at each other and my hand goes to my belly.

"Shall I—"

"Yeah, go for it."

"Well, we're pregnant."

"Congratulations." Again, with the smile that doesn't quite reach her eyes.

"And... we've had some... challenges and I guess I thought it would be good for us to resolve those, so we'd be in the best position to have a baby. I want everything to be perfect." I squeeze Ollie's hand and smile up at him.

"That sounds very thoughtful of you, a baby is a huge life change and, even for the most secure couples, can cause tension and rifts. I'm interested to hear your use of the word perfect,

Evie, I'd like to come back to that later. Ollie – how about you –
what do you hope to get out of these sessions?"

He starts at this, takes his hand out of mine and runs it
through his hair, sighs.

"Yeah, same as Evie really. Just want to make sure we're all
good before the screaming starts – the baby, that is!" Dr
Lucinda politely laughs along with him before making some
notes.

"Okay. Thank you. I think it's always good to be really clear
and upfront about what our objective is here – and it's so great
that you two are aligned on that. What's often slightly harder
though, is seeing if the challenges you – Evie – alluded to are
perceived the same way by Ollie. Could you expand a little bit
on them, Evie? It's good to be clear what we're dealing with
here."

Wow. I see what Nina meant. I take a sip of water – much
like I do at work for similar reasons, to buy me some thinking
time. *How to phrase this...*

"I think that we have... trust issues. Sometimes I feel like
Ollie isn't as committed to this relationship as I am... anymore. I
know we've been together a long time, but it feels like recently,
he's been distracted and unavailable." I don't add my big fear –
that he'll leave me for one of his flings to raise the baby alone.
Next to me Ollie mutters "ouch" under his breath, takes his arm
off the back of the sofa and leans away from me.

I remember all too well Mama telling me how hard having a
newborn was. How I didn't stop screaming, how she didn't
sleep for months. How she was on her knees, broken with it all.
The isolation, the loneliness. *I had no family, Evie, no one over
here to help me. I was all alone. Never let that happen to you.
Ever.*

Part of me really pities her. Back then, being a single
mother, no one around to help – with limited financial support.
I don't know how she did it, to be honest. And I was unplanned

– and she was so young, only twenty-one – *the peak of my modelling career, Evie! It all collapsed after you.* She did a shoot when she was heavily pregnant with me, it was everywhere at the time, her body, naked, silhouetted, bump, boobs, legs. She still got royalties from it when I was a teenager. But that was the last of it, apparently. Her career was over when I arrived. All her friends melted away.

So I am determined to do whatever it takes to stay together with Ollie, during this pregnancy. To raise this baby together. I will not turn into my mother. And I will shower this baby with love. I will always be there for them.

"Thank you, Evie, for being so open and honest. I know that can be hard, but it's so good that you feel comfortable to share. Because this is a safe space. It's a place for you to both move forward.

"Ollie, what do you feel the issues are in your marriage?"

He takes a big gulp of water too. I learned all my best delaying tactics from him.

"My wife... I've always felt that she's keeping me at arm's length. I mean, she's a private person and always has been. And I know she has trust issues. But these days it's more than that. She doesn't talk to anyone about how she really feels. Never has."

He looks at me and shakes his head.

"I feel like there's something she's not telling me. There's a part of her that's off limits to me, and it's hard, you know? Knowing your wife doesn't love you totally, no matter what you do. She's paranoid too... even this morning, she wanted to check my phone messages, worrying I'm cheating on her with every woman we know."

I have to stop myself rolling my eyes at that.

Dr Lucinda scribbles in her notebook, the indigo scrawl almost luminous – from here I can see the words *trust* and *commitment* underlined.

"I can see there is a yin and yang to your thoughts about the relationship. Ollie, you feel your wife doesn't trust you and is withholding love. Evie, you feel your husband is untrustworthy. Both of these say more about you both as individuals than it does about your marriage.

"If we only see these issues through the lens of your relationship then, Ollie, you'll always be feeling like you need to prove yourself to Evie – and equally, you, Evie, will always be second-guessing everything. Trust is the glue to any successful relationship. But to work on that, we first need to look at you as individuals.

"Ollie, why do you feel Evie is withholding from you and have you felt people have withheld love from you in the past?

"Evie, why don't you trust Ollie and where have you learned that those you love can betray you – where has your fear come from?"

We sit on the sofa in stunned silence. It's as if she's lobbed a hand grenade into the room, her analysis more precise than a surgeon's knife.

"This is a lot to think about, I know. Therapy and marriage counselling is not for the faint-hearted. You need to commit to working through these issues but, I promise you, things can be so much better when you put the effort in. But that's crucial here – your commitment. It's not going to be easy. Things that are shared in these sessions – both as individuals and in the couple sessions – will be hard for you to hear. You'll need to sit with the uncomfortable truths, not only about each other – but about yourself. It takes resilience and patience – and kindness, with yourselves and each other, to work through it."

She pulls a binder from her tan leather tote and places it in front of us, opening it up to reveal two copies of the same document, marked with pink sticky tabs where we need to sign.

"Do... do we need our lawyer to look at these?" Always business, Ollie, thinking with his wallet.

"No. This is not for me. This is for you both, as a sign of your commitment to this process and to each other. I want you to agree what you think success looks like after these sessions, write it on these sheets and sign it. I want you to be working towards the same goal, even if that goal isn't to stay together."

Ollie and I look at each other, but he speaks first.

"I don't think we can sign this right now – I certainly need some time to reflect on this."

"That's not a problem. These are for you to keep and bring back to the next session for us to discuss the objective you've agreed on."

"There's homework?" Typical of my husband, wanting the easy route. I frown at him, he mouths *sorry* at me.

"You don't *have* to do it, Ollie. But it's worth considering what that says about your commitment to this."

My husband, not easily ashamed, takes the file off the table and places it on the sofa between us, silenced.

A wave of exhaustion hits me. "So, um... what do we do for the rest of the session? That was a lot to take in, already I feel wrung out and I need to be careful, this is a high-risk pregnancy."

"I'd like to spend the remaining time hearing a little more about your backgrounds and how you met – only briefly as we'll go into more detail in the individual sessions. It helps me build a baseline picture. Evie, would you be comfortable to go first?"

"Um...sure. I... how far back do you want me to go?"

"Perhaps if you can tell me a little about your childhood? Your background?"

"I grew up just outside London. It was just me and my mum."

"And your father?"

"Never met him. And my mother never told me anything about him either – before you ask."

Her pen scritches across a fresh page.

Sorry, honey, Mama used to say, *I was hangin' around with a coupla guys back then. Coulda been either of them. But, baby, why do you want a daddy? Is your mama not enough for you?*

"And how did that make you feel, growing up without a father?"

"It didn't make me feel anything. You can't miss what you never had."

"Is an absence of feeling not a feeling in itself?"

"No, I don't think so." *Besides, I'm pretty sure having a father wouldn't have made the blindest bit of difference to what happened to me.*

Ollie stops flicking through the papers in the binder and pats my leg.

"Okay, then. And what about your wider family – your mother's family?"

"My mum was from Texas, but her family disowned her when she got pregnant with me. She'd run off to be a model in the 1970s, ended up in London trying to get discovered, that was bad enough. But a single mum too – that was unforgivable."

"So, you never met them – they never came to your wedding, nothing?"

"Nope. No family, just me and Mama."

"Darling, what about those people you told me about – the ones you grew up next door to? You said they were like family... they were this couple that had a kid your age?"

Ollie knows a little bit about Alice.

"We weren't that close."

"You told me you practically lived in their house. You went on holiday with them and all sorts."

"We did, but only a couple of times, not a lot."

I know Dr Lucinda will be drinking in this little discussion. It's not what we say, it's what we *don't* say.

I look at the time on my phone. "So, I met Ollie at university, we were both on the same course – Law. We bonded over the terrible photocopier there. I mean, this was well before everything was digital."

Ollie smiles, I know he's thinking about what happened after that. The tame little version of our relationship I've given her.

"And that was it?"

"Yes, pretty much. We were inseparable from the start, weren't we, babe?"

We were. Suddenly, I wonder where the Evie who Ollie fell in love with went, and if she'll ever come back. She certainly wouldn't put up with a cheating husband.

"What do you think bonded you?"

Things that I can't say in polite conversation. Things that Dr Lucinda looks like she'd never understand.

"We had similar interests." Ollie winks at me. "Liked the same kind of music."

The next time, after the photocopier, was in a club. He'd come with another girl. I'm not proud of myself. I know I behaved badly back then. But it was worth it.

"But what *bonded* you? What made it more than just a fling?"

This time we look at each other. I can't tell what he's thinking.

"She got me. She wasn't like the girls I went to school with. She didn't talk about ponies and skiing – and she didn't want to move to the country and turn into her mother. She wasn't at university to find a husband."

All those Rebeccas and Sarahs and Emmas, identical in their diesel jeans and silky handkerchief tops. Although I know now that it's not really a compliment, to be told that you're not like the other girls. I'm cross with myself that I fell for it then.

"I wanted to reinvent myself at university," I say. *And I did.*

When I meet Ollie's eyes now, there's an almost audible crack of electricity.

Lucinda watches us, head swivelling like she's at a tennis match, and then checks her watch.

"I appreciate this detail. Perhaps, Ollie, you might tell us a little about your childhood before we wrap up?"

"I grew up in south west London – Wimbledon. My parents are still together. Went to a half-decent school and then on to uni – not Oxford though, much to the parents' disappointment. I mean, it's all good really, I don't know what to tell you... I've got a younger brother, he lives with his boyfriend in Australia now, and does 'something in media'."

He makes air quote marks with his fingers and I cringe internally. He struggles so much with his parents, always disappointing them.

"And what did your parents do?"

"Dad was a banker and Mum looked after us. Standard, really. I mean, we didn't really worry about stuff. I saw my grandparents pretty regularly, aunts and uncles too."

"I see. I'm interested to know, given your different upbringings, what you saw in each other?"

Well, it's quite simple. We were both obsessed with Ollie. Not sure that's the answer she wants though. And I want to know what Ollie says here.

"It's hard to explain. Sometimes there's a connection, unspoken."

"Eyes meeting across a photocopier?"

"Yes... sort of."

I was driven and focused – I was determined to escape where I came from and so was he. But mostly he wanted me to start with because I didn't want him, not for anything meaningful. He wasn't used to that.

I jump into save him.

"When I went to university I was adamant I wasn't going to fall for some boy. I wanted to have some fun, yes, but I wanted to get what I was paying for. I didn't want to live how I had growing up. I didn't want to be reliant on handouts from a man. I didn't want a job, I wanted a career, I wanted to excel at something, be better than everyone else."

Dr Lucinda is scribbling away again, even though we only have another five minutes. She'll be interrogating me at the next session, I suspect.

"I wasn't at university for the social side. I didn't want to make friends. I'd tried that before and been burned. So, when I met Ollie, it wasn't meant to be anything serious."

I'm looking at Lucinda, but I can feel Ollie's eyes on me. From his hand on my leg, I know what he's thinking about.

"Why do you think it turned serious then?"

I'm scared to answer these questions honestly, make myself vulnerable – but if I don't, nothing will change. Sometimes you have to lose a battle to win a war.

"I – we – fell in love."

When I look at Ollie, he's nodding.

"I didn't want Evie only at certain times, I wanted her all the time. And it didn't wear off. Not after a month, or six months – or a year."

We must be out of time by now. It's hard to stop my leg jittering again, a wave of nausea passes over me and I reach for my water.

Dr Lucinda checks her watch again and leans forward.

"I think we'll stop there. Thank you both for sharing so much with me. I know it's not easy to be honest but already you're making progress—" Suddenly my glass tips.

"Oh goodness, I'm so sorry! Let me get you a cloth," I cry.

The water has soaked our file and caught the edge of Dr Lucinda's skirt.

"Honestly, please don't worry, it's fine."

Ollie shakes his head but smiles. "She's so jumpy these days. I blame the hormones."

I smile tightly, grit my teeth.

After we've closed the door behind her, he starts.

"What was that all about?"

"What was what?"

"Your little act with the water?"

"I don't know what you're talking about. Why do you always think the worst of me?"

"And you don't of me? Whatever, Evie. You acting like this, isn't healthy. For someone who wanted a baby so much, you're the one causing it loads of stress. What kind of mother are you?"

We're back in the kitchen now. He's pouring a glass of wine.

"You're such a bastard. Don't you even care how that makes me feel?"

"I didn't want to try again. I told you that. And I'm not cut out for this... this parenting stuff. I liked our life the way it was."

"You mean you like *your life* the way it was. What about what I want?"

"Oh, come on. You've got what you wanted – you always do."

"You think I wanted to be here, miles from home, no real friends, no family, my career stalled?"

He promised me that our move stateside was temporary, *max five years, darling.* But that became ten and now it's nearly fifteen years and I've hopped consultancies as much as I can but where we live, options are limited.

"If your career stalled, that's your own fault, messing about with IVF treatments and taking time off. I told you, these people don't give a shit about feminism. So don't blame your crappy career trajectory on me."

"You wouldn't even have a career if your daddy hadn't bankrolled it. After you failed your degree, you couldn't even get a job in the post room at one of the banks."

He puts his wine glass down on the side and walks away.

"At least I know who my dad is. At least my mum wasn't a total *whore.*"

"What did you just say?"

"You heard me."

"You asshole!"

When the glass hits the wall behind him it makes a satisfying crunch. Even if the wine stain will be an absolute nightmare to remove.

"You're crazy, you know that?" He disappears down the corridor and the study door shuts behind him.

I didn't mean to throw the glass. I'm so much moodier recently, Ollie wasn't wrong. But he can't say things like that and get away with that. My mother was far from perfect, but what he called her was unforgivable.

I end up having a bath and catching up on *Succession*. My phone chimes periodically – I've messaged the girls for recommendations for good cleaning companies. I might not have much in common with them but they always know the right people for the job.

> Hey, Evie, hadn't heard from you in a while. Just thought I'd say hi.

It's Alice. I've not spoken to her in a couple of weeks. The last thing we talked about was Brighton. I wonder if she's been thinking about things back then too? I wonder if that's what made her think of me? Or maybe he's told her I'm following him on Instagram. I don't think he would though, somehow.

I've pored over every picture on his grid. Not that there are many. Typical of him. Mostly blurry shots of food or drinks, the odd sporting activity, none of his kids or his wife. And nothing in the last six months or so.

Not like Alice, who seems to be adding new stories almost every day now.

Hey, right back atcha. How's things on your side?

Not too bad. Bored out of my skull at work though. Kids driving me mad. Same old same old. You?

Well, I threw a glass of Rioja at my husband's head this evening...

She sends a cry-laugh emoji before typing her reply.

Gotta confess to considering doing the same a few times, but kudos on actually following through.

Jake and I never fought, back then. He was the alkaline to my acid. When I tried to make him argue with me, he would find a way to pull me out of my funk, to make me see that it wasn't me against him, it was the world against us.

Yeah, kinda surprised at myself.

LOL the Evie I remember wouldn't think twice about throwing things at men.

Ouch. I wasn't that bad, I don't think? I had a lot going on. She was in her ivory tower the whole time, oblivious. I had reasons.

The Evie you remember is long gone.

I do miss her sometimes though. Well, parts of her.

Shame. I quite liked her.

It didn't always seem that way. Alice only liked things that were useful and or beautiful. Sometimes I was both, mostly I was neither.

We all like stupid things as teens. Sun-in, butterfly clips, frosted lipstick.

Come on, Heather Shimmer was the best shade ever!

Not for all of us.

I favoured Black Cherry, Rouge Noir knock offs, trips to Camden Market in north London to pick up clunky boots, fishnet tights, cobwebbed tops. Alice never came with – TopShop was more her scene, spending hours in its labyrinth floors, then going for milkshakes in McDonalds.

True. So why the wine throwing? Unless that's some new cool thing you're doing out there?

He was rude about my mother. Only I'm allowed to do that.

I don't know why I'm being honest here with Alice. It's like a compulsion to come clean, to tell her everything, the way I used to. She doesn't need to know all this. I wouldn't normally tell anyone this.

Okay...

We're having a few problems and it was the last straw. Plus, I'm pregnant so you know – hormones...

Shit, I didn't mean to tell her that. I don't want her to tell Jake.

Oh my god – that's amazing news! Congratulations! How many weeks are you?

Just gone twelve weeks.

Ahhhhh so you've had your scan. All okay?

Yeah, all good thanks.

How are you feeling?

It's a good question. I feel like I can tell her the truth about this. She's far away enough not to judge me. Or for me not to care if she does. I sink deeper in the bath, top up the hot water, and feel my muscles begin to relax.

Fed up. Sick. Scared.

That's normal.

Is it though? I wanted this baby so much and now I don't know how I can do another six months of spots and aches and heartburn and mood swings.

We've not spoken in years and now she knows things I haven't told anyone else.

Honestly, all that glowing mama stuff is total bullshit. I hated being pregnant. Hated the lack of energy, losing my looks, my sleep, my figure. And don't get me started on birth.

I don't want to even think about giving birth. It doesn't seem physically possible that something so big can come out of something so small. And I'm not good with pain.

But you loved them when you had them right?

Grey dots start and stop again. The bath water is cooling. I shouldn't have had it so hot in the first place, but I'm fed up with the pregnancy police telling me what to do.

Yes... most of the time.

Yeah?

It's hard to explain. I love them but there are times when I don't particularly like them. No one tells you how hard it is, how relentless. Not everyone is cut out for this.

Mama sure wasn't. Leaving me alone when I was maybe twelve with twenty quid for pizza and disappearing for the weekend more than once. The times I put her to bed as she sobbed about the mistakes she'd made, the house stinking sweet and smoky.

Your kids look so happy in your pics though – I'm sure you're doing a great job.

I don't actually know what she's like as a mum. But I know that this is what she needs to hear.

Yeah, they're fine. But me, not so much. Everything is just... it's a lot right now. Everything is a lot.

But you seemed so well at that conference?

Which one?

The tech one. A few months ago. You were with a law firm?

OMG – are you kidding? You were there? Why didn't you say hi?

Oops. Forgot I hadn't told her that. I couldn't speak to her back then, though. What would I have said?

Had to dash off – but you were great.

Thanks. Didn't feel it. It's all so fake, that whole have it all, do it all schtick. I'm juggling plates like crazy and to be honest some of them are crashing. But the thing is you can't tell anyone, or they'll tell you it's your own fault. You need to work smarter or plan better or use this app or lean in or step up. But shit... I can't keep up with everything.

I'm taken aback by her raw honesty. I thought she'd be all humble-brag and waving off the comments but really knowing how good she was.

You're a role model for so many women though, Alice – seeing you up there. Kids, work, husband. You're doing it. You're living the dream!

Hah, thanks. Not sure it's quite the dream I thought it'd be. I haven't slept properly in ten years, my tits look like oranges in socks, my husband doesn't fancy me anymore, the PTA are like the mafia on HRT and I think I'm going to be made redundant soon.

I don't know what to think about her comment about Jake. She looks great and she knows it. She must know that I know they're together – that I've seen her wedding pictures. Already I'm on the back foot, with her games. Nothing's changed. Or maybe it's the hormones, making me paranoid.

Well from the outside, it looks like you're smashing it.

It's a pathetic response and I know it. It's all I have for her right now. I didn't expect this vulnerability. This didn't exist all those years ago. Or, if it did, I didn't see it.

I guess so...

Alice, you should look at everything you've achieved and be super proud of it. It's amazing!

I am, I am...

I feel briefly sorry for her before I remember how she has three children, a gorgeous husband, an amazing job. She should be able to see how lucky she is – she's not stuck with an unfaithful man-child and pregnant, in a job where they write her off because she doesn't have a penis.

We exchange a few more messages, but it's clear we've run out of things to talk about.

She says she has to go – one of the kids needs something, unspecified – and we leave it at that.

Funny how it's come to this, seeing her at the conference, becoming a client, work bringing us back together after all these years.

The last time we saw each other – not at the conference, but as teenagers – changed everything. Set us on this trajectory. Me to that other place, her onwards and upwards. I don't believe in fate, but something has brought us back together, and I'm not letting go of her so easily this time.

ELEVEN

Ollie wasn't wrong. I have kept things from him. But to be honest I've kept them from myself too. There was a time, early on when we were first together, that I might have told him, but it was never the right time and then it was too late, I couldn't tell him. I couldn't find the words. And even if I did, what difference would it make? I couldn't bear his kindness, or worse, his pity.

The Evie who those things happened to – who did those things – that's not the Evie he knows. I liked the way I looked in his eyes when we got together – the admiration, the desire. He praised my strength, my drive. And I fed off that power. I didn't need looking after, I wasn't waiting for a prince, I was my own salvation – and more.

But I guess over the years, as he hears me tell the same stories over and over again, he's spotted the gaps. And, to paraphrase someone famous, the gaps are where the truth gets out.

Then

Miss me?

Uncle John had a shed in the garden, ostensibly for doing DIY and gardening. But really it was a hiding place. He had folding chairs, a picnic rug, and a radio. Every Saturday morning he'd go out there. Mum and Aunty Meredith were at the tennis club, Alice with them, being coached in the fine art of looking good in white Aertex and pleated skirts and flirting with wealthy boys. I wasn't invited.

The shed smelt of whisky and cigarettes. Uncle John was always drunk and clumsy.

The shift in our relationship started small. At first it was invites to come and sit in the shed, have a hot chocolate, bring a book, keep him company as he tinkered with his seedlings and re-potted various plants. We had a little routine where I'd make us some crumpets or toast for elevenses.

What would I do without my Evie-Lynn? Such a treat.

I know, it seems weird – why would I, the moodiest teenager alive, want to sit in a cold shed with a middle-aged man? But this was before Jake, before I learned that love didn't have to hurt, before I knew I deserved better. And Uncle John knew that, as a teenage girl, all you want is for someone to recognise how special you are, how different from the other girls you are. Now I know that's a red flag. But back then, back then it was... everything.

Uncle John suckered me in with music, my true love. He had an old radio with a cassette deck and he'd play me old bootlegs – illegal recordings of Nirvana's set at Reading in 1992. Radiohead performing "Creep" live. The first time I heard Oasis was with him, in that shed, music making fragments of gold in the air, shivering down my spine. He'd take a break, sit next to me. Ask me what I thought about the bassline, the chords, if the lyrics were too much. He'd tell me how smart I was, how lucky some boy was going to be, how beautiful I was.

And although I know, in hindsight, it sounds creepy, it didn't feel that way at the time. Uncle John had something far more dangerous, he had charisma. Even at work I've never met anyone so charming, so handsome. The way his eyes crinkled when he smiled at me, when he played me a new song, it felt like he was offering up something special just for me. He made me feel unique, as if I was the only person in the world, right then, that he wanted to talk to. As if I was the only person who understood him. These days I can see what he was doing, the game he was playing, the way he'd waited years for me.

I don't remember the first time, or even the fifth time. It just became how it was.

Transactional. I had something and he wanted it. Even if he knew I had value in a way I was only just starting to discover. He'd mould me into the shape of his desire, lie me down beneath him on the picnic rug, the music still playing. I can't listen to those songs now. Even when it was happening, he was always avuncular, pretending that it was nothing out of the ordinary. But sometimes the mask slipped.

Once, he asked about my scars,

Burned myself making dinner.

In the rare times we talked like this, he told me he saw me for who I was, that no one got me like he could, that he could see through to the darkness inside me – didn't he know I was just like him?

Always, to clear up after, he handed me a washcloth, watched me get up carefully, as if I were made of glass, filled up with water that I mustn't spill.

And you know, the thing is, he wasn't the only one. I wasn't the only one. Everywhere I looked this sort of thing seemed to be happening. The dentist Alice and I used to see – praising us for our lack of cavities:

I can tell you brush with fluoride.

And then he'd put his hand on my bare leg, my summer shorts riding high, and loom over me again.

Open wide please. Even now, sausages remind me of the taste of his fingers in my mouth.

Or the catcalling from building sites, the beeping from vans. The warnings about walking home alone. The stories about teachers and students. Sex was everywhere. Men were everywhere. Nothing and nowhere was safe. Not even home.

TWELVE

NOW

The notification comes through when I'm in a client meeting. An innocuous white envelope. I didn't often message people on Instagram, there were only a handful of possible senders. I knew though, that it was him.

Hi

Hi yourself, I type furiously, and then turn back to the meeting.

My phone vibrates again within seconds.

How are you?

What to say?

"Evie? Is there something more interesting happening?" Freddie and Rupert are staring at me. "We were discussing when your secondment in London should start."

I put my phone back in my bag and pay attention for the rest of the meeting, but Rupert glares at me periodically. I know what he's going to say afterwards. Reminding me about calibration and bonuses and how I've been trusted with this project.

But I'm still not sure I'm even going to London. I've not told them about the pregnancy yet. Can I agree to go and back out afterwards? If I do, Rupert will kill me and I'll blow any chances of promotion I have left.

I can't think about it right now. After the meeting I scurry back to my desk, ditch my laptop and head out for some lunch, and check my phone.

It's still there. His message, asking me how I am. As if we'd only spoken yesterday, or a week ago.

I'm pregnant.

I need him to know this straight off the bat. That my messaging him is platonic. I would never. No matter our past. Dakota and Ronnie are always going on about setting boundaries. They'd be proud of me, I think.

Congratulations?

Thanks. How are you?

Thinking about you.

My heart skips a beat.

I don't know what to say.

I know it's been a long time, Evie.

You don't even know me, not anymore.

Are you sure?

I see you finally got a tattoo

I did indeed.

He sends another picture through. He does have a full sleeve. Intricate vintage style tattoos, pin-ups and clocks and hearts and skulls, woven together with vines.

Wow. Bet that hurt.

A little...

I don't know what to say but I can't put my phone down.
Where are you? he asks me.

At work – well, grabbing lunch currently.

Wait... where are you?

The US – Boston.

Wow, okay. It's nighttime here.

Not here – obviously 😊

Send me a picture.

Of what?

Anything – your view, your lunch, whatever you like.

Okay, hold on.

I snap a picture fast, don't give myself time to think about it too much.

Nice bagel!

I wonder if he noticed the wedding ring on the hand holding the bagel.

It tastes good. Though I'm so fussy right now.

Have you been sick much?

A little.

That's rough. When are you due?

Six months from now.

So still early days.

Yeah, it is.

Have you got a bump? I can't imagine you pregnant.

He'll be picturing me, a lanky teenager, badly dyed black shaggy hair, chipped polish, studded bracelets, school uniform or baggy jeans and a band tee. So no, a bump won't fit his image.

I don't look the way I used to.

And then he takes my breath away.

You're still beautiful

I don't know what to say.

Thank you.

I don't tell him that I have since googled him, found his LinkedIn profile shot. He's a creative director at an ad agency now. He's grown into himself. That gangly, awkward boy, now cool, and charismatic. Neat dark stubble, short cropped hair, greying at the edges, a slight tan, setting off his green eyes. Even in a crumpled, rust coloured T-shirt, battered old jeans, his clothes hang off his 6"4' frame as if they were custom made for him. Always slight, his arms are now tight with wiry muscle, his shoulders broader, his legs long and lean. No longer the boy I knew. And he thinks I'm beautiful.

If only he knew the truth.

My phone then rings, breaking the spell. For a moment I think it's him, calling me, but it's not, it's Rupert, summoning me back to the office and demanding *a scalding hot grande Americano* on my way.

All afternoon I'm useless, accidentally deleting emails, unable to open files. When I get up to go to the bathroom I bang my hip on the door handle and spill paperwork on the floor. Eventually I tell Freddie I'm unwell and I'm going home to work there.

He looks at me, narrows his eyes.

"What's wrong with you? You'd better not be pregnant."

I shake my head, but for some reason I can't lie to Freddie and I'm sure my fiery cheeks give the game away. Even so, I head home.

But it's not the pregnancy that's thrown me.

Despite his failings, I've never cheated on Ollie. Not even come close – and it's not like I haven't had the opportunity. Working in the industry I'm in, frequent travelling, socialising, late nights... But I made my vows and I focused on the end goal – the house, the job, the kids, the lifestyle. I wasn't about to screw things up for myself over some sweaty grapple with a Patrick Bateman wannabe in a Hilton.

When I get home, I try to work. I correct the emails I sent in error, do some month-end analysis and forecasts, and prepare a deck for tomorrow. But all the while I'm pretending not to look at my phone. I tell myself to remember the time difference, that it's the middle of the night where he is, that he's asleep. And he's lying in bed next to his wife, my old friend.

There are no more messages. I pick at my supper and Ollie asks me what's wrong, offering to run me a bath or give me a shoulder massage. I blame my mood on hormones, nausea, and he gives me a hug and settles me on the sofa with another chamomile tea. I can't tell him what's really wrong.

When I wake up in the morning, I see that familiar white envelope notification. I wonder if Ollie feels like this when Cassie messages? A strange mix of guilt and excitement, adrenalin spiking his blood. I'm dizzy with anticipation, fumbling with my phone.

It's a photo of a photo. One of those images from a strip taken in a photo booth.

I'm sitting on Jake's lap, our arms wrapped around each other, as we gaze into each other's eyes, grinning like the absolute fools in love we were, back then.

I can't believe you kept this, Jake.

Of course.

We look so young.

We were so young!

I wonder if he has the full strip, the photos after this one I remember being slightly less family friendly. We couldn't keep our hands off each other. Typical teenagers in love.

And yet... and yet, I miss him despite myself, despite all the years.

Out of everyone I left behind, he is the one I regret leaving the most, the one who never hurt me, who was always on my side, had my back. Believed in me, supported me – even when I was horrible to him, when I screamed and shouted and told him to leave me alone. He stayed, steadfast, loyal.

So I have to wonder, now, how did that free-spirited boy, who loved me and hated Alice, hated what she turned me into, how did he end up being the man who married her?

For the rest of the week, we message sporadically. Photos of our views, our lunches. Stupid memes. Things to entertain and delight. I try not to read too much into it all. *I don't need to feel guilty*, I tell myself. *It's fine to reconnect with someone from my past. A bit of harmless banter is fine.* I don't think about how I'd feel if Ollie was messaging an ex, pretending I'd be cool with it. We're all adults now. But deep down I know that's part of the problem.

I don't know if it's that work is crazy this week – back-to-back calls, ten-hour days – or that Alice is also messaging me, or that Ollie and I are bickering again, but by Friday I'm worn out and my back aches. I know I need to rest. I message Ollie to tell him to sleep in the spare room. Typically, he's out partying – apparently it's someone's leaving drinks, whatever – and I don't want to be woken by him, stinking of booze and sweat, when he crashes in at silly o'clock.

But when I go to bed that night, I dream I'm on the deck of a boat.

Not a super yacht – nothing that fancy – but something still sleek and glossy, polished wood, white and chrome. I'm leaning against the railing on the stern, wind blowing in my hair, facing into the sun. We're not travelling fast, but we're going somewhere.

A man with his back to me is holding a tray of champagne. He's wearing a neat navy polo and pressed chinos. When he turns to hands me a glass of champagne, I see it's Jake. even when I resist, he presses it into my hand, won't leave me alone until I accept it.

I take a sip – because what the hell, one glass won't hurt.

I close my eyes and when I reopen them, Ollie is in front of me. He's talking but I can't hear him, he gets closer, points behind me, pulls at my hand, tries to get me to come with him. But I can't move, won't move.

I take another sip, blink again and this time Dr Lucinda is there. Half my champagne is gone. I can't hear her either, but she pulls me round and shows the clouds building on the horizon behind me, gathering fast. She tries to get me to go with her, below deck. When I won't, she passes me a life ring, but I discard it.

Another sip and this time the glass is empty. Alice is in front of me. Not Alice from the conference though. She's the Alice from school, from when I was sixteen. In immaculate uniform. She points upwards and the clouds are above us now, full and black. With the other hand she holds out an apple.

Bite it.

Although her lips don't move, her voice is in my head.

Go on.

Do it.

I blink again and she's gone. The apple is in my hand, the glass is gone. I bring the apple to my lips and bite.

I open my eyes again and this time I am awake and in bed, alone, with a pain unlike any other spearing through me. When I lift the sheet, all I see is crimson.

"I'm sorry, I'm so sorry."

I wake to the sound of Ollie's voice as he repeats himself over and over again.

"Sweetheart, you scared me so much."

And he cries into my hand, which hurts because there's something in it, a giant needle by the feel of it.

"I can't believe I nearly lost you too."

He's sobbing, big messy snotty snobs, everywhere.

I open my mouth, but all that comes out is a parched rasp.

"Oh, darling, don't try to speak, let me get you a drink."

He calls a nurse, who hurries over, presses a magic button that makes the head of the bed move up, and inserts a plastic straw into my mouth. The water is ice cold and I suck gratefully.

"Sip slowly, hun."

When she takes the beaker away, she reads from a clipboard before taking my pulse and blood pressure, checks my temperature.

"How are you feeling?"

"Um. Like I've been hit by a truck? Sore... tired."

"Do you remember what happened?"

"Kind of."

I remember crawling on my knees to the bathroom and vomiting. I remember calling Ollie, over and over and him not answering. I remember struggling downstairs, blood running down my legs, to let the paramedics in. I remember the sweet relief of a needle.

And then nothing.

"Where were you?" I look at Ollie. "I called you and you didn't pick up. I needed you."

He doesn't answer, only presses his lips together.

"What? What is it?" Tears creep into the corner of my eyes. My hand moves to my belly and I know, before the nurse tells me, her voice soft and solemn. Telling me it's very rare at this stage, as if that's any consolation.

"I'm so sorry for your loss. We've given you something for the pain and the consultant will be in to see you soon."

The irony of thinking this pain can be medicated away.

I try to roll onto my side, ignoring the twinges and muscle aches, I want to face the wall. I don't want to be here. Not again.

"Sweetheart. I should have been there. I know I should have. You have to forgive me. You do. I promise things will be different, I promise." His voice is screechy and scratchy. I'm guessing he's on his knees, he always liked a dramatic gesture.

"Mr Robinson, your wife has had a severe haemorrhage, she needs rest and quiet. In addition, we have other patients here. If you can't lower your voice, I'm going to have to ask you to leave."

The door closes.

"Darling, I'm here. Whatever you need."

He's whispering now.

How many times has he whispered to me in the dark? Making promises his body couldn't keep. Promised he only wanted me, no one else was like me, he couldn't live without me.

But words mean nothing without actions.

If someone shows you who they are, Mama once told me, *believe them the first time*.

They let me go home the next day. They explain what happened, a late miscarriage, placental rupture, haemorrhage, nothing to be done. That they basically hoovered my baby out of me. I want to fall to my knees and howl. Instead, I fold myself into the Uber Ollie has ordered. Lean my head against the window, feel nothing but numb from the neck up and the waist down.

"Straight to bed with you when we get home, okay? I'm going to wait on you hand and foot."

I let him manoeuvre me into our bed. He's replaced the sheets with brand new ones, all coordinated shades of grey and green. Like Alice's eyes. I roll over into a ball and fall away into a dream in which a little girl in a pink bathing suit and a girl in a red bathing suit run through a sunlit garden, over and over again. Every time I wake, I taste apples, and then I sink back down again.

"Darling? Can you hear me? I need to pop out to grab some stuff, are you going to be okay?"

Ollie's face looms over me, large pored and grey with stubble.

A garbled noise of assent makes its way out of me.

"I'll be quick, yeah? Like 10-15 minutes?"

He's out of the room before I can ask for a drink, a hand, painkillers, sanity.

I don't know how long I've slept for. My head feels synthetic, my mouth tastes metallic. Sounds are too bright, the sunlight is too noisy.

And then a phone starts ringing somewhere.

I flap around on the nightstand, patting aimlessly, objects clattering to the floor.

I don't look at the phone, just put it to my ear as I accept the call.

"Hey. What the hell is going on? Have you told her yet? This is freaking ridiculous. You said you'd tell her and then you go AWOL for like, three days! It's been like, months and months!"

Whoever she is, I'm pretty sure that she's drunk, or high, or both. If it's as early in the morning as I think it might be, I'm almost impressed. Or I would be, if it weren't for the fact that I've answered Ollie's phone, not mine.

"Well? Aren't you gonna say anything?"

And she disconnects. When I look at the phone, I see the caller was Cassie.

When Ollie gets back, I want to play it cool, pretend I don't know. But I can't.

Instead, when he walks in, I tell him two things: that Cassie called – to which he doesn't bat an eyelid – and that I know everything.

While he grovels and begs – and then shouts and screams and punches the wall and calls me a heartless bitch, unworthy of bearing his child – even as I stand there with blood-stained legs, I know what I need to do.

PART 2

THREE MONTHS LATER

THIRTEEN

NOW

It's been two weeks since I returned from Las Vegas – time spent finalising the divorce paperwork, negotiating with Ollie, hashing out the details. Now there's nothing left to discuss – our life together is over. I gave Ollie what he deserved and nothing more.

I'm a free woman now, I can do what I want, I tell myself, as I shove pairs of heels into another suitcase, sit on it and zip it closed.

I cast my eye around my bedroom. The blank spaces on the units where pictures and ornaments sat, now in some strangers' house. The empty wardrobe, the odd forlorn hanger still dangling – both on my side and Ollie's. He took all his stuff when he went to Cassie's. I might have helped a little by putting it in bin liners, texting him to come get it and then changing the locks. I enjoyed selling his golf clubs on Facebook and donating the proceeds to a women's refuge charity. He ended up having to get his lawyer to pick up the rest of his stuff before I sold that too.

I can't explain what's happened to me since the miscarriage, but it's like part of me went with my baby. And I'll never get that back now. It's gone. Sloughing off a skin. The doctor keeps encouraging me to see someone, to speak to them. But I can't forget that one session with Dr Lucinda, and wonder if it triggered something that caused all of this. Digging up the past like that. I don't want some stranger poking around in there, telling me I have daddy issues and fears of abandonment. I know those things already.

Alice is worried too. After I didn't respond to her for two weeks and then impulsively sent her a photo of me in a hospital gown, she started messaging me daily to check in. We've even had a couple of calls. She isn't sure a move right now is the best thing for me.

You've already had so much upheaval, you need to let your body heal.

But she doesn't realise that the secondment in London is exactly what I need. I can't stay in this city any longer. I always was on borrowed time here, and I need to come home.

I'll be fine. I've got private healthcare. I'm even flying business class.

Well I'm glad you'll be nearby at least, so I can keep an eye on you.

I'll expect dinner on the table every night.

For sure 😕

I know I'm ready because most nights now, I dream I'm back there, in the garden, eating apples with Alice. It's a side effect of the antidepressants they prescribed me after the miscarriage – vivid dreams. So, I relive my childhood night after night. Wake up and smell Shalimar and smoke. The echo of my mother's Texan accent fading in my ear. It bothered me at first, waking with tears crusted on my face, but now I'm used to it.

I'm tired of being in limbo out here. I'm closing down a life I don't want to be living any longer. Transferring bank accounts, selling the house, the furniture, the cars. I'm itching for the next stage to happen, to open that new chapter.

Of course, Alice isn't aware of my other motivation to come home. I've promised myself I'll behave, though. I've been cheated on, I know the betrayal. I've always thought I'd never do that to someone else, no matter how great the temptation. And Alice is my friend, the past is just that: the past. I know it's just the dopamine receptors in my brain and not anything real. But that doesn't stop the way I feel when I see he's messaged me again. In fact, he messages me as much as she does.

It's all tame. Nothing he couldn't show her. But it's the volume, the times he does it. In bed at night, alone in the car, at work, in the bathroom. Sometimes they message me at the same time. I think of them lying in bed together, me the single thread connecting them both, from thousands of miles away.

I want to see you Evie, when you're back

Sure. We can do drinks.

Only drinks...

It's tricky.

What can she say? You're an old friend.

Is she really going to be okay with us reconnecting? Have you told her?

What she doesn't know won't hurt her.

He's fooling himself if he thinks Alice won't be bothered. She never liked sharing. And I'm less sure about seeing him in person, now it's getting nearer. I don't know how it's going to work. It's one thing messaging from the other side of the world, lighting up the satellites with our chemistry. But if there's nothing in person then that's going to be a disappointment. And if there is? I need to be careful. I know it's a slippery slope.

What if I'm a disappointment? I'm not fifteen anymore.

It would be weird if you were. And besides, I know what you look like now.

He adds a flame emoji.

Although he's not said it in so many words, he's making it very clear how he feels. This isn't a simple friends' reunion, this is more – if I want it. And I do, despite myself, I'm struggling not to think about him all the time now. Stalking all his social profiles for pictures and snippets of information to build a pattern of the man he is now, the shadow of the boy hiding behind it all.

Besides, you're not the only one who's older now.

Older and wiser?

Definitely not!

But he does look after himself. He goes to the gym. Sends me pictures post run, sweaty faces, grinning with the endorphin high. And he posted a shirtless pic to his Insta stories, hashtagged it #ThirstTrap. I wonder who else is thirsting over him, even though I know the picture is meant for me.

> Seriously though, it's going to be different when I'm back. She's already inviting me round for drinks and dinner.

He has no idea how much she messages me. That I know so much about their life – her life – already. Which school mums she hates, who her celeb crush is, when she has a sneaky glass of wine before pick-up, the times she pretends to have to work late so he has to do bedtime.

She writes,

> It's weird. When we first connected again, I wasn't sure. Not after how everything ended. But now I can't wait for you to come home! I'm so excited to see you 😀

> Me too. But it's almost weird how not-weird it's been? I feel like I can always talk to you.

> Make sure you send me your flight details. And where is it you're staying again? I can send you directions to our house.

We arrange for us to have a girls' dinner and catch up the Friday after I fly over, so that I can "get over jet lag and settle in". I have to restrain her from insisting we have dinner the night I get there, at hers. When I tell her I have other plans, she is incredulous. But it's not a lie.

I'm moving the last of the rubbish bags into the basement when I see it. Just a scrap of wallpaper with rosebuds, like Alice had in her profile picture, tells me I'm doing the right thing uprooting myself. It's in a box of who-knows-what, probably been here since before we moved in, most likely it'll still be here when the next owners move out.

I put the scrap of paper back in the box and go to put the lid back on – it amuses me that this particular rosebud wallpaper even made it over here. But then I pause. Whoever it belonged to isn't coming back any time soon, we've been in this house almost a decade. Prime real estate and no one cares what's in the basement – the new owners will probably remodel it. Ollie had planned to turn this room into a rec room with a full-size pool table, La-Z-boys, a wet bar, fully retro. I was less keen, hoping to make it into more of a family den. Either way it's another bright, shiny dream, now lying tarnished and consigned to history.

And the clock is ticking, I know. No one has mentioned it to my face, but I'm in my late thirties. The chances of finding someone now, to build that basement conversion, is slim. I know I've got a lot going for me, but most single men my age, especially out here, are either divorced with kids and don't want any more, or, only date women under thirty or with a BMI less than 1.9 or some other arbitrary rule.

I've looked at the apps, I've even downloaded them. Made drunken attempts at scrolling and swiping. But in the morning, I always regret it. I know what I really want.

I grab my phone and snap a picture of the wallpaper, send it to Alice.

Look what I found in our basement!

I know it's the wrong time there. But it's something whilst I'm travelling – through space and time – to get back there.

I leave the wallpaper where I found it, head upstairs and lock the basement door. I don't need to go back down there again. In fact, all the rooms are clear now. My suitcases are packed and ready by the front door. The house is empty – and yet full. I never realised how light it was before. It's ready for someone else to love it, to create the happy family we never could. I know I should be remembering dinners and parties, Halloween and Easter. Summer BBQs and winter get-togethers. But the novelty wore off. The fun when most people were single or unmarried at least – the messy nights that then segued into more sophisticated evenings, with multiple courses and wine pairings and expensive whiskies. Even if we did still end up doing karaoke. The next stage never really happened, because of nap times and babysitters and people not drinking or on special diets. Our lives fizzled out. We ran out of things to say to each other and everyone else. I often wondered if other people sensed our failure too, as if the house was cursed and they would be too if they came over.

I'm rarely sad to say goodbye, and this time is no different – because what's waiting for me is so much better than anything here. There's nothing really left here at all.

The Uber I ordered is late – the time of arrival changing by five minutes at a time and I'm hanging around on the porch, Samsonite cases next to me like a girl stood up on prom night. I've pushed my keys under the door. The new people have their own set – and if they've any sense they'll change the locks.

When we first moved in, there was a proper community here – and we got the house as a fixer-upper. The old lady who lived here before us actually died in the house, she'd been here fifty years, seen her babies become children, then adults and flee the nest – and her husband had died six months earlier. The realtor told us she'd died of a broken heart. Either way, we got the house for a steal because her kids just wanted the probate done and dusted. I remember the day we moved in, seeing husbands out mowing their lawns, kids on their bikes, our neighbour even brought over a muffin basket. Ollie said to me afterwards, were we sure this wasn't Wisteria Lane we'd moved to – and not to go having affairs with the gardener! I was so glad that I'd found somewhere to put down roots, to settle and make a life together.

It's changed over the years though, as people got priced out of the city centre, trying to find big old family homes for a bargain – but rich people stay rich by keeping the money to themselves, so eventually people bought houses out here and now they're worth a fortune.

But even when people buy them, intending to stay and build their lives, they're still always somewhere else – summering in the Hamptons, wintering in the Caribbean, skiing in Aspen at Easter. It's not unknown for houses to stand empty for months – years even – the owners travelling across the world, never stopping to wonder if what they're looking for is right in front of them. Just one long treadmill from plane, Uber, hotel over and over again. They never open their eyes, never realise they're holding the key to their own freedom.

The driver struggles putting my stuff in the trunk. I half-heartedly apologise, then slide into the back seat instead, the leather cool against my arms and my neck. Connecting my AirPods, I drift off as the car eats up the white lines on the road, the first step on my journey home.

My Uber leaves me at departures just in time.

I wheel my cases into the concourse. I checked in online already for my flight, so I go straight through into the business class lounge. I settle in an armchair with a glass of champagne. I probably shouldn't – flights are dehydrating as it is, I'll look like a prune by the time I get to Gatwick, but I don't care.

My phone vibrates, notifications coming through now we're off the freeway – I always get terrible reception there.

Wow that wallpaper pic is a blast from the past.

And then:

Are you on your way yet?

I snap a picture of the lounge and send it to both of them.

Alice: Nice! Who's paying for that?

Him: Sure you don't want me to pick you up?

There are papers and magazines available, but who reads those still?

I dig out my iPad and stick in my headphones. I haven't had much of an attention span recently, but I figure it'll distract me from my thoughts and also act as a buffer from anyone trying to talk to me. Already the man sitting opposite me in a matching armchair is checking me out. By the time we board I'm itching to be somewhere familiar, to sink into a plump goose down duvet. Some darkness, some silence, a bed, some respite from the voices in my head.

I settle myself into the cabin bed, ignore the man still trying to get my attention from across the cabin. Turning out the lights, pulling on my eye mask, closing my eyes. I think briefly, again, about the end of my marriage, before drifting into another dream about that sunny garden, on that long-ago day.

When I arrive at Gatwick Airport, even after all these years, even as a stranger twice over, there is still the sense of the familiar. If I have ever belonged anywhere, it is here. London is the real thing. I was made here and still part of this place is under my skin, in my DNA.

There's another Uber waiting here for me. It's all slick and shiny and this one isn't late. He takes my luggage, asks me how my flight was. As the Surrey hills rush past us in a blur of green and gold, I breathe in good and deep. *I'm here, I can relax, I did it.*

It was easy enough to just take the secondment – it's what work wanted me to do and I'm not pregnant anymore. Rupert couldn't get rid of me fast enough, though goodness knows what he and Freddie will do without me. But I won't be missing them. The secondment itself is six months to start with but probably longer – which, to be honest, suits me just fine. I don't know where my head will be in six months. But I'm not going back to Boston.

The driver is pulling off the motorway; we're in the countryside, trees grasping at the windows, winding country lanes pulling us into a maze. Somewhere at the centre is Alice.

And Jake.

FOURTEEN

The only thing about going back, I realise, as I settle into my new life, new routines, new ways of living, is that at every turn, there is a reminder of before.

In that first week, I join the tide of commuters from the suburbs, swarming like rats into London. The density of houses increases as we get closer to the city, the flashing windows of the Shard like the eye of Sauron in the distance. When I change trains, I go past my old stop. I almost expect to see a phantom of myself standing on the platform.

When I get home, I fill the kitchen of my serviced apartment with the food I ate as a child – Marmite, Ribena, custard creams, Mars bars, Jaffa cakes, baked beans. I drink tea the way Alice's mother used to make it, the colour of bricks, and I eat rounds of buttered toast as if they are going out of fashion.

When I'm in the office, I'm distracted, stretching myself between Boston hours and London hours, but the jet lag gets me in the night and I find myself awake and watching my phone clock countdown the hours from one am to two am and on until three.

So it's inevitable that with everything – the reminders, the messages – that other memories start coming to the surface, things long buried.

They are first triggered by something completely innocuous. I'm coming home late, after drinks with the new team that first week. I'm at the station figuring out how to get a cab when I see them – two teenage girls. One of them is crying and storming off, the other one following behind, telling her she's sorry, she didn't mean it, it was an accident, please come back.

When it's clear the other girl isn't coming back, I check on her friend.

"Are you okay? Do you need money for a cab?"

When she turns her face to me, I see she's been crying too. And despite the immaculate make-up – no over-plucked eyebrows and lilac shadow for these teens – she is barely fifteen, if that. I want to hug her, feed her tea and toast. Where is her family, don't they care about her wandering around at night like this?

"I'm okay, I'm okay – but thanks."

"Are you sure? Where are you going?"

"Home."

"Well, how will you get there?"

"It's fine, thank you." She sniffs and wipes her nose on the back of her hand. "I've messaged my mum, she's coming now."

I wait with her at the station until a Porsche Cayenne pulls up and a woman with long blonde hair, skinny jeans and pristine Uggs walks towards us.

"Baby! Are you okay?"

As she draws nearer, she gives me a narrow-eyed look. "Who are you?"

"She's no one, Mum, she was trying to help me."

"What have I told you about talking to strangers? Let's go."

And she hustles her daughter away, but not before shooting me another dirty look.

I never cried much as a teenager. And neither did Alice, so it was all the more eventful when either one of us did.

Then

Shortly after the trip to Brighton, when I'd been duly grounded for a week, I'd gone over to Alice's and been turned away by her mother. Apparently she was sick and didn't want visitors. After three days of this I barged past Aunty Meredith and headed upstairs to find Alice lying on her bed, crying, surrounded by tissues and listening to Magic FM. There were no packets of paracetamol, no sick buckets.

"Leave me alone."

"What's wrong?"

"None of your business."

"Wow."

"I said, leave me alone." She lay on her bed, her body the shape of a question mark. "Can't you hear? Get. Out. Of. My. Room."

"Okay, okay, I'm going."

"Yeah, fuck off to the shed with my dad, like you always do."

I froze.

"What's that supposed to mean?"

"What do you think it means?"

"I don't know, that's why I asked."

"You're pathetic, you know that right? Just because you haven't got a dad, doesn't mean you can take mine. What makes you think he even gives a shit about you?"

"What are you talking about?"

"You're old enough to do your homework by yourself at your house. So why are you always here? Go home. No one wants you around. Especially not him. It's just such bullshit. Leave us alone."

"You don't know what you're talking about. And your sainted daddy. He's not so perfect you know."

"Shut up. Just get out!"

"With pleasure."

I was halfway down the stairs when she called me back. "Actually..."

She was peering down at me, on the stairs. Just the way she looked when we were kids, that first time. Long loose hair, pastel pyjamas, the light beaming out behind her in a halo.

"What?"

"Look... I'm sorry."

"Whatever."

"No, please – my head's a mess."

"No kidding."

"I shouldn't have taken it out on you."

Like she could just undo the last few minutes. But she also knew how hard she was to resist.

"It's fine. Forget about it."

"Can you meet me tomorrow? After dinner – in the park? I really need to talk to you, I can't trust anyone else."

Her request takes me by surprise. But then I remember what she told me in Brighton.

"Yeah, of course."

She'd never been one for heart to hearts before. I knew Jake would warn me off going. Tell me to stay out of her schoolgirl politics. But Alice was just like her daddy – persuasive, good at finding someone's weak spots; there was never a chance I'd say no to her, and she knew that.

She was sitting on the swings when I got to the park. We had come here so much as kids, once the swimming pool incident happened and we were banned from using it unsupervised. Never occurred to anyone that we weren't any safer here. Or maybe we were. Somehow things always happened when we were together, but not to us.

She was moving slowly, dragging her feet back and forth along the ground. It was late – maybe nine-ish and the sky was a rich navy blue.

From the park entrance, I watched the lit end of her cigarette glow with each drag, then darken. She wasn't in her usual perfect princess clothes, no short skirt, knee-high socks. Just a big hoodie, old jeans, battered Chucks that I didn't even know she owned.

I swung next to her, but when I asked her what was wrong, she only cut her eyes away and down. So I pulled out my Walkman, stuck my headphones on, and relaxed into my music. Sometimes Alice was like a cat, you had to pretend you weren't interested, to get her attention.

As I watched each star prick out its place in the sky she began talking.

"I trusted her. I trusted him."

The Stone Roses came on my mixtape, the opening chords of "I Wanna Be Adored" raised goosebumps down my spine.

"And this is how she repays me."

Our swings went back and forth. Somewhere I could smell roses.

"Richard was mine."

I took her cigarette, took a long drag. Expelled the smoke away from me.

"I know, Alice. You told me. So what are you gonna do about it?"

When our eyes met, I saw our childhood in their reflection, everything else fell away.

"Don't you mean what are *we* going to do?" And she looked at me, something in her eyes shifting, a flicker of a smile curving her lips. "You're the only one I can trust. The only person I can rely on."

"What do you want to do?"

"Teach her a lesson."

She swung back and forth, head down, scuffing her feet.

"Okay. But how?"

She looked at me. "I don't know yet. But when I do, you're in, right?"

"Yes. Of course." And I was. Because still, I could not say no to Alice.

And then she faced me and smiled, lighting up her whole face.

Getting off her swing, she pulled me by the hand into the encroaching darkness, whispered into my ear, "I'm sorry – for what I said, before. About you and dad. I didn't mean it."

And that was everything I needed. We walked home, arm in arm. Except, I didn't need to go anywhere, because for me, on a good day, Alice was my home.

And it didn't matter that I didn't know what was coming next, even though I did know that Jake wouldn't like it. But I didn't care.

I knew to wait for Alice to let me know her plan. But then when we saw Rosie at a party, it all just fell into our lap.

"Does Rosie know that you know – about her and Richard?"

Alice smirked into her plastic cup of fruit punch. It was heavily spiked with vodka.

"Yeah. She actually tried to ask me if it was okay. And then asked me for advice on how to keep him."

"Is she worrying about that already?"

"Yes, but that's good! I've set up the plan – it's perfect. I told her you'd take some pics of her, on your Polaroid. She's totally up for it.

I look at Alice, narrow my eyes at her. "Are you sure about this?"

"Yes! Don't worry. It'll be fine okay, untraceable. Meet me tomorrow, we'll sort it out."

The next day, in Aunty Meredith's kitchen, Alice was more determined than ever. And I saw why Uncle John always joked about how Alice would end up in politics when she grew up – either that or in prison. But she never found that funny.

"How long do you think they've been together?" I ask.

"Oh, I don't care. But she needs to be taught a lesson. Let's go out, I don't want to talk about it here."

Uncle John was in the hall, asking where I'd been, where we were going.

"Out." Alice rolled her eyes at me.

Uncle John shot me a look, but I couldn't decipher it.

I think she knows, I'd said to him the other week.

How? What did you say to her?

Nothing, I would never... But he was worried. Not that I cared. How much worse could he make my life?

Alice walked outside, then took a loop around the houses, taking angry drags of her cigarette, not caring if the neighbours saw and ratted her out.

"Should we mess with Richard? I think we should screw with his head too."

I was unsure. I couldn't afford more trouble. "Umm... it depends if you want to get back with him. And what would we even do to him?"

"Oh, never mind, you're right, let's stick with her – she's gonna freak out when she sees."

Alice laughed and ran ahead, then spun around with her arms out, to face me. It was early evening, early spring, cherry blossoms in the air, the scent of mown grass. We were at the top of the road we lived on, a steep hill. Behind Alice was the golden glow of the setting sun, she looked like she might fall backwards into that pink tinged sky, take off to anywhere. She looked like an angel, fallen from heaven.

"Yeah." I smiled at her glad to be back on her good side. "She'll want to die."

FIFTEEN

NOW

It was a last-minute invite. But then all the best things often are.

Almost a month on from returning and I am still living out of a suitcase. Still to try everything on the room-service menu. Not on first name terms with the maids yet. Still haven't been to Alice and Jake's. Why does coordinating diaries when you're in your thirties turn into a military operation? Alice kept suggesting dates, I kept rejecting them. We were both tiptoeing around setting a date like teenagers not wanting to be the first to say I love you.

It's our old school's bi-centennial. Fancy it?

What a place for a reunion.

When is it?

Tonight.

I couldn't tell if this was a trap. The old Alice would do this.

The new one, I'm less sure of. No one would recognise me. There might not even be anyone I knew there – well, except Alice. By some miracle, I was actually free on a Friday evening. I finished work early, made excuses about having an off-site meeting. So I was sitting back in my bedroom when Alice messaged. I was planning on bingeing *Killing Eve* and ordering steak for dinner, asking for a nice red with it.

Not much notice there.

Sorry, thought you'd have been invited.

No.

Are you not a member of the alumni club?

Yes.

How odd you didn't get an invite. Anyway, it might be fun – free booze at least. And we'd get to see each other! At last!

I couldn't think of a good excuse. I was bored. I wasn't that tired. And I was intrigued. Nothing like returning to the scene of the crime.

Let me just check something.

I'd do it. I'd go. Nothing ventured, nothing gained.

Yep, all good, I'm free.

Excellent, I'll pick you up later!

And that was that. And now I'm here, on a terrace in the early evening sunshine, drinking champagne – the real stuff – feet away from where the art block was. They've rebuilt it all now. Obviously. They couldn't keep it the same, I guess. Not after what happened.

In the end Alice didn't pick me up. I was running late – a work thing, or that's what I told her anyway. I couldn't face seeing her and the school at the same time. I needed to dip my toe in slowly.

Now I'm here, but I can't spot her anywhere. Looking at the guests tonight, everyone looks very well-to-do, very glamorous. Intelligent, wealthy, successful – exactly the crowd the school wanted to be known for. They've got all types of alumni – old chaps with medals pinned on in wheelchairs, city types in suits and signet rings, women in big hats as if they'd stumbled in from Ascot.

It's no surprise. My school has some prestigious ex-pupils: Hollywood stars, minor royalty, kids of rock stars, entrepreneurs. And the odd sporting champion. They love a bit of rugby and lacrosse. Rowing, tennis and swimming too. Anything that poor people can't afford to do. I shouldn't even have attended, but for reasons I've never properly understood, Alice's family paid for my education. Something to do with a favour Mama did for them before I was born and in return they paid for my schooling. Seems like it must have been a pretty big favour – the termly fees were thousands of pounds. The only problem was that the rest of Mama's income didn't match up. There's nothing like being the one poor person at a rich-person school. Nothing like the humiliation of having Alice's hand-me-down uniform.

I take out my phone.

Where are you? Are you here yet?

She tells me she's on the terrace.

Me too! I'll come find you.

But I don't. Not yet.

I snaffle a canapé from a black-clad waiter – current students pressed into service. They've all got a QR code on their name badge, ready for prospective mentors to scan and review their CVs, book in work experience at law firms and consultancies.

I don't know where anyone from my year ended up. Except for Alice, I didn't look up anyone else on social media. I told myself I was better than that, fishing around in their mediocre lives and comparing myself to them, to people that didn't matter then and sure as hell don't matter now.

I suddenly spot Alice's creamy blonde bob several feet away from me. She doesn't see me. She's surrounded by ex-teachers and the current headmaster. Just like at the conference, I recognise her immediately. When you grow up with someone it's not the way they look that you know and recognise. It's the way they move, hold themselves, speak. The tiny mannerisms and tells that a person can't change – not without a lot of hard work.

She's loving the adoration right now, standing with one arm across her chest, pushing up her boobs, one leg crossed over the other, sipping from a crystalline flute.

She's here. Right here in front of me, seconds away. My past and present on a collision course.

I used to be the shadow to her light.

But now I can shine too.

I message:

Hey, I'm just going inside for a bit.

I see her glance at her phone, type out a message.

Sure, I'll come and find you.

I don't know why, but I am compelled to prolong our reunion even more. I am Ariadne, leaving Perseus twine at the labyrinth door. Inviting him in to find the monster at the heart of his story.

It's shady and quiet inside. There's a receptionist behind the desk, glass of champagne in one hand, clipboard in another. I wonder if they still have favourite students. If they give them access to photocopiers and keys out of school hours? I wonder if anyone realised that the rulebreakers in a school aren't just the students.

There's a rope barring the entrance to the main stairs of the house, but I just unclip it and glide upwards, as if motorised. Here, more than anywhere, if you look like you belong some-where, no one will question it. I leave something behind for Alice, so she'll know where to find me.

The main part of the school is a former mansion house, built in the early 1900s. Apparently Wallis Simpson came to tea here before it was turned into a school. The ballroom became the library, the bedrooms, common rooms, the smaller guest rooms, classrooms. It's all been modernised now, big new wings of glass and steel added on, housing laboratories and the prep school.

Back when we were here, they held our classes in shoddy old pre-fabricated annexes, put up after the war – not intended to be permanent. They were always cold and mouldy. Smelled of feet and cabbage and distantly of bleach. The grounds have also been done up, the acres of woods we clambered and hid in, walled off. The open-air swimming pool, covered up. The ruined cellars and icehouses and coal pits that we made dens in, that we thought were haunted, dug up and concreted over.

You can't fundamentally change a building though. Not without razing it to the ground and starting again. It'll always be haunted by its past, just like people are. And around every corner here, there are spectres lurking. The phantoms of the girls Alice, Rosie and I used to be. Except Alice and I grew up, escaped. But Rosie never did.

I reach the top of the stairs, where it divides, and take the left-hand flight. The right one won't take me where I want to be. And besides, I can't walk along there anywhere. Even now, seeing the route to the headmaster's office makes me nauseous, thinking back to that day. Being asked to leave. The pointing fingers. The screaming and crying.

No, I go the way I know. Up. Higher and higher. The rooms get smaller, originally only servants would come up here, not anyone important. And interestingly, the higher up the school, the less they've changed. These are still the music rooms. Back then, if you had a secret, this was the place to come. My phone vibrates.

Hey, I'm coming to find you. What a place for a reunion!

These rooms were always my favourite place. At the very top of the school. Tiny low doorways, tiny rooms, tiny windows – and then some bigger, the original sash windows still in place.

There were rumours of ghosts up here, creaking floorboards, instruments playing themselves. But I wasn't scared of the dead. Indeed, I hoped that around me, invisible, were long dead scullery maids and butlers, enjoying scaring children, no longer responding to a bell, falling victim to hideous diseases wiped out by modern medicine. And besides, I knew all too well that only one person had the power to hurt me.

I walk down the corridor, heels clipping on the floorboards. It's the room at the end I want.

It's all changed so much here, I can't believe it. Just chatting to the lovely receptionist – she remembers me, can you believe it!

There's not much time now. Distantly I think I hear my name, or voices, or music. But I keep going. The door opens smoothly. It used to creak like crazy. How can a room be both full and empty at the same time? So much light, so many memories.

The window is the only part that's different. They've put bars across it now. And a strong catch. And a note that says the key for the lock is in reception and to check with the music teacher before opening it.

I'm nearly there. God, I forgot how many stairs there were.

One of the few things I learned when I was taken away was how to pick locks. This one is tough, but I manage it all the same.

Then I put down the things I brought with me. And take a photo.

Waiting for you – just popping the cork now!

And then I leave, slip quickly down the back stairs on the other side of the corridor even as I hear her footsteps reaching the room.

I'm sliding into the seat of a taxi when she messages.

Hey! I'm here – where are you???

Soz, had to run – work emergency. Typical, huh!

I was so looking forward to catching up. Thanks for the champers though. Nice one!

Enjoy!

I wonder what she thinks of the apple I left her. I wonder if she saw Rosie's memorial plaque. I wonder if she's scared too.

SIXTEEN

One of the best things about Jake was that he never needed to prove himself, compare himself. I loved that about him. I loved that I was the dark and he was the light. With Ollie I was the dark and he was... he was the abyss. In hindsight, it was never healthy.

I worry about whether Jake has changed. It's hard to tell from our messages. It's not the same as when you meet in person. Their body language, the things they reveal without speaking. What if he's changed – and not for the better? Or maybe I'm just making excuses. Covering up how I really feel about him, finding ways to put off the inevitable. That nothing will have changed and when I see him, I'll fall right back in love with him. I'm halfway there already, truth be told.

Reunions are supposed to be dreamy, romantic. For us it's more like lighting a match during a gas leak. It's been seeping out, colourless, odourless, for so long. Invisible to everyone. But it only takes one spark to cause an explosion.

"I can't believe you're back. I can't believe you're here."

I realise it was a mistake to meet here, in my suite, alone. I thought we'd be able to chat without an audience – like we do in our messages. But as soon as I see him, my body remembers him, heat pools inside me.

He's standing on the other side of the room, looking out of the window, admiring the view of the road and further up, the retail park, proudly home to not only a McDonalds but also a Burger King.

"You're sorted for hangover food."

Immediately I am picturing us in bed, the morning after. Clothes in a trail from the door to the bed, sheets awry, the room smelling of us. Of what we've done.

"I'm not sure this was a good idea, Jake."

"What do you mean? It's fine. Come over here." He walks across the room, casting a long shadow across the floor and perches on the edge of the bed. The maids have been in, the room is immaculate. He pats the crisp white cotton quilt next to him. "I won't bite… unless you ask nicely."

He's got game, as Nina would say. The Jake I knew had many things, but he didn't have this.

I sit down, despite myself. Aware of how close he is, his size. His height. The crisp smell of expensive aftershave, the way his tan is fading on his arms, but he still has the remains of a golden summer glow. He turns to me, so close I can see my reflection in his pupils.

He's loosened his tie, and without thinking, I stroke the silk. It's amazing how your body remembers how to be so at ease with someone. That their body, their clothes, feel like an extension of your own.

"Who still wears ties to work?"

He smiles, still that lopsided, shy boy smile. I try to pull myself together. This is Alice's husband. Our history is irrelevant. I've come back here for answers, not to create more complications.

"I do, clearly. Had a client meeting, thought I should make an effort."

"You look like a real estate agent."

"I do not!" he says, mock affronted, and laughs, and then, "Do I?"

"No, not really. I just... yeah, I would never have imagined you this way, with ties and suits."

"We've grown up, that's what it is."

It's so good to be around him, I can't explain it, but it's like my whole body has relaxed for the first time in who knows how long.

"We have." And I reach up and touch the corner of his eyes, his face, trace with my fingertip the lines that have appeared since I last saw him. He sits very still, as if I'm a wild beast that could bite at any time.

"Evie..." His voice is a sigh. He swallows. Time moves treacle slow as he reaches for my wrist, pulls my hand away and presses his forehead to mine, but then pulls away slightly to look at me again.

"What are we doing?" I say.

"I don't know, I don't know – but I can't stop, Evie... I've thought about this moment for so long. What I'd do, what I'd say... what you'd do and say."

"And is this like what you thought?" I indicate our clasped hands, our closeness. We are teetering on the brink of something.

"Almost." He looks at my mouth when he says this.

I feel like I'm in a car going too fast, but where I'd normally wonder if it's possible to brake in time, now I wonder if it's possible to go faster – to fly, even.

If recent events have taught me anything, it's that people will take things from you. You can fight them, or you can give it to them or you can negotiate, but either way they're coming for you. So I've learned not only to fight for what I want but sometimes, to simply take it. That if an opportunity comes your way, it's meant to be. You'll only ever regret the things you don't do.

He bites his lip. I think of how gas causes an explosion, that relentless build up, invisible but so very much there and present. I lean forward, close my eyes and kiss him.

Boom.

SEVENTEEN

THEN

"Did you bring the camera?"

Rosie gets straight to the point when she answers the door. Back then we didn't have smart phones or social media. And if you wanted photos developed you had to send them away and wait weeks to see if all your hard work was actually just pictures of someone's thumb. But Alice, of course, had a polaroid camera.

"Yup."

"Are you sure this is going to work?"

"How could it not?"

Rosie had asked us to do it – that was the one thing Alice and I agreed on, stuck to in our stories. She told us to take photos. And it was true – I didn't have to persuade her. She wanted to do it. She couldn't wait to get me in the door. We didn't know how they got everywhere, we later insisted. Or at least, that's what I insisted. I didn't get a chance to speak to Alice, after, to get our stories straight.

I still remember her room, though I wanted to forget it, forget my part in all of it. But it's been seared into my mind. All pink and frilly as if Barbie had too many Malibu and cokes and vomited everywhere.

When I got there she had all her make-up out, her curling wand, lots of lacy and sheer lingerie laid out, ready on her bed. If she rubbed her thighs together she stood a good chance of self-immolation.

But I was sure that her mum still bought her five-packs of M&S floral briefs, that somewhere she even had the odd faded pair with My Little Pony on, or Care Bears. We were still such children, even as we believed ourselves on the cusp of adult-hood, the last few years of our teens all that stood between us and our futures.

She sat at a white melamine desk and applied wobbly eyeliner and layered on pastel shimmery eyeshadow, RImmel or Seventeen or Cover Girl. Shaped a clumsy seduction on her face.

Passing me a Rainbow Brite water bottle filled with a peach liquid, we both gulped back warm, acidic mouthfuls of archers and lemonade.

Alice had persuaded her that all she needed to secure Richard as a bona fide boyfriend was to show him exactly what he'd be missing out on. God knows how she made her think it was a good idea. Probably because Rosie had such low confi-dence and self-belief that she didn't doubt for a moment Alice's loyalty and friendship. In that moment even I despised her vulnerability and her naked desire for validation and approval. It was something I wanted too, but I would never admit it.

I tried to persuade myself that, actually, she deserved every-thing that was coming to her – given she was making a play for Alice's ex. She knew exes were off limits, surely, even if Alice had given her the okay?

Rosie curled her hair into sausagey ringlets, sprayed them liberally with Elnett hairspray. In hindsight, that was the moment where I could have saved her – asked her what the hell she thought she was doing. This wasn't her. Told her to wipe all the make-up off, comb her hair back into French braids, slip into PJs. We could have ordered pizza and rented a film, had a sleep-over. If I'd done that, my entire life would be different. But I didn't.

She was pathetic, kneeling on the bed, giving it her best sexy pose. But soon she had finished the contents of the water bottle, and was slurring her words, sprawled in a mess.

I turned off the overhead light, put a red scarf over the bedside lamp.

In my head, I heard something my mother used to say whenever there were cameras around.

I'm ready for my close-up Mister De Mille.

Rosie pushed her breasts together, let one strap drop, looked up at me from under spidery mascara.

"How do I look?"

"Hot. Really hot."

And I picked up my camera.

"He's going to love it."

The rest of it was easy. All of it. Alice got permission to use the school office from the secretary. They all loved her there, with her tins of chocolate and Christmas bottles of wine. She could have been caught photocopying her bum and they'd still let her in.

"You did a great job with the pictures," she told me.

The printer chewed up and spat out sheets and sheets of paper. I squinted at the Polaroids we'd rejected. Over-exposed, they still showed everything we needed. Rosie had developed early. The first in her class to wear a bra. The first to get her period. She was always in the epicentre, always the focus. And she never wanted the spotlight, I know that now. But she drew it, looking the way she did. Part of me wondered if Alice was punishing her for that, for taking attention that should have been hers.

Even though I'd gone through with everything so far, unquestioning, seeing the pictures and prints now, I was less sure.

"Where did you tell her you'd put them?" I asked.

"His locker. I said I'd slip them in as it's next to mine."

I knew that if I was going to say anything to Alice, it would have to be now. But I wasn't sure how to word it, I'd been on the receiving end of her anger before. And what's to say she wouldn't do something worse to me?

But then I thought of Rosie, crouched on her bed, posing for me, the sound of her little sister splashing in the bath next door, their mum singing to her. I tried to imagine how I'd feel. Although with Mama, the shame would be for different reasons. I bit my lip, imagined Jake finding out what we were doing.

"Alice, are you sure about doing all this? I mean, why don't you just let her have him? And if we get caught – we'll get in so much shit."

Alice held up one particularly explicit picture, examining each freckle and curve, the way Rosie held her legs akimbo. She didn't look at me as she replied. But the tone in her voice wasn't like anything I'd heard from her before. Cold, hard – forbidding.

"*She's a* slut. She deserves everything she's got coming to her. You're either with me, or against me. Which is it, Evie?"

I didn't reply, but she took my silence as I shuffled and collated the images, for the compliance it was.

I still don't know how Alice got into school so early to do what she did. She never did tell me about that part when we planned it.

And it was only ever meant to be a joke. Certainly, I just

wanted to scare Rosie a little, warn her off stealing other people's boyfriends. Show her how it wasn't very sisterly to do what she did. We believed in girl power and some people needed to be taught a lesson. And if I'm honest, I liked that Alice had chosen me, of all her friends, to help. To know that I was the only one she could trust. That I had what she needed.

"You've got to help me. Please."

Rosie found us quickly, tears streaming down her face. We were in our usual hang out, the music rooms, at the top of the main building. Low ceilings, dimly lit, cobwebs lacing up the corners, not often patrolled by the teachers. It was hot up here, and we'd opened the window to catch the breeze.

"They're going to expel me. My parents will find out."

She ran around the room, like a hamster on a wheel, frantically pulling down the pictures that covered every wall.

"Oh God... I want to die."

It was no good. Alice had done a thorough job. The pictures were all over the school. Everyone had seen them.

I spoke up. "Alice... You need to get her to calm down. This has gone too far. Alice?"

Alice inspected her cuticles. "Rosie, Rosie, Rose. What did you think would happen? You shouldn't take things that belong to other people."

Rosie went white, her hand flying to her mouth as she began to realise who was behind the pictures.

"I'm sorry, I'm so sorry. I didn't mean for it to happen."

Alice raised an eyebrow.

"Okay, I did. I wanted him. I didn't think you'd mind. He said you'd broken up. You said—"

"You know, in other countries they stone women for committing adultery with someone else's man."

Politicians could learn a thing or two from teenage girl machinations.

I cleared my throat. "Alice, chill out, you're scaring her."

Rosie was the year below, only just fifteen. But it was no good.

"Didn't your parents ever teach you not to steal?"

Alice stepped forward, Rosie stepped backwards. The open mouth of the window yawning behind her. One second she was there. The next, she was gone. Leaving us both behind, hanging over the windowsill.

After what seemed like hours, but of course could only be seconds, Alice ran out of the room, but I simply stood there, frozen. Staring down at Rosie's shattered body.

By the time we got outside, everyone knew, the police and an ambulance had been called. But it was too late.

Alice got to the teachers before me, said she couldn't be sure if Rosie had fallen or if she'd been pushed. And then she told everyone that it was my idea. That I'd put up the pictures. That I'd lured Rosie up there. That she'd been afraid to go against me.

And, over the hours that followed, Alice kept talking. She told them I was always trying to get her to listen to Marilyn Manson and to come smoke weed with her, that I wore a necklace with a pentagram and dyed my hair black. And although she didn't say it in so many words, she said how she felt sorry for me, with just my mum at home. No one to look after me after school or on weekends. I couldn't fight back. People saw what they wanted to see. Including Mama, who didn't wait for the post mortem or to hear my side or to judge me. And neither did the school. I was hauled in front of the headteacher later that week and told I'd been expelled. With Alice's witness testimony there was no doubt, Rosie's death was my fault and they couldn't possibly keep me at the school. I would have to sit my exams somewhere else.

I still think about that day. About the truth of it. Who did what, where and when?

I run it through my mind again and again, how Alice had Rosie backed up against the window frame. She bent and whispered something in her ear. Alice had put her hand out – I don't think she really meant to push Rosie, she was just angry. She needed to let it out somehow. We all have moments like that, don't we? It was an accident. That's all. Alice isn't a killer. And neither am I. Right?

EIGHTEEN

NOW

When can I see you again?

Jake messages me all the time. I wonder if this is how it was for Ollie, cheating on me. I thought perhaps he wouldn't turn so fast, that he'd have some loyalty to Alice. I don't want to consider that maybe he's done this before. Or is it just the novelty of being reunited with his teenage girlfriend?

I can't help myself, I reply.

Do you miss me?

Always, he says, always.

And the three dots on messenger wriggle across the screen. I idly browse through the Coco de Mer website, La Perla. Look at overpriced scraps of satin and lace. And then quickly close the open tabs on my laptop, even though there's no one to catch me. We're a long way from teenage fumbles and losing our virginity to each other in my single bed. *I shouldn't be thinking like this.*

I've thought about you so often, he tells me.

Oh yeah?

I want to know every single time he thinks about me. I want to know how he felt, where he was, what he did about it. I can't get enough. I try to persuade myself that we haven't really crossed a line. We haven't slept together yet. And I'm not cheating on anyone.

Did you think about me, Evie?

Yes, no, maybe, sometimes, always, almost never, every day. There are no right answers, there are no wrong answers.

Do you want me to think about you?

I don't know where the words are coming from. An untapped well inside of me, straight into my phone, filter free.

You haven't changed.

Are you sure about that?

Let's play a game.

He video calls me. To answer or not to answer? It's a Saturday morning. I'm not sure I'm ready for this. But will I ever be. I swipe to connect us. There's a rustle and then there he is, stubbly, sleepy looking. *Shit.*

"Where are you?"

"Walking the dog."

Of course he has a dog.

"Wow. Look at you. Two-point-four kids, dog, big house, big car..."

There's that crooked smile. *Damn it.*

"Happens to the best of us."

"Not all of us."

"Well, we can't all marry rich men and move to Boston."

There's that twist of his mouth again.

He's still so beautiful. It hurts. I want to cry. All this time, wasted. Everything we could have achieved. Despite myself, a part of me hopes it's not too late for us. I adjust the angle of the phone, I'm not reminding him of what he's missing, I'm simply making sure that the laundry and used coffee cups are out of shot, that's all.

"Evie..."

"Yes."

"What are you trying to do to me?"

One of my colleagues once described me as mercurial. I don't see that as a bad thing. If you want to have some fun with me, you have to be able to keep up with me.

"Let me make it up to you, Jake."

I know the quickest way to a man's heart. It's through his belly. I know what to give him, to be heart-stopping.

"Where in the park are you?"

"By the brambles. Where the kids pick blackberries."

"Watch out for nettles."

"Oh, there's masses of those. And those spiky thistle head things."

Nature makes the most dangerous plants, the most seductive. All shiny berries and glossy leaves, huge flowers.

"I wish you were here, Evie."

"I wish I was too."

There's a scuffling noise. His jaw twitches, if you didn't know him, you'd think he was so unhappy right now. I change the angle of my phone again. I learned some tricks from Cassie, reading the messages she sent Ollie, the carefully edited photos. He sighs loudly and swallows. His phone goes black and the call disconnects.

Some people think it's weird to notice this stuff, these micro-reactions. I read somewhere that it's called hyper-vigilance, from trauma. But I think it's the sales training I've had – learning how to predict and read customer behaviour, if everything is one long poker game, your tells can cost you your life.

It's after lunch when Alice messages. I'm used to them both messaging me throughout the day now. It's almost like my own personal soap opera. Before I moved back, I did think about creating a chat group. But I quickly realised that wasn't sensible.

Hey.

Hey! How's your weekend going?

Not bad. Being spared the usual three-ring circus that is the kids' social life this weekend.

I don't understand why she constantly complains about these things. Surely she knew kids came with responsibilities? She should be proud of their achievements. Jake never moans about the kids. Nevertheless I reply as required.

Hope you've got your feet up with a cup of tea and some trash telly then?

More like a G+T.

Some would say it's a tad early to start drinking, but of all the things Alice could do wrong, that's the least of them.

She sends me a shot of a glass full of chunks of ice and cucumber and clear liquid. Insta-ready of course.

Cheers babe, I type.

So sorry I missed you at the school reunion – what a shame you had to work *sad face emoji*

LOL it's just the way it is. It's why they pay me the big bucks, baby!

Hahaha

Did you have fun?

Yeah – it was all right. Bit boring without you though. So, what are you up to today?

I imagine telling her the truth. I feel a pang though. I never used to be so indecisive, flip-flopping over where my loyalties lie. They are both tied to me in different ways and different levels of complexity. And it may be a cliché but when you have nothing, you have nothing to lose.

Ah just chilling at home as well. Probs seeing a friend later.

God it sounds blissful. I wish...

What do you wish?

Ah, nothing. Just being silly. So how are you finding being back home? Missing Boston much?

Sounds like a touch of the grass is greener here – I'm intrigued as to what she can possibly feel is lacking in her life.

Nah. It was time. What with the divorce and everything...I just wanted to be home. I never really put down proper roots over there anyway. Maybe if we'd had kids it might have been different but Ollie was always so weird about that.

I'm really sorry it ended so badly. You guys had been together a while right? I did a bit of snooping on your pics!

Ha, you stalker.

I knew she'd be hooked. It's all on there just for her. The blue sky, the cherry lips, his tanned six-pack, our life. The one she wanted all those years ago. The one she taught me to want.

How did you guys meet?

University. Cliché, I know. I knew he was the one from the start.

Aw, how romantic. I never had you as the type!

Neither did I, to be honest. But Ollie just... got me. He understood me. And then it allllllll went to hell.

The dots wiggle on my screen. Is she thinking of pretending her marriage is as perfect as her Instagram makes it look? How happy and smiley and #blessed they all are?

And then the buzzer goes.

Got to go, sorry, Alice. Someone's at the door. But I was thinking, let's get a date in for a proper reunion.

Love to! I was thinking the same. Are you free this week at all? I was wondering if you fancied dinner?

I read her reply before throwing my phone onto the bed and

heading for the door, as my buzzer goes again. I frown and pull open the door.

"I don't know why I'm here."

I only stare at him.

"I'll go. I'm sorry."

But before he can turn, I grab the sleeve of his coat.

"Stay. Please."

And I usher him in. The apartment I'm in is basically one big open-plan living space with a tiny shower room attached. Jake loiters by the kitchen area this time. At least he's not headed straight for the bed.

"Where does she think you are?"

"Helping a mate with something. I mean... it's not a total lie." His eyes catch mine as he says this. The word something lingers in the air, holding a multitude of sins.

"Did you bring me any blackberries?"

"Blackberries?"

"Yeah! From your walk?"

"Wha... oh, no." But he's laughing now. I wonder where he's left the dog – tied up outside or did he make a quick detour home?

I hover by the sofa still though. He bites his lip. He always used to do that when he was nervous. I don't want to think about why he might be nervous.

"Do you..." I have to swallow, my mouth is dry. "Do you want a cup of tea?"

"No, thank you. I don't want a cup of tea."

His voice is calm though.

"Why are you here then? Really?"

"Why do you think?"

My whole body is wired so tight. I can't think of anything to break this tension. Well, I can, but I need him to be the one who does it.

"You tell me."

The entire world seems to hold its breath as he gets up, walks over to the sofa.

"I feel like I'm drowning here." He sits down and pulls me down next to him, holding my hands in his. "I can't help it. I can't stop thinking about you, all the time."

He drops my hands and turns to face me. "Please tell me you feel it too. I know you do."

"I do."

But we both looked at the ring on his left hand.

"I know, I know, I'm just weak and pathetic."

He slams his hand against the wall next to me. He wasn't like this before. I like it. I want his hands around my neck. I want to give him everything.

"Sure you don't want a drink?" For some reason my nerves are dissipating.

"Yes... no... yes... I don't know."

"I'll get us something."

When I come back out, he's sitting on the bed. I feel a tremor run through me. The bottle of whisky and the shot glasses clink in my hands.

I take a step towards him.

"Are you sure?"

I know it's not the drinks he's asking me about.

"I'm sure." My voice catches, but I'm certain. I don't care anymore. "But I don't play games."

"I know. I haven't forgotten. I remember everything."

Another step closer. I was always the feral cat in the relationship, allowing him to tame me, coaxing me towards him.

"We're not kids anymore. This is real life now."

"I know."

"Please." I make my voice quiet and small. "Please."

"What are you asking me for?" But I can tell he knows.

The apartment is quiet. Outside, there is little traffic. No one walks past. No one to see us, no one to hear us.

It's as if every part of me is a storm, waiting to break and crack and spit and burn. All it'll take is him. It was like this the first time. It was like this the last time.

And then he stands and reaches for me, pulls me onto his lap. His tongue is hot and sweet and slow on my neck. I don't move, I don't touch him. I might not come back this time.

"I'm scared, Jake."

"Don't be scared."

It's never like this with anyone else. With him, I think about how it all might get taken away. How everything got taken away before. I have fought to be here. Fought to be alive.

I can't look at him. Can't see what I know he feels. It's against the rules. It's against everything I'm working to achieve, everything I came back for.

I can't wait any longer and close my eyes as he pulls me close against him, down onto the bed.

When I replay it in my mind, after, it is in snapshots. His skin burning against mine, his hands holding me tight, our breathing becoming ragged and fast. And all I could do was hold him tight and wait for the fireworks to explode behind my eyelids. Because that's all I can do, all that can keep me here, on course.

I love you. I love you, I love you, I love you.

The words are a memory, but maybe, one day soon, they'll be real again.

Sorry, got sidetracked. Dinner this week sounds great, where and when?

Wednesday? Want to come here first and then we can walk down to the pub? Shall we say about 7:30? Jake will have to manage bedtime solo for once.

Haha, perfect, looking forward to catching up properly! It's been soooooo long.

She sends me her address and it's that simple. As if it hasn't been twenty years, three kids, two weddings, several hundred-thousand miles and a handful of secrets.

NINETEEN

THEN

When I was younger, my mother used to tell me I wasn't capable of love. But if that was true, maybe I wasn't capable of hate either? As I sit in the Uber to Alice's, she is all I can think about. How she made me feel – how she still makes me feel, and how close love and hate really are. Because I want to know where she is and what she's doing at every moment, I want to know if she's happy or sad, rich or poor, healthy or sick. I care about these things, I need to know them. Maybe more than I ever did with anyone else. Alice and I, we're like the two wolves in the Russian proverb about good and evil; the one you feed is the one that wins.

So much of my future hinges on tonight. By the same token, so does my past. We could write enough messages to fill the library at Alexandria, but they still wouldn't have the power generated by us laying eyes on each other. If he is a slow gas leak and an explosion, she is a black hole, a vacuum. Everything before now will disappear. At least, she hopes it will.

When I dress, I dress for her – expensive lingerie, the kind women love, delicate embroidery, straps to flatter, a wide band of silk trim, a vintage look in navy and bottle green. Worn jeans and an embroidered, draped top that sits in the right places; the top even has pockets. What woman doesn't love pockets in their clothes?

Groomed brows, glowing skin, glossy hair, teeth, nails, winged liner – the kind of look that she'll notice. And will know is almost impossible to pull off without either a lot of expensive products, genetics and help – or a combination of all three. No matter what she does tonight, I'll still be the one her husband wants.

When she sees me, she'll be thinking what I'm thinking. Of that mirrored wardrobe in her bedroom and how we used to score each other. If she's anything like me, she's still scoring people, she's still comparing and judging and ranking.

Hey, running a bit late, can we make it 8? she messages.

Sure, no worries.

Outside the houses and the roads, the cars and the garages and playgrounds are identical. No doubt they are on the inside also. When I get to her road, I can tell her house is going to be all fifty shades of grey and upcycled furniture. There will be a row of matching muddy Hunter boots in different sizes by the front door. Her kitchen will be wall-to-wall fitted appliances, and subway tiles as a splashback, though she thinks those are getting a bit passé now, it might be time for a refurb. She has an apple tree in her back garden. She wants to get it cut down, it overshadows the house, the apples are a nightmare, rotting in the grass, more than she can deal with.

"Hey! You found us. Oh my God, you've changed so much, Evie."

"Hey yourself! Had to grow up sometime. Can't look miserable forever."

There's a pause and we both remember the last time we saw each other. The hot smell of fear.

I lean forward and hug her, wonder if she'll remember my scent, the feeling of my body against hers.

"Oh... you shocked me!"

Her fingers fly off my arms and she steps back. We're standing on a nylon doormat, so I expect that's what's caused it.

"Anyway, come in, come in! God, I can't believe you're really here."

Once we're inside, I look at her properly. She's perfect. Of course she is, she always was. Ruffled blonde bob, immaculate skin and brows, even teeth and that wide, inviting smile. Her lips still a little too full. At least she'll have no need for filler.

The slip dress and white T-shirt combo that I remember so well have been replaced by clinging cashmere and leather. The Heather Shimmer lipstick replaced by a matte pillarbox red. And on her feet, buffed black Dr Marten boots. The kind she was always so dismissive of, back then. She has a heavy beaten silver bangle on one arm, her ring fingers on both hands glitter with diamonds as do her ears, and a tiny crystal winks at me from the hair-fine chain around that slim neck. It's disappointing sometimes, always being right. Why can't people try harder, why are they all so predictable?

"You look fabulous. Wow, Alice, you're all grown up..."

She turns me to look in a mirror in the hall.

"*We're* all grown up. God, us two, adults!"

"You're an actual mother."

"I know, right? It's insane when you think about it. I'm sure it was only yesterday that—"

"The kids are asleep," and there's a voice I know well, too well, coming down the stairs, "So I'm just going to... oh... hi."

He is dark to her light, rangy and spare, dark stubble, silver-flecked cropped hair, tall and jittery in the hall.

"Oh, Jake, you remember Evie, don't you? From school?"

He looks baffled, scruffs his hand through his hair.

"We're going out for dinner? I said last week? It's on the calendar."

"Sure. Hi Evie, nice to see you again." His smile is different now, perfectly even, showing off straight white teeth. He reaches out a hand to shake mine. His palm is dry and cool against mine. When Alice turns to get something, he winks at me.

"Nice to see you too."

I don't want to let go of him. I remember his fingers brushing my skin. Rough and urgent. I remember the salty taste of the back of his neck, the smell of the hollow of his hips, before the lines of muscle that bracket his lower belly and down. His shiver when I licked him.

He looks at me quizzically.

"Oh, we had a class together, right?"

Alice butts in.

"Babe, we all went to the same school – but we were the year below."

"Yes, that's it, now I remember. Although you looked a little different then, no?"

"A touch. But wow, this is amazing, a proper reunion!" I throw my arms out and embrace them both. It gives me an excuse to press my body against his.

When I let go, he runs his hands back through his hair again, pushes his hands into his pockets, looks at me, away, at Alice, back at me. *Compel, repel, attract, distract.*

"Right, well you ladies have a great evening – lovely to see you again, Evie." And he lopes off down the hall, disappearing behind a door.

"I'll be two seconds."

Alice is rummaging in a cupboard, pulling out gloves and a scarf. I check my phone while she gets her coat on. Sure enough there's a message from him.

WTF are you up to? Pls be careful.

I'm hiding in plain sight, that's what I'm doing. He's the one blushing like a teenager with a hard-on in maths class. I put my phone back in my bag.

"Right," and she rolls her eyes at me. "Well, I'd meant to offer you a drink here and a gossip before we head out, but thanks to my darling children, there's no time for that—"

"Don't worry about it, I'm starving anyway and I'm sure Jake wants some time to play on the... what is it? The Xbox?"

"Yeah, something like that. Men – can't live with them, can't kill them either."

I can't help but laugh. "Good to see he hasn't changed."

Alice doesn't turn around from where she is faffing around with her bag.

"From before, I mean."

When she faces me again, she's biting her lip. "I wondered if you'd remember him."

I have to give it to her, she plays her hand well. As if she hadn't walked in on us that one time. Seen us walking home hand in hand after school. Watched me disappear in front of her eyes, into his arms. She slings her bag over her shoulder.

"I don't really remember him to be honest."

She doesn't reply, just slams the door behind us.

"Oops, that'll wake the kids. Oh, wait, I don't care, do I? Jake can deal with it."

"It's like that, is it then?" And I wink at her now. "I won't tell, I promise."

We walk up the road. Past the Mercedes and Beamers and Range Rovers. They're all so shiny I could do my make-up in the reflection. There's no litter, no weeds, no people – except us.

"How was your day?" she asks.

"Ugh, full of meetings with complete morons. Everyone I work with is completely incompetent."

We're chatting as if we see each other regularly. But I guess because of the messaging, it does feel like that.

"Are they? That sounds very frustrating. Can you put them on performance management?"

"Probably. Too much paperwork though. Better to make them cry and work harder."

"Interesting management technique there."

"It's trained into us on the graduate programme."

"Is it? Really?"

"No!"

When she laughs, I laugh too. She's easy to be with; I find myself relaxing, unwinding, slipping into old habits. If Jake makes me tense and jittery, Alice is the opposite. It's like coming home. I want to be wary of her – and when I'm with Jake it's easy to be. But in person, it's different.

We reach the pub. It's a gastropub – serving gourmet twists on classics like burgers and pie. Since I've been gone it seems every pub is now a gastropub.

"Nice," I say, when we step inside, looking at the exposed brickwork and worn velveteen booths with artwork and knick-knacks that have been bought in bulk by every pub chain in the UK.

"Fancy a gin and tonic to start?" she asks.

I like the idea that there will be more drinks. "Why not."

We sit in the corner, near the fire, in snug chairs, a table between us with condiments and cutlery.

"I'll just leave some menus here." The barmaid, with Sharpied-on eyebrows and extensions down to her bum, sneaks off, probably to sext some spotty youth on her phone. We clink glasses.

"Cheers."

Alice looks so happy, a big smile, relaxing in her chair. Skin clear, not a wrinkle to trouble her.

"Our first legal drink together. Who'd have thought we'd have to wait so long?"

I can't tell if she's baiting me or genuinely doesn't remember what happened the last time we got drunk together. *Pushing buttons is fun, Evie, you should try it sometime. One little press and off they go, crying and wailing. It's human fireworks.*

"Right, where should we start?" she continues.

"Twenty years is a long time. I didn't know I had to prepare a presentation."

"Haha, at least you're still creating presentations, not stuck at home with the rug rats."

"It all looks amazing on the 'gram."

"You should know not to believe everything you see."

We order garlic bread and wine from the barmaid, when we can tear her away from her phone.

Alice wants to know all about my divorce, about Ollie, about work. She doesn't ask about anything before then. I've drip fed her bits of information when we'd messaged over the last few months, but like any married person she wants the gore, she wants to know about every snarky email, every irate text, how we battled over cutlery or plates or saucepans.

I wonder if she knows what happened to me after I left school, where I was sent? If Mama or John or Meredith ever told her anything. I wonder if she tried to write to me? For a long time, I was convinced she was writing to me but the letters were being intercepted. After a few months in that place, I had to accept the painful truth.

"How long are you back in the UK for then?"

"Well, I'm on secondment to the UK office, so minimum six months, but probably more like a year..."

"Wow – we can meet up again then? You can come out with me and the school mums."

"Sure, sounds good," I lie.

"What is it that you do exactly that means you get to travel around like this?"

She tops up my glass, we're almost a bottle down already.

"Well... you know how everyone hates real estate agents?"

"Yeah..."

"It's worse than that."

"Worse than an estate agent? Is that even possible? Are you human pond scum?" She giggles at her own joke.

"Even worse than that."

"Worse than that? What's worse than that?" She's laughing now. "Oh God, don't tell me you're a corporate lawyer too?"

"Nope. Close though. I mean, what does a management consultant do anyway?"

"You're not...?"

"Yep, leading on Human Resources for Fleshfield Dorringer."

She blinks rapidly. "Oh yes! You mentioned – you're working with my old firm, Smallfield & Grace."

I wonder if she's working it out. That the restructuring she's a victim of is partly because of me? Obviously, it wasn't deliberate, I didn't know she'd be impacted, I didn't specify who should be put at risk. I didn't identify individuals or teams. I simply talked about costs. I need to be careful what I say now though. I don't want to be the enemy.

"Are you not still with them?"

"Well, the company is going through a restructure at the moment – with your firm."

"Ah... well I don't advise on restructures specifically, it's all strategy and best practice, not actual delivery."

I'm lying. Why else would I be over here? But she's too distracted to ask me more. I need to tread cautiously. I put my hand over my wine when the waitress comes to top us up.

"Well anyway, I took paid redundancy last month. So I

guess I'm a full-time stay at home mum now." She takes a big gulp of wine.

"It's always women – and part-time women affected the most, isn't it?"

"Apparently so. I mean I'm sure it was all above board. But they've been looking for a reason to get rid of me for years. All the snide comments about leaving early when I finish at five to go and get the kids, without seeing all the extra hours I did, working late and on weekends."

"My boss loves part-time workers, says they're all the work for half the price."

"That's exactly what my manager was like. Happy to approve my flexible working request, talking about being output focused, aligning targets appropriately. But then scheduling key meetings on my days off or at the end of the day – and making me out to be awkward and unreasonable."

"Do you even miss it that much, then? The real answer, not for Instagram."

"I do love being with my kids, being there for the moments that matter."

I raise an eyebrow at her, at this.

"But... it's the admin I hate. The emotional workload of having to remember the minutiae of everyone's life – the sports kits, the birthdays, the presents, the medical appointments. Easter, Halloween, Christmas. Holidays, food shopping, food prepping. Laundry, cleaning, DIY. Dealing with every call and piece of paperwork. Being the person who knows where everything is and the only person who puts it there. Being chief cook, cleaner and bottle washer."

"The Alice I remember wasn't anyone's skivvy."

"The Alice you remember doesn't exist anymore."

"I doubt that." And I smile at her, pat her hand. She looks me in the eye and shakes her head. Rueful? Admonishing? All part of Alice's game.

"It's so long ago now, I wouldn't even know where to start, finding her."

"Oh, I'm sure if you looked hard enough, you'd find her again."

After all, every day we pull on different outfits, depending on who we want to be. The Alice I knew is just waiting in the wardrobe, waiting to be selected. I've already seen glimpses of her, no matter how much the now-Alice pretends.

"So, tell me how you and Jake ended up together?"

I need this map of their history, the route to how they got here. I don't care about the story coming out of her mouth, I want to see what her eyes tell me, the slant of her head, the way she holds her body – how easy it is for her to lie to me.

"It's a funny story actually." Sip of wine, hair toss, quick glance up to the right as she thinks of the right answer. "We met at work, on a grad scheme."

"Well, you didn't exactly meet at work."

"What do you mean?"

"You knew each other already – from when we were kids, remember?"

"Oh yeah but, I just meant we didn't really meet properly then." She fiddles with her hair, scans the room.

"Did you go to uni together as well then?"

"God, no. He went to some redbrick in the Midlands." She waves a hand as if indicating anywhere above the Watford Gap.

"Where did you go?"

"Durham." She dips her head, looks up at me, gauging my reaction.

"Oooh, fancy."

"Yeah... I didn't love it."

I bet. All the proper posh types frowning at Alice's new money *faux pas*.

"Had to be done though, Daddy was so keen."

I don't remember Uncle John giving a crap about Alice going to uni, but okay then.

"You must have walked into a job after that then?"

"Pretty much yeah."

"So... Jake?"

"It's pretty boring, we went on one of those inductee socials, drank too much, slept together, found each other tolerable, been together pretty much ever since."

There's a lot to unpick there. The guilt I feel about sleeping with him starts to erode. It's hardly the love story of the century from the sounds of it.

"I can't imagine working with my husband."

"Oh, we don't any more. He had a bit of a wobble – decided life was too short to be a boring stuff-shirt forever. He got poached by one of his media clients actually, so now he's a Creative Director. Weird, I know."

I nod.

"Don't get me wrong, we love each other, you just get a little jaded after ten years and three kids. He's zooming ahead in his career and I'm just... stagnating." She shakes her head, her eyes hard and flat.

That Alice I remember is just below the surface; one little crack and pressure in the right place is all it takes to shatter glass. I top up her glass.

"The irony is, I was actually better than him at work. Got promoted faster, got better clients, got better grades at school even. But then I got knocked-up, didn't I?" Another big gulp of wine.

The waitress hovers into my eyeline clutching dessert menus, but I wave her off, I don't want her distracting Alice.

"Did you not want kids then?"

"No, I did, I did, I just didn't know... I didn't know what it would really be like. I didn't know I'd become invisible?"

"I mean, you're pretty visible to me."

"Oh, I'm just sick of it all. You think it's bad when you're pregnant and it's constant do-this, do that – and then you have them and everyone wants to know if they're eating and sleeping and if you've snapped back. And just as you get over that, the little terrors start school."

She must know how insensitive she's being, surely? But then she always was the victim, somehow.

"Why did you have three, then?"

Even though I know it's rude to ask, I'm intrigued by her attempts to get me to feel sorry for her. That I have it better.

"Contraceptive failure. Sounds ridiculous I know, like we're teenagers without a clue." Is that a glimmer of tears? She used to be able to cry on cue.

"Although we've learned our lesson – I don't think we've had sex since and Sebastian is nearly two!"

Alice's voice seems loud and around me the waiters are stacking chairs or gossiping behind the bar. We're the only people left here.

"Looks like they're going to chuck us out in a minute, but I think we need another night out again. Booze and therapy combined!"

"Sorry, I've gone on, haven't I? I don't know why."

The waitress comes over with the card machine and I pay.

"Oh! You didn't have to do that."

"I wanted to, my treat."

Outside it's chilly, perhaps a hint of frost. Maybe the alcohol has removed any inhibition but we huddle up close, Alice links her arm in mine, looks up at me with those blue eyes, giggles again.

"Why have you come back, Evie?" She stumbles and looks down. I wonder what she'd say if I told her the truth. A truth I haven't even really admitted to myself yet.

"I told you, work... and the divorce."

"Yeah! Time for a new man."

"For some fresh meat, definitely." I curl my mouth into a tight little smile.

A car rushes past us, its red rear lights leaving a vapour trail.

"How long does it take to walk from your place to mine?"

"Not sure. I got a taxi."

"Are you staying in those new apartments?"

"Yeah, just a short-term let. They're serviced though so I don't need to do too much."

"Surprised you're not based in London though – bit rubbish, being out here in the sticks, having to commute."

"It's so I can fly out to the other offices easily. I'm not only working with the UK firm."

I don't want to tell her I chose where to stay, that I could have been in the city, but I wanted to be out here, near her and Jake.

"So you'll be staying here then?"

"For now, yes, but once the work with the European offices finishes, I might get moved into the city to be closer to their main office. We could have a night out on the town!"

"Sounds great, how soon can we go?"

It's not a bad idea, actually.

"I'll message you."

We've been walking fast and we're at her gate now.

"Sure you don't want to come in for one more?"

It's tempting. "Probably better not to – I've got work in the morning, need my beauty sleep!"

"No worries..." But she's giving me that Princess Di look. Why does she want me to come in, what else does she need to tell me? Alice was never so friendly without good reason.

A quick peck on the cheek, a whiff of roses and musk and she's gone.

All done then? Wanna hook up?

It's him. He must be watching from a window.

Does anyone even still call it that?

Apparently I do.

I loiter on the pavement. If anyone asks, I'm waiting for a cab.

The glow from my phone fades but I'm not scared.

There's movement in the alley way running along the side of Alice's house.

In the streetlight a shadow appears, forms the shape of a man.

The end of his cigarette glows, a beacon in the night. My lighthouse, my safe harbour, my home.

TWENTY

NOW

"God, I missed you," he's mumbling into my hair, running his hands down the shape of me. "Don't go away for so long again."

After dinner with Alice, it's Sod's law that work sends me off on a trip to the US, and then for a week in Switzerland. All because the client needed me there to handhold them it seems. So I haven't seen Jake or Alice in almost a month.

"You managed without me for twenty years..."

"I didn't know what I was missing."

Twenty years is a long time though. It's people and places and experiences and it changes a person. I'm not the same person and whether he knows it or not, neither is he. I can see the cracks in him too. His soft edges are all worn away now; he is hard and bright like a diamond. The Jake I knew didn't cheat or mess around. The Jake I knew wanted to be alone with me, his music, his art. I miss that boy, but I want the man.

"Did you never wonder about me?"

"All the time." He's kissing his way down my neck, ferreting up my top. I don't believe him.

"Why didn't you try to get in touch?"

"I didn't know where you were. There wasn't any Facebook for me back then. You just disappeared."

"Did you try though?"

He sighs loudly. "Of course I did. I sent you letters. And Alice kept me updated too..."

His eyes slide away from my face.

"She did? How?" I wonder what lies Alice fed Jake, back then. Just to have something because I couldn't.

"Have you forgotten we lived on the same road?"

"Of course not." *But I thought they barely knew each other back then.*

"When did you see her then?" I pull his face up to mine, pull back as he leans in to kiss me.

"Just... around, you know?"

He loops his fingers into my waistband, backs me up against the wall in this soulless serviced apartment. I'm not afraid of him this time, I'm ready for us. Something in my mind has set, like cement. The line we've crossed is so far behind us, it's no longer visible. The guilt I should feel dissolving in the wake of another, stronger emotion. People say you never forget your first love. And if it's not a meaningless hook-up, then is it so wrong, what we're doing? She doesn't love him. Not like I do. We're meant to be together. Otherwise why would it feel so good, after all this time?

"What did she tell you?"

"Oh... just that you'd gone away, she didn't know when you'd be back." He goes back to kissing my neck, untucking my top, running his hands up my body, squeezing and cupping me against him. "Why are we wasting time talking?"

I let him carry on, but all the time he's unzipping my jeans, tugging them down, dropping to his knees, burying his face between my thighs, I can't help but think of him. And her. And what happened after I left.

Even as my legs tremble and he lifts me onto the bed, makes

it so that there is nothing between us but skin, I think to myself, *Evie, this is important.*

When he's gone, I message her.

Fancy meeting up again soon?

Definitely, what about that night out in London you promised me?

On it now. I'll message you deets. Let me know any days you can't do.

She sends me the most complicated mix of times and days. I don't know why I asked her for them. I'm not her PA. I resolve to ignore them. Find the best day for me. Which honestly would be as soon as humanly possible because when I know someone is withholding something from me, I can't rest until I've uncovered the truth. I've always been one to pick at scabs, rip off the plaster. Even so, I remind myself to breathe, to be patient. *You catch more flies with honey, Evie,* Mama whispers in my ear.

He sends me poems. Pictures of broken things, run-down buildings, graffiti tags. I come home to gifts – leather covered notebooks, tiny sequinned purses, expensive gin, lingerie made from eyelash lace in the darkest navy.

I'm doing everything I wanted to do then.

I take pictures of myself in odd locations. With clothes on, some without. I send him Spotify playlists with obscure covers by Nirvana, like "My Sharona" and "Bad Moon Rising". I send him The Pixies. I send him Sonic Youth. I send him Patti Smith and PJ Harvey.

You're breaking my heart all over again.

Do you remember? I type out. Do you remember where we were when we first heard this?

I remember your T-shirt

I remember your bed.

Oh yeah?

Yeah...

Sometimes he calls me. Tiny tortured minutes in an alleyway in the city, the rumble of other lives in the background. His voice a mumble of words that, strung together say *I want you* in one light and *save me* in another. There is never enough time. Never.

Do you think she suspects?

I don't care.

I don't ask where this is going. I know where it's going. This time I'm the one in control. I'm just not quite sure what I'm in control of – but that's what I love, what I've missed. Ollie never gave me this. And now I see how although I wasn't ready for this as a teenager, I am now. I am ready to be adored, to be worshipped, to be loved.

Why are you friends with her? I don't get it.

He's not happy that Alice and I are meeting up again. He still doesn't know how much we message, but he doesn't need to know.

I'm just intrigued, you know? There's stuff I need to ask her.

Be careful though. Some things are best left in the past. She's not what she seems.

I can handle her. Thanks though.

I know you can.

Worried I'll find out all your dirty little secrets?

You are my dirty little secret.

Always.

This is how it starts; this is not how it will end. He leaves stuff at mine. His shirt, a toothbrush, loose change. I leave nothing with him. Just faint marks on his skin, his back, his wrists.

Doesn't she notice?

It's not like that anymore.

It's such a cliché that I think maybe she just doesn't care. I wonder why. The Alice I know doesn't give up on her possessions and she doesn't share them. But then maybe she doesn't love him anymore, so she doesn't notice? If she's discarded him, then he's mine, guilt-free.

It goes on. We talk, we text, we have sex. I text his wife. I make plans with her. I lie to her when I'm with him and I lie to him when I'm with her.

Can't wait to see you, she says, a week out from our "girls' night out" as she keeps calling it. I really need to let my hair down.

Happy to help :)

I have plans for her for sure. For both of us – well, all of us really. Some are short term and some are long term. But in the meantime, I keep on sleeping with her husband and lying to everyone.

TWENTY-ONE

It's difficult being back, because it's reminding me constantly of when I left. I think they call it intrusive thoughts. But I can't help it. After a long day at work, when my head is messy and burned out, the memories come for me.

I know it's all a long time ago now, but when I'm weak and vulnerable, it's easy to remember how I felt back then. Now, sitting in the dark, with a glass of wine, indulging in my retro playlists, the darkness creeps in, the thoughts about how I'm unlovable, broken, wrong. That's why Ollie cheated, it's why I can't stay pregnant, it's why I was sent away.

It's not helping that I'm staying so close to where it all happened. Travelling down the same road, passing by the same buildings, the school. Time travel feels truly possible.

I wake up early most mornings, mostly to crack on with work, but sometimes to go for a run. The sky at this time of year is shades of blood red, peach, orange, but on crisper, colder days it changes to a pale pink.

The day they took me away, all those years ago, the sky was the same colour. I'd packed the night before. My suitcase was in the hall. I had to get up at the ungodly hour of six am.

I'd played Radiohead at top volume that morning, to comfort myself – and to piss off my mother.

"There's no need for that, Evie-Lynn."

"If I've got a flair for the dramatic, you've only yourself to blame."

Despite the early start, my mother was in full make-up, hair done. I'm not sure who she thought she was going to impress. But that was typical – standards had to be maintained.

As for me, I was almost looking forward to going away. Surely it couldn't be any worse than living with her – cooking my own food, washing my own clothes, no one caring if I did my schoolwork?

On the table my papers waited – the checklist, the letter of welcome. Stepford Hall Independent School. Although, what sort of school collects its pupils in a car?

"This is for the best. It's the only way to protect you."

"Protect me? From what... you?"

She only shook her head. If this was her attempt at empathy, at caring, it was too little too late.

"I know I should have done more, seen more. Been a better mother—"

"Oh yes, it's always about you. About how hard it is for you. Maybe you should have kept your legs crossed. Or even better, had an abortion!"

Tears welled in her eyes.

"I know you don't mean to be so cruel. I did the best I could for you."

"If that was your best, I'd hate to see your worst. You protected me from nothing!"

A car pulled onto the drive. The doorbell rang. There was no time for further goodbyes. I hoped someone would get a message to Jake.

Everything had moved so fast since Rosie's body was found and seemingly, Mama couldn't get rid of me fast enough. Now I know she thought she was doing the right thing, and it's not like she had any role models. But sending your child away, rejecting them when they need you most? I would never do that to a child of mine.

Being back here now, so close to being a mother myself so many times, I just can't understand her. Why didn't she want me? Why didn't she love me? Why didn't she care? I suspect she even knew about Uncle John. She probably knew about everything.

In the end she could only be my enemy; she didn't even try to understand what had happened. She never once hugged me, you know? Not properly, not for reassurance.

Oh sure, she would beckon me over when she was half cut in her chair, fling her arms around me, slobber into my neck that she loved me and I was the best. But then she'd disappear for a few days or a long weekend, telling me to call next door to Aunty Meredith if I needed anything.

I only allowed myself to see her one more time before she died. She took me to university after I left that school. In her clapped-out old Mini, my suitcases in the back, a big bag of old books and bits and pieces. I remember arriving and everyone else had a mum and dad, and what seemed like the whole of a department store to decorate their rooms. But I only had her. And just like when I went to that school, she didn't even stay to watch me go. Everything was always on her terms. Always being left behind. Empty.

I never even went to her funeral. She died after I'd already moved to Boston. It wasn't worth the time and money. I lost my mother the day she sent me away. There was nothing left for me to mourn.

TWENTY-TWO

NOW

I'm so excited. I'm so done with PTA nights out.

Alice wanted to go out in London, so we're going out in London. She dropped enough hints about the last trains and cabs that I knew what she really wanted though, so I've arranged a client meeting and booked a hotel room in London for us. I'll claim it back later.

In the city, it's office party hell everywhere – unbuttoned shirts and ties as headbands, every corner paints a picture of the modern corporate work – finance assistants puking into their handbags, sales executives doing coke in the men's bathrooms, florid-faced directors dad-dancing with their PAs, wondering why their wives don't want to wind and grind against them like that.

The bar I meet Callum in is all exposed brick and graffiti art. Not sure how it justifies the twenty-pound cocktails but it's not my problem, I'm not paying. We're in Shoreditch – east London. I thought it was a bit cliché to come here, but given Alice is used to gastropubs and piano bars, this'll be a walk on the wild side for her. I bet she didn't party at university. I bet she never partied. Apart from at school. I want my Alice back.

Callum is an old friend of Ollie's, but he's always had a soft spot for me. And of all Ollie's friends, he's the least idiotic. The only one not privately educated. I was never really sure of his place in Ollie's friendship group. I know he had useful contacts for them too, but sometimes Ollie made comments about him, behind his back, about his accent, where his clothes were from. I never said anything, but it didn't surprise me – it was Ollie's attitude to anyone who wasn't like him or didn't ingratiate themselves with him. Often on nights out, I'd end up dancing with Callum, doing shots.

He wanted to meet for a drink and as I was in town, I didn't see the harm in catching up with him first. I guess it's a bit of a confidence boost.

"Who are you out with tonight then?"

"An old friend – from school." I don't want to explain the intricacies to Callum, though I feel like he is one of the few people I might confide the truth in.

"Yeah?"

"She doesn't get out much – she's got kids – and she just got made redundant."

"That's rubbish."

"Yeah, I'm not the biggest fan of girls' night's out, but I couldn't say no."

"Sure, I get it." He watches the office group in front of us do shots, screeching about thirsty Thursday. "Are you planning to party hard?"

"Like... what?"

"Like Ollie does? You can hit me up if you need anything. I can get it for you."

I'd be lying if I said I'd never dabbled with drugs before. Ollie's friends, when we first moved to the US, loved their coke, but I stayed away – they all sounded like complete twats when they were on it, I didn't want to be like them.

"No, we're okay – but thank you."

"No worries." He drains his pint.

"Want another?"

"Nah. I'll leave you to it. Your mate'll be here soon. I'm not going to crash your girls' night out." His foot nudges mine under the table. "But, maybe call me later?" He brushes his hand against mine.

Callum is a handsome man, striking. At university, he was the one, out of Ollie's crowd, the girls I knew wanted to be introduced to. Even tonight he turns heads – men and women. But I'm not interested, I might have been once, but not anymore. And Alice would ask too many questions. "I'm not sure what time we'll be out until…"

"Sure, don't do me any favours." He snatches his hand away, his face flushing. He's never so openly tried it on before. I guess because I was always taken then. "It's not like I don't have options."

I laugh. "Poor baby, so many women wanting you."

"A guy's got to keep busy," and then he winks. "You heard from Ollie?"

"Why would I?"

"Yeah… I guess not. He's just gone a bit off the radar, that's all."

"Probably too busy shacking up with Cassie."

"Hey, don't get bitter. And besides… it's not like you don't have alternatives." Underneath the table his thigh bumps mine, when our eyes meet, there's a small charge of electricity.

My phone lights up. It's Alice.

Just off the tube!

Callum stands up. "Right, better be off." And I lose his

attention to his phone which is bleeping insistently. "Call me. Don't call me. Whatever."

I watch him as he leaves, fist bumping people, shaking hands. He's a popular boy Callum is, friends everywhere.

I almost don't recognise Alice when she walks in.

"Is this seat taken?"

"Yes... oh, Alice!" I stand up and clash cheekbones with her. She smells of my usual perfume. And cigarette smoke. Her hair is shorter and blonder, her lips shiny red. Tonight is going to be different.

"You look fab!" And she does. A blue satin jumpsuit, with buttons down the front, short sleeves, military detailing.

She fiddles with a pendant that hangs above her cleavage, artfully exposed by undone buttons. I pour out a glass of fizz, pass it to her.

"It's new... I might have given Jake's credit card a bashing."

"Oh yeah...?" I raise an eyebrow.

"I don't want to think about it anyway. Not tonight. Tonight is for fun." And she raises her glass to me. "Chin-chin," knocks back the champagne in one go.

"So, that's how it is?"

"That's how it is." I refill our glasses and settle back in my seat. I wasn't expecting this tonight, but I can work with it.

"Good week at work?"

"Just the usual. I don't want to talk about it."

"Trust me, it's better than the alternative."

"Touché."

And she goes on to bore me with the minutiae of the bickering on the WhatsApp groups, the humblebrag of the mums whose kids have read *Harry Potter* whilst others, like Alice's, have barely mastered the alphabet from the sounds of it. By the time we've sunk a bottle of champagne, I tell Alice I need the bathroom.

. . .

It's so busy in the bar and there's a long line for the bathrooms. When I get to the front, before I can say anything, Alice pushes into the cubicle with me when one becomes free.

"Sorry – I couldn't wait for another cubicle! God, I needed a night out!"

I'm aware of how close she is. The physicality of someone I left behind, tried to forget. But right here her flesh is luminous and scented. I can almost hear her blood humming in her veins, her heartbeat pounding in my ear.

"I needed to find the old Alice – so I did. No more slummy mummy, more like yummy mummy!"

In the cubicle next to us a voice yells "Preach sister!" Alice laughs, her pupils tiny black dots inside her pale irises, a new type of thousand-yard stare.

"You're more than just a mummy, Alice."

"Ha. Sure, if you say so – this life, it's like being back at school."

"Yeah?"

"It's one big pressure cooker of needing the right clothes and the right friends and the right house."

I'm not sure why I'm supposed to be feeling sorry for her this time.

"And the politics are just insane. Who's in, who's out, changes hourly sometimes. They post such shit online. Such blatant lies."

"Like what?"

"Hang on."

And then she flips open the toilet seat and pees. "Sorry, needs must, after three kids."

"Sure..."

She wipes and flushes and then we exit the cubicle. No one bats an eyelid as we muscle our way to the sinks where we're nudged to the side by a woman in a bandage dress that looks like it was stolen from her teen daughter's wardrobe. As she pushes past, I note her VPL and the toilet paper stuck to her heel.

Alice is swiping at her phone. "Look at this nonsense."

"It's a bouquet of flowers...?"

"Yeah, from her husband. But he's a total creep. He stands too close, makes jokes about mummy-swapping. Thinks he's so hot but he's just scum. She knows it, too, but she still posts that, trying to pretend everything is perfect."

"Sounds grim."

"It is. I can't stand all the crap. I wish I could teach that guy a lesson."

We go out back to the bar, queue for a round of drinks.

"Why don't you?"

But she's too busy scrolling – "And this one, look at this dinner – looks great right? She'll be throwing it up right after, otherwise she won't get invited to the designer sample sales she likes to go to."

I couldn't care less about all this stuff.

"Here, this bag right, and all this make-up. She's a klepto. She takes stuff from people's houses. No one will have her kid over for playdates anymore. And everyone just turns a blind eye to it all. Pretends it's all real."

As if Alice never posts picture of her happy little family, even though her husband loves me. I'd call it the price you have to pay for perfection.

"Have you ever had a bit of fun – you know, like... trolled them?"

"How?"

"Show me some more."

She shoves Facebook in front of me. There's a picture of a smug looking blonde woman with her daughters.

"I don't get what you mean." Alice bumps against me as we reach the front of the bar queue.

"Look at the caption. *Perfect reports all of them, so blessed to have such talented daughters, beautiful and intelligent who love to do their homework and work so hard on their extra-curriculars.*" Underneath are rows of comments about how it's all down to her parenting.

"Yes, love?" the barman wants our orders. I look up at the cocktail menu, drawn in chalk behind the bar.

Alice is still engrossed in her phone. "I'll get these, yeah?"

I roll my eyes at the barman. "I'll have two of those," and I point behind him at the illustration.

When it arrives, it's a lurid green drink, red cherry, straw, parasol, all the tack.

"What is this, Evie?"

"Limoncello, lemonade, lime, vodka and soda."

"No, what's it called, so I can order it again."

"I Dare You."

Her eyes widen, freezes with her drink halfway to her mouth. "I Dare You?"

"Yep. That's the one."

She starts laughing. "Are you kidding me? Seriously? I Dare You?!"

"I'm not kidding."

She takes a big sip.

"Give me your phone."

I open Facebook and find the post, tap quickly.

"What have you done?" She tries to grab the phone, but I stop her.

"Just having a little fun. Your turn now."

"What?" She looks at what I've written, snorts.

"Go on – you try it!

I've hooked her.

"What should I write?"

"I don't know, anything you like."

"Not now. Tomorrow."

"That's a promise. Live a little. I dare you."

At that she laughs and I make her pinky promise.

"I'm holding you to this."

"I won't let you down."

And then she grabs my hand and pulls me onto the sweaty, heaving dance floor. We throw our arms up and let our hair down, we wind and grind and shake what our mamas gave us.

There is a moment out there, under the light and the glitter, just before the beat drops. Alice seems to wave and weave in slow motion, like life is on go-slow. And in that freeze-frame of pink then white then blue then black then back to pink again, I see something else.

I see I am in the eye of the storm, I see I am the catalyst, I see I am everything and everyone. I see that the future is in my hands. I see that I have offered Alice the red pill and the blue pill and really her choice is her fault. And as the beat thuds back to life, in that split second, I see that in order to get the truth from Alice, I will need to take it from her.

TWENTY-THREE

"Is this how it's going to be then?"

"What do you mean?"

Jake has come in, flung me on the bed, no hello, no nothing. Which admittedly I enjoyed. He always was good with his hands, even as a teen. I blame all the guitar practice.

"I'm not just some toy for you to screw whenever you like."

Inside, I cringe a little. I sound like a needy, clingy girlfriend needing reassurance and cuddles, desperate to know where we stand. I can't deal with being messed around. With Callum, his offer in the bar was very clear. But I'm not interested in playing those kinds of games with Jake.

"Did I say you were?"

"There's no hello, no nothing. Do I mean nothing to you, just someone to play with when you're bored?"

There's that muscle twitching in his jaw, stubble that burned against my neck. His eyes flit around the room, not landing on anything.

"That's not true."

"Whatever." I turn over in bed, pull the sheets over me, pull my eye mask down. "If you're done then you can leave."

"Don't be like that."

"I'm not being like anything. You've made it perfectly clear how you feel."

He's standing up, buttoning his jeans, shoving his T-shirt back on.

"What? It's all right for you, Evie, swanning back in here as if nothing's changed, stirring up shit, screwing with people's heads and then disappearing off again for ages."

"I had another work trip. It's my *job*. You knew that. You've got a nice little wifey at home, remember? You don't get to have both of us under the thumb."

"Shut up." He pushes his feet into his shoes, not looking at me.

"What's the matter? Not quite so under control then, is she?"

His fist thuds into the wall above the shoe cupboard.

"Maybe you should smack her about a bit?" I'm goading him but I can't help it.

"Go to hell." He's wincing now, clutching his hand. "I shouldn't have come over. Shit." Blood seeps from between his fingers, but he makes for the door anyway.

"Jake."

"What?" His voice is so brittle, I know it won't take much.

"Sit down." I can't be too kind; he's like me, it'll break him.

"Fine."

I get an ice pack, wrap it in a towel. Find some painkillers and the whisky. Approach him like a wildcat, waiting for the hissing and hackles to lower. I crouch between his legs, soothing him. He doesn't say a word but doesn't take his eyes off me. Every time I look up.

"I'm sorry, Jake. It's just hard. Being back here, seeing you, realising what I lost, when I got sent away. And now she's got you. It's so unfair. I wanted this life with you – and now I have nothing and you have everything."

"I don't have everything. Not without you."

"But you're with her. Not me."

He hangs his head.

"I need to know that this isn't just a fling for you, Jake. Being away from you, and being back. I can't give you up again – not this time."

"No one's asking you to give me up."

"Prove it though. Prove how much I mean to you."

"Evie..."

He looks at me, jaw clenched.

"It's not that easy."

"It's as easy – or as hard – as you make it."

"There's the kids to consider."

And then he huffs to himself.

"What?"

"Just... the irony, that kids are keeping me with her – again."

"What do you mean?"

"Nothing... shit, my hand hurts – forget I said anything, it's not worth it."

"Okay then. But next time something isn't worth it, maybe you could try not to break either the wall or your hand?" He wasn't angry like this before. She's done this to him.

"I'm sorry about that."

"It's okay." I reach up, stroke his cheek.

"She's so difficult sometimes. I feel like I'm suffocating." He's shaking his head now. "It's all a big mistake and it's too late now."

"Marriages have their ups and downs, it's normal."

He's so out of it, so lost inside himself, he doesn't even question my sympathy.

"There's something wrong with her though. She's not right in the head."

Tell me something I don't know, I think.

"She always was kinda intense. But that's pretty strong..."

"She's obsessed. She won't put her phone down. She's always on it. I think she's up to something."

"Sure she's not having an affair?"

He sniffs, cocks an eyebrow at me. "That would be preferable. Nah, she's messing with someone's head. I just feel it. Why does she have to be like that? She's got everything she could want."

"Want me to have a word with her?"

"What?"

"Well, I'm seeing her this week. I can try and find out what she's up to." As if I don't know already, as if I didn't set her on this track.

"I didn't realise you were seeing her."

"She's so excited I'm back."

He shakes his head now. I get up from my knees, sit on the bed next to him. Some conversations are better had when you're not face to face. His thigh twitches incessantly.

"It's weird, you guys hanging out like this."

"How's your hand feeling?"

"Give me the painkillers." I pop them out, pass him a tumbler with two fingers of whisky – but he adds another before gulping it all down.

"Look, you've got nothing to worry about. She has no idea about us and I'm not planning to tell her. You're safe." He doesn't need to know about the messaging, the planning, the stirring up of long-forgotten things.

I try to still the hammering of his leg, move my hand towards his crotch, but he picks my hand up and interlaces his fingers with mine, rests his injured hand on his other leg.

"I meant what I said, Jake. You coming back has stirred up a bunch of stuff, okay? It's not your fault but some things were best left where they were, in the past."

The thing with wounds, if they don't heal properly, they fester and rot. It might look all scabbed over, scarred on the surface, but underneath things are still moving. I've always been one to pick and pick and pick.

"I never wanted to hurt you, Evie. I never thought this would happen."

"I know." In fact, he drove this, he messaged, he wanted to meet up, he made the first move. And he's the married one. It's dangerous, when you're playing with people's feelings. I can't help but feel that if anyone is the victim here, it's me – not him. "You can trust me, you know that? Always." And I kiss him, slow, gentle, tender, coaxing out the words he can't say. He pulls away, tips his forehead against mine.

"Don't you ever wonder about it, Evie? If things hadn't gone the way they had. If we were together all the time. If I could wake up next to you. I'm so tired of everything. That's all."

"I know, baby. I know."

This isn't what I was expecting, but it's reassuring. We're on the same path, as ever. Wanting the same things. He's still wavering but it won't take much, to bring him over to my side.

"I just can't help thinking about alternatives. About... the life I might have had. If we hadn't... if I hadn't..." He puts his head in his hands, winces.

"If you hadn't what?" What *is* he saying – what did he do? What did we do – or does he mean Alice and him? This scab needs working loose, needs picking at, otherwise I will never heal. None of us will heal.

"Just... we made a mistake and we paid for it. And now look where we are." His face twists with anger. "Sometimes though, I hate this – all of this. I'm tired of it all, it hurts. Even being with you."

"Right. Well, if you feel like that then you can go home – back to your safe little wife and your safe little life." I spit the words out. "If you hate us so much."

He gets off the bed. Gets his stuff together, phone in pocket, patting for his keys.

"Where did you tell her you were tonight? What's she going to say about that?" I point at his hand, bloodied and bruised. A broken thing between us.

"I don't know. Football. The pub."

"Where's your kit?"

"In the car."

"You're not safe to drive. Not in this mood."

"Since when do you care if I'm safe to drive?"

"I don't want to be responsible for you running someone over. You can't drive home."

He squints at me in the dim light. I wonder what he's really seeing, because I don't think it's me now. He breaks up the distance between us, runs his hands through my hair. Pulls me up close to him. Looks me in the eye.

"I hate this and I love this. Shit... why is this so hard?" His voice cracks. I know he was remembering. "I wish you'd never left me."

"I didn't leave you. Not deliberately. I was taken from you – think of it like that."

I wonder what it'll take to make him commit, this time. "And I'm back, I'm here now, with you."

"I know what I want, I do. I need some time. That's all."

"And I need to know that this means something to you."

"You do, I promise. I mean it. I swear, Evie..."

But he takes his arms away. Steps away from me. Closes the door behind him. He's the one leaving me this time. But he said one more thing, before he went.

So quiet, I could think I imagined it.

But I hold it to me like a treasure.

I love you, Evie.

PART 3

TWENTY-FOUR

"And then she uninvited her to the barbeque!"

Alice is midway through some endless story about people I don't know and don't care about. She always did take forever to get to the point. Also, who has a barbeque in January? My phone buzzes in my hand, flashing RUPERT in big letters.

"Sorry, I need to get this, hang on."

Alice clunks her cup onto its saucer.

Work won't leave me in peace at the minute. Something about my expenses and written warnings. It's all right when Rupert wants to take people out to Gaucho for Wagyu steaks, but I treat myself to a few drinks or a luxury hotel stay and they lose it. Do *they* want to go to Tokyo or Sao Paulo or Dubai with no notice?

"Yes?"

"Evie, you still on for lunch today?" Rupert is in London for a meeting with the higher ups. He doesn't come over often, so I know I should be worried, but I'm too distracted to care.

"Yep."

"Good. Rosamund is joining us."

It's not great, being summoned to Head Office, for a

lunchtime meeting with HR. Although maybe it's a promotion? The client feedback is positive. Maybe this is a good thing. I don't know.

I hang up and check my calendar again, scrolling down on my phone to see all the details, in case there's a clue I've missed.

"Everything okay?"

Alice doesn't have to pretend, I know she's busy playing chess with people's social lives. Manoeuvring herself into the centre position, just like at school. This is what I wanted though, to see if that Alice is still here.

"Yeah, just boring work stuff."

"Huh. Well, at least you've got a job."

"Hmm."

Since our night out, since I laid my bait, she's been a good girl and walked straight into my trap. She's been worming her way into people's affections, booting other people out of favour, enjoying her power. I gave her this, the confidence to see who she could be. But it's not enough.

I think about her, at night. When my dreams are pulling me back there, taking me back to that other place and time.

Jake is right – coming back is stirring everything up again, the memories buried by silt in the riverbed of my mind, are starting to swirl up and around again. She feels it all too. Last time we reached a tipping point, bad things happened. But they gave me an escape route. So where are we running to this time?

She's looking at her phone again now, smirking.

"It's working."

"What's working?"

"The stuff you told me to do, you dared me to do. It's genius."

She shows me her phone, her fake accounts, the trolling, the comments.

"It's so easy. And they're like kids." She's so dismissive of their stupidity, how malleable they are. How she's spread rumours of infidelity, gay husbands, redundancy, miscarriages. Cracking lives apart, word by word. But this is small fry. It doesn't have the repercussions I need it to. This isn't enough.

"Do you ever think about the stuff we did?"

She turns a blank face to me, blank eyes, no soul, carefully forms words. "What stuff, when?"

"When we were younger?"

"What did we do?"

She's going to make this hard. She's playing me. She can't have forgotten. "The swimming pool?"

Hurry, hurry says my heartbeat, it remembers. The scent of roses, silver bubbles drifting past my face. She's switching places with me, memories slide about, loose files, silt spinning.

"I'm not sure what you're talking about." She's fiddling with her phone again.

"I dream about it all the time."

"Dream about what?" She's so absorbed in her task, she's forgotten why she's doing it.

"That I'm back there. In the pool, in your room, under your sheets. At school, in the music room."

She winces, looks around. I can't believe this.

"What? No one's listening."

"Look, it's painful for me, that's all. It was hard for me too. With you gone. Stuff happened."

"What stuff? With who – Jake? School?"

"Oh, come on. Why are you asking all this now?"

This is who I remember. This is the Alice only I saw. The mask is slipping. Everything we knew to be true is just perception. Here is the answer coming, I feel it. I need it. This is the calm before the storm.

"Because I feel like you're hiding something from me, Alice."

"What? That's bullshit. It wasn't easy for me, you know. My parents got divorced after you left. What you said to your mum

– about my dad, him being inappropriate... they couldn't carry on. Not with the rumours. I still don't get why you did that. Stuff like that ruins lives."

"So, it's my fault?"

"No, I don't blame you. All I'm saying is that... shit, it's working!"

"Alice, what are you up to?"

"This mum is such a stupid cow, right? She thinks she's so perfect, with her perfect house and kids and husband."

Much like you, Alice, I think.

"She needs to be taught a lesson. It's not nice to rub everyone's nose in it."

I raise my eyebrows.

"I don't know why you're looking at me like that, you told me to have fun, stop taking all these people so seriously. So, I am. She doesn't need all these freebies, it's not going to hurt, spreading a few rumours."

She always needed a fall guy, clearly nothing has changed.

"Well, isn't she paid to do her posts – isn't that her job?"

"Look, I know you're living the high life, jetting about, but some of us are very fed up. Maybe Jake and I have just been together too long, I don't know."

"It happens to everyone though."

"Maybe it's how we got together then, we were so young."

"It was at work, right?"

"No... what? We were teenagers. It was after you left."

"I thought—"

"Look, I know you had a crush on him back then, but it just happened okay."

In a blink she's rewritten history to suit her.

I let the silence stretch out, wait for her to fill the gap.

"I missed you. You were my best friend, practically my sister. You were there and then you were gone. And Jake was there and I needed someone, something." All that time I was in that place, far away from home, struggling to finish school, crying myself to sleep and worrying I'd find my roommate dead in her own bed, Alice and Jake were shagging and living it up. Jake was mine, *is mine*. And she took him. Just like she takes everything.

"The baby was an accident – it just happened... Evie, say something, anything, please."

"What baby?"

The deluge of information – that they were together then, and now a baby – is leaving me cold. My brain can't compute this. A baby. A fucking baby?

When she looks at me, her eyes are glassy. "I lost it."

Pain pulses through my chest. I want to empathise. I can't imagine going through a miscarriage as a teenager. It was unbearable even as an adult.

"Alice, did you even know you were pregnant?"

I mean, if she wasn't trying to get pregnant, if it was an early loss...

"Yes."

"And you wanted to keep—"

"I didn't know. I didn't really get the chance to think about it properly. Before... before I lost it." She casts her hands out to her sides, as if trying to convey her confusion back then.

I hate her for calling her baby – their baby – it. The ease with which she can discard, dehumanise something so precious. I can't bear it. But I know I need to pretend. To grin and bear it. And I do feel sorry for her, back then.

"I'm so sorry. That must have been so tough. You were so young. I can't imagine."

I force myself to lean across and hug her. "I know how hard a loss like that is."

She nods, presses her lips together in a bloodless line.

"But," – I am compelled to ask, needing the truth – "you stayed together after?"

"Yes. I loved him, he was an escape route. My parents were... well, everything was so messy and I just wanted to get out of there. And he was having a tough time with his family too – you know what they were like about his brother and him. So I – we – did. We left."

"What do you mean, you left?"

"Well, Jake and I... we went to university together."

"You definitely told me you met at work." If she's lied to me about this, what else has she lied to me about? And I can picture them now, arms entwined on campus, sleeping in a single bed, that couple everyone aspires to be, dreamy and perfect, smug. Relationship goals. *We've been together since school.*

"Look, I understand you're upset, maybe this is a shock – but we were only kids. Jake told me that you guys were never serious, that it was always me he wanted."

I tilt my head towards her. Meet that perfect gaze. So many lies now – Alice and Jake, Alice and Rosie, Uncle John, Ollie. The numbness I felt has turned to a strange ringing noise in my ears and my head, my whole body throbbing with it.

I thought coming back would make things simple. But it's only made things worse.

"Where are you going? Evie? Aren't you going to say anything?"

"I've got a migraine," I gasp out and gather my bag and coat, almost knocking the wine bottle flying as I go, imagining the pool of viscous red it would cause, staining Alice's carpet, impossible to cover up or remove.

But before the door closes behind me, I hear her tapping away on her phone already, gossiping, spinning, weaving her web. Telling the story that suits her best. I've had enough, I don't care about the baby she lost, I've lost so much more and now, now not only do I want answers, I want something else. I want everything. It's my turn now.

TWENTY-FIVE

I call in sick to work, and cancel my lunch at Head Office. Tell them I've been signed off by a doctor. *Gynaecological problems* – Rupert can't put the phone down fast enough. I lie on my bed, waking only to refill my water bottle, lulling myself into a hazy artificial peace.

Where are you?

Answer your phone

I need to see you

Pick up

I'm sorry, okay.

Her words are just faint bleats, cries for help that I don't have the desire to give. *That'll teach you* and it will.

It's not just her messaging me. He is too. I picture them in their house, together but alone. I am the only person who can save them. But I can't save them both. I won't save them both. I might not save either of them. I need to save myself first. I wish I knew how.

Days pass – I don't know how many. Time is blurry and fluid, and irrelevant. I'm obliterating myself. Dr Lucinda would have a lot to say I'm sure, but I definitely don't want to talk to her. There is more than one way out, there is more than one ending here. I just need to figure out exactly what I want and then how to get it. It should be simple. But for some reason, it's not.

Sometimes I lean out of the Juliet balcony and smoke a cigarette I don't even want. *I'm not a smoker*, I tell myself. But then I take another drag, watch the way it dangles from my unmanicured nails, breathe smoke out of my nostril and it wakes the dragon inside.

It all goes around and around in my head. *Ollie's affair, my baby, Jake's betrayal, Alice's baby*. And somehow, I'm the one to have come out empty-handed. Everything I give to people, everything they take from me. Uncle John, Mama, Rupert, it's all about them, never about me.

It's never my turn, no matter how hard I try. Even if he left Alice for me, there would always be that doubt within him. Did I mean so little back then? When I was going through the worst a person can survive, he simply changed lanes. That life we planned, he kept to it, just changed the girl he lived it with.

Even now, how do I know I'm not a plaything, easily dropped when someone younger, prettier appears? When the novelty of rediscovering his teenage sweetheart fades. What would he do if I told him the truth about his wife and me? That she's a killer. That I helped.

One night I perch on the edge of the balcony, thighs clenched to avoid falling, legs crossed, balancing. Time is still branching away from me, all those alternative possibilities, alternative worlds. It's up to me to choose one. I weigh up the pros and cons. I think about what might happen if I jumped, how I'd say goodbye, waiting for those wings to spread out, the message I'd leave behind. And think about how I wouldn't be falling but flying.

On another night I'm sitting there again, on the edge. It starts raining. Not dramatic, movie ending rain, just drizzle that soaks you apathetically. Not even the weather is on my side. A grey blanket that makes me shift, step down, go back inside. *Dry off, warm up.*

It does the trick though, a message from the heavens. How British, that it's in the form of the weather. When push comes to shove, I'll save myself every time. And that's what I forgot – I let myself get distracted, get too involved in other people's dramas.

Alice taught me one thing, that it's always worth playing a long game. To be patient, controlled, keep my eyes on the prize. Jake was the same, all those years ago – waiting for the pay-off when we could leave everyone. It didn't work then, so I allowed my head to be turned. I'm not making that mistake again. *Fool me once, shame on you, fool me twice – shame on me.*

I make myself say it out loud, the things I want. An incantation, a spell, a wish, I didn't believe it when I wanted a baby. But it worked then. It will work now. I will it into being. The life I should have had, the life I lost because of her – and him. It's my turn for perfection now. I'm tired of running, trying to mould people that don't want to be moulded. I deserve to be looked after. I deserve to be loved on my terms. I deserve everything she has. And I'm going to get it.

There's a hammering at the door the next day, a delivery boy with flowers, but I ignore it. They're not for me, I am not the person they are looking for, she's not here anymore. Someone else is here instead, and this time, she knows what she wants and what she'll do to get it.

TWENTY-SIX

THEN

The thing with Ollie was that he had a very short attention span. I always knew that if I wasn't on top form, there would be someone hotter, dirtier, newer. I needed to keep that novelty factor alive. Some ways were easy. We fought a lot. Not in a physical sense, but we were always messing with each other's heads, breaking each other down, to build each other up again.

But I needed security, I didn't know any different. I couldn't imagine a life without him. He played on that, of course. He wasn't faithful. Though he was at least discreet. I had something though, something that kept him coming back for more, something that made him see a future together.

He liked that I was damaged. I was unpredictable. I didn't have tantrums, I didn't react. I didn't play the type of games he expected. But in return, he didn't either. He pushed me constantly, to do better, to be better. To fight for better grades, better experiences, better friendships. So, I knew, when my mother's letter arrived, he'd want me to go.

I don't know how she found my address. I hadn't spoken to her since she'd dropped me at university in the first term of my first year. I didn't go back home during the holidays, I stayed in halls and earned my rent by cleaning and waitressing and acting as bar staff for all the conferences.

Even at Christmas, I stayed. *You'll be all alone, there's no catering.* The support staff were concerned about me. But they didn't realise that Christmas alone was still a safer place than Christmas at home. I enjoyed walking through a deserted, snow-topped campus, like something from a survivor movie, where I was the last one alive. Walking down endless corridors to find my room, the kitchens, the bathroom, expecting ghostly twin girls to come after me. It was still preferable. *Autonomy, choice, peace.*

Once I met Ollie though, it was different, I went home with him most holidays, to his family chalet at Christmas, Scotland at Easter, and anywhere he fancied in the summer. I had some money, but it was irrelevant whether I could afford anything because everything came paid for in any case. Even with clothes, I borrowed his sister's or he gave me his credit card. He didn't care, it wasn't him paying the bill each month.

Mama's letter was short. Uncle John was dying, would I visit him? He was asking for me.

"You have to go." Ollie was adamant. "You need to face him. This is your chance to confront him."

Ollie knew what had happened to me, what Uncle John did. He often asked about it. I think he thought he was helping. That he was being supportive. He encouraged me to see a therapist. To talk it through. But sometimes I think he just liked hearing about it.

"He probably doesn't even remember, Ollie."

"Why else would he be asking for you? It's the usual deathbed apology. You need to throw it back in his face."

I often wonder if Ollie had ulterior motives, even then. If he knew what his encouragement would lead to? If you make a monster, you can't complain if it behaves monstrously. But in the end, it was too late for Ollie. Just like it was for Uncle John.

. . .

The staff at the nurses' station fell quiet as I walked in. His room was blinding, white and harsh with the smell of bleach. I hurt when I saw him. I didn't expect it. A ripping sensation, a falling away inside. In my heart.

"Don't cry, princess."

His voice took me back in an instant. Back to the shed, with its dirty, sweet, sour salty smell.

"It's not as bad as it looks."

I was expecting the Uncle John I knew, from almost a decade ago. The matinee idol looks, the luxuriant moustache, big and beefy. But only his eyes were the same. Silver grey. When he closed them, I saw how the unspeakable had its claws in him. All over, everywhere. It had eaten him away, back to the bone.

"It's been a while, Uncle John. You're... you look different."

"So do you."

In his attempt at a smile, I saw a shadow of the charming man he used to be. I sat on the edge of his bed, the balance of power shifting. His palms were callused. Tubes ran down into his elbow, his wrist, holding him between this life and the next.

"It's okay, the morphine's pretty good."

"Gonna share some?"

His mouth crooked up again at the easy banter we shared. Or easy for him, not forced. I felt sick, the air in the room was too close, dirty. I wanted a shower, still needed to wash him away, even after all that time.

I've never cried like I did that day. Not before, not since. Involuntary, the tears kept coming, running down my face, quicker than I could wipe them away.

"You gotta stop crying, baby girl. You're breaking me apart."

Outside, on the window ledge, all these stories up, there was a tiny nest, a little brown bird tapping on the window.

"He's there every day."

His arm trembled as he pointed.

I wondered if he remembered about the sparrows in his garden, how the cats got to them that one time. How he told me we have to be cruel to be kind. Even when I was so small, all the time we spent together, teaching me the names of plants and animals, potting seeds, watching them grow delicate shoots.

"I missed you, Evie."

He still stole the breath from my body. I had thought it was love. But now I knew better. That fear can be breathtaking too.

"Don't. You have no right." I hated him – and yet, I didn't. I couldn't, I wanted his approval, his validation. The complexity of feelings. Muddy and twisted.

"I did miss you. I never wanted you to leave."

I laughed, but it came out as a sob.

"It was wrong, what happened to you," he said. I knew straight away he wasn't talking about what he did to me. He was talking about school. Something inside me uncoiled at his words, though. The validation I needed to continue with this – whatever it was. *Reunion?*

From nowhere my tears stopped.

"Why did you let it, then?"

He told me not to ask questions I didn't want answers to. But I wasn't sure which question I was asking and what answer I wanted.

A nurse came in then, interrupting us, did something with a clipboard and his machines.

"How are you feeling, Mr Robinson? Lovely to have your daughter visit."

Turning to me she said, "He's such a charmer, your dad. Has all of us in stitches! All he has to do is smile, even in his condition, and they're all under his spell."

She hurried out then, but not before he gave her a wink, leaving her blushing and giggling.

"My daughter..." He raised an eyebrow.

"Like you care."

"Just... surprised, that's all."

He sipped from a beaker, awkwardly, bending the straw into his mouth. He wanted to know why I had agreed to come.

His tone pushed me back into my chair. Pushed me back onto the floor of the shed. Despite my blow-out and my Chanel and nude mani-pedi it seemed I'd never be rid of that girl, that girl that was his. Scruffy and dishevelled, ladders in my tights, chipped nails, unbrushed hair.

Seeing him again made it hard to believe Ollie – and Jake originally – when they said that I was blameless. Because he made me need it. Didn't that make me culpable too?

"Don't talk to me like that, I'm not some stupid teenager anymore."

"I can see that."

I told him it was a mistake. I shouldn't have come. That I'd hoped he'd changed.

"Why? Because you've changed, is that what you're going to tell me? That you're a big girl now and you know what we did was wrong and your Uncle John is a dirty old man?"

His words were a hiss. He sounded just like Alice, the same serpent tongue. He grabbed my wrist, his strength startling, superhuman. A part of me longed for more, for worse. I hated myself for needing it still, to know I was his favourite.

"Let go. You're hurting me."

"You'll always be mine."

"I was never yours."

He let go and laughed, a raspy, painful sound. "You keep telling yourself that."

I got up and almost made it to the door – but he stopped me there. A dying man in his bed could still bar my exit.

"I know you didn't do it – to that girl. You didn't have that in you."

"You know nothing about me."

"Please. Don't insult my intelligence."

"I'm not. But don't presume to know me. And anyway... if you truly believed that you could have saved me – but you didn't." Suddenly, I was breathless. As if a trapdoor had opened under me, that I was in freefall.

"Don't be like that, baby girl." He switched the charm off and on with ease.

"I'm not your baby girl. I'm not your princess or your angel or your anything, anymore. Whoever that Evie was, she went away, a long time ago. She's never coming back."

That day at the hospital, I think a part of me was destroyed. A part that I didn't know was still alive. The part of me that maybe had hope? Later on, I realised that if Ollie hadn't convinced me to go, if I hadn't needed his validation too, I could have avoided all of it. Again, life branching out ahead of me, but with the headlights only illuminating a few feet.

When I got home, Ollie was waiting for me.

"How was it? Did you get him to grovel? Did he apologise?"

"I don't want to talk about it."

"It's the perfect opportunity. You need to face your fears, darling. He's a sick old man, what can he do to you now?"

"I said" – putting my hands around his neck – "I don't want to talk about it."

Ollie dead-eyed me and then peeled my fingers away one by one, pushed me down backwards onto the bed. Gave me all his attention.

I'd called the hospital every day, waiting for the words I needed. And then I got them.

"Oh, hello, Mrs Robinson, did you forget something?"

I had called every morning, pretending to be Auntie Mered-ith. So far, I'd been lucky and she'd not been visiting at the same time.

"Oh, what am I like – brain like a sieve."

"It's to be expected in the circumstances."

"I'm so sorry, do you mind repeating what you said earlier?" The brief silence on the line told me I'd slipped up, but never mind, I pressed forward. "How is he today?"

"There's – there's no change I'm afraid. And with the pallia-tive care plan we've put in place..."

The friendly nurse gave me everything I needed to know. It was my turn to show Uncle John who I was. To show Ollie too. Prove myself to him. I was no victim. I was worthy of him.

When I got to the ward, there was no one at the nurses' station. Curtains were being pulled around beds and there was much bustling and rustling in the bays. It was ward rounds time but, luckily for me, Uncle John had already been seen.

I sat down by his side, but this time there was no chat, no sly parry and thrust of words. He'd withered further in my absence and despite myself, grief flailed in my chest, a wild bird, wings beating for release. I clasped his hand, bent my head. I didn't even know why I was crying but he still lifted his hand, placed it on me, giving me all the blessings I never needed and never wanted.

I don't think I'd ever flinched from his touch. No matter how much it hurt, how heavy the burden of his love. Even when he'd hurt me, I wanted it, lived for it, asked for it, needed it. Or so I thought, back then.

Time was fluid in that room, dissolving away the hours. When I next looked up, they were bringing around the lunch trays. But nothing was brought for him, because I had shut his door. *Privacy* I mouthed at a passing medical person.

His room was a spaceship, the day darkened into the dim light of a mid-winter afternoon. The machines keeping him alive were mission control. If he didn't know where he was going, it was my turn to be the guide, to help.

The sparrow outside was back. His nest was complete, but bare of eggs, I couldn't stop crying again.

We're all bits of star.

He had told me that once.

And even dead stars burn.

Stars are just an illusion. By the time the light reaches us, its source is gone, a supernova. Anything that was once good in me, by the time it reached him, it was gone. I was a supernova too.

I wanted a sign from him. Some acknowledgement of what he'd done to me. And for once he gave me something that I asked for, not just something he made me think I wanted. He opened his eyes.

I could see it at once, still there, inside him. He always was the type to chew his own leg off, rather than stay and face the music.

Those silver-grey eyes, just like Alice's. Just like mine.

I didn't want to know. I don't want to know. There was nothing to know. There was just dirt and dust and somewhere in the wild broken place that held my heart, a cinder smoked and crumbled to ash.

The sparrow outside was getting ready. Its little wings were flapping. It was time for it to go and for me to go – for us all to go. It was my turn to be a hero, to be cruel, to be kind, to rescue myself. I was never a princess. That dress was never a dress. It was always a cape.

The machines beeped and hummed, the room grew close and dim. The scent of bleach and death around us as I leaned over him. Whispered in his ear, said the words I'd always needed to hear from him.

And then I did one more thing. The thing I came to do all along, that Ollie knew I'd do, before I realised myself. And then I kissed his head, walked away, and closed the door behind me.

Before I left, I went to the bathroom. Smoothed my hair, met my own steady gaze in the mirror, greeted myself, that new person, newly risen from the dead.

By the time I reached the nurses station I could hear the steady whine of a machine, of a life, pleading for release. *Do not resuscitate*, it said on your notes.

"How did he get his mask off?" Nurses passed me, but they didn't see me in their hurry, as I slipped out of the ward.

I knew they'd call when I got home, and I knew what I'd say.

That I had just stepped away for a moment. That I didn't see.

Just like he did, to me, when I needed him.

I'm sorry. I'd whispered to him. *I'm sorry I didn't do this sooner*.

TWENTY-SEVEN

NOW

I wait until Alice is drunk. Another night out.

"Doesn't Jake mind?" I yell into the black void of her ear, imagining the air vibrating through the bones and nerves coiled up in her mind, conjuring up pictures in her eyes. Magic.

"Don't know, don't care." And she loops her arm around my neck, sways gently, wine glass in one hand.

We're out with her new BFF, Sadie, queen-bee school mum. She's been angling to get in with her for ages and I see her machinations have paid off. No doubt tomorrow, when the pictures from tonight go up on social media, some woman will be crying into her latte wondering what she did to be uninvited. And all she did was run into Alice, have something Alice wanted. And we all know what happens then.

Sadie is at the bar, being winked at by some hipster dad with a man bun and a massive beard. She's loving it. Not surprised given the uber-preppy lawyer Alice told me Sadie is married to. Apparently he pays more attention to his dog than his kids or wife.

True to form when she returns, she tells us his name is Ed and he's in digital marketing, single dad, she's got his number.

Still got it, and she winks at us, *I'm deleting it now*. I know she's pretending though, keeping it for the days when things are more bad than good and she needs a little pick-me-up.

She's got shots for us, so she can feel free to indulge in a spot of emotional infidelity if the drinks keep coming. I need Alice to be less than sober for this plan to work.

We've been drinking for awhile already, though. I met Callum straight after work, another casual drink. He mentioned he's still not heard anything from Ollie. I'm not fussed though. We're divorced, I'm just the ex-wife. Why should I care what he's up to? Thankfully, Alice's arrival interrupted Callum's inquisition.

"Hi." Alice looked from him to me and back again. Her eyes are sparkling. They're all the same, these Surrey Mummies, keen to see everyone married off like them. She's so transparent.

"Callum – meet Alice. Alice, this is Callum."

She shook his hand, he smirked, masking it behind his pint.

"So how do you two know each other?"

"Oh we go way back... don't we, Alice?"

He drained his pint and stood up.

"Leaving so soon?" I asked.

Alice watched us. Fascinated.

"Yeah, babe, catch you later."

And then Sadie arrived, distracting her, but I knew the seed was sown. Time to water it.

In the bathrooms – again, always the bathrooms – I ask her.

"Have you ever been tempted?"

"What?"

We leave the bathroom, walk back out.

"You know..."

And I nod my head at Sadie, back over with Ed, on the other side of the section of the floor this overpriced bar has deemed a dance floor. I guess you could call what they're doing dancing, at a push.

"Mmmmph. I should be so lucky."

"You never know." I coax her ego back to life, stroke it. "Jake's a lucky man."

This time she looks at me. "Doesn't feel like he knows it."

"Maybe you should show him."

"How?"

"Remember what we used to do?"

"We did a lot of things, babe, you'll have to be more specific."

This time I pull her close, wind and grind, like teenage sluts.

"Remember now?"

She leans into me, there's that scent of roses again, and underneath it sweat and booze.

"I can't, Evie. We're all grown up now."

"Are you? I could call Callum..."

She's considering it.

"I couldn't. Anyway, Jake's not interested in me. He wouldn't care about competition."

"What? Sure he would."

At this point, I'm even fooling myself that I care about Alice. But I also know that she doesn't always tell me the truth.

"No, he's not. He's got someone else."

"Oh come on, he wouldn't do that to you. He loves you."

"Love me or not, I'm pretty sure he's screwing someone else. He's done it before."

I freeze. Well, I guess I shouldn't be surprised. It all came so naturally to him, the subterfuge, the deception. Still, I'm breathless, winded. I don't want to be that woman again, bleating about how he told me he loved me, but somehow I am.

I try to stay calm. Remind myself of the way he is with me, our history, our shared past. The ties that bind us. Try to convince myself that this time, for him, it's different. I'm not just another notch on his bedpost.

"What an asshole. Aren't you angry, Alice?"

"I'm too tired to be angry. I'm trapped. It's easier to turn a blind eye."

"Do you want to win him back or figure out if he's actually cheating?"

"I don't know. Both."

"I don't get why you're being so passive about this. The old Alice didn't take this shit."

I look her dead in the eye, but she shakes her head.

"You don't get it. It's got to be worth the upheaval. Sometimes ignorance is bliss. If I knew for sure, maybe then I'd do something. But with just suspicions, it's pointless. Why am I the one having to take responsibility for our marriage?"

"Don't you think you deserve more?"

"Maybe. But it's okay for you – you're hot and perfect, babies haven't wrecked your body. No wonder you're sleeping with a millennial."

"I'm not sleeping with Callum. And we're all millennials – *cusp millennials*, that's what I keep telling myself! And besides, your body looks pretty good from where I'm standing."

"It's not though. The stretch marks, the loose skin, the scars. I pee every time I sneeze."

She's riling me up.

"What if I could do it for you?"

"Do what?"

"Find out if he's cheating again?"

"How would you even do that?"

"Oh, I have ways, believe me."

"I don't know. This isn't a game."

"Do you want to be in limbo forever?"

Her apathy sickens me.

"Just... I can't, not now."

"You can't live like this. Don't you want to know?"

Something shifts behind her eyes – guilt, desire, shame. But before I get an answer, we have to intervene because Sadie is being sick in the bathrooms and Ed wants to know if she's okay.

Three days later she messages me.

Okay. Do it. Don't tell me anything.

And five minutes after that my phone rings.

"I lied. Tell me everything."

"It's just a honey trap. Chill. It's no big deal. To see how he responds. And then you'll know either way."

"But if he's having an affair, won't he worry about cheating on *her*? Shit – what if it's with a guy?"

"Can probably get one of Callum's mates to hit on him, if you're worried about that? Do you think that's likely?"

"No. I'm being silly, I know. Ignore me."

"I know it's difficult, but don't overthink it. Leave it all to me. It'll be fine."

"I want to be there."

"You do?"

This scuppers my plans a little – but actually, maybe it's not such a bad idea?

"Yes. I want to catch him red-handed."

Her anger seems to come from nowhere. She always was slippery, mercurial in her mood.

"Okay. Let me sort it out. I'll message you the details."

"One thing. Can you not use some barely legal hottie? At least try and get someone nearer our age."

Barely legal's not his type, I want to say. *That's your father's.* But I don't.

"I've got the perfect person in mind."

After that it's easy. I book dinner and a hotel room. I make some calls. I do some shopping.

When? She wants to know. I say *soon.*

I need to travel, I need distance, need time and space to think.

Where? She needs to plan too. I say *hotel room.* She's pleased with that. Can't risk the kids catching us.

How? How it's always done. Dinner, drinks, lingerie and a surprise guest.

What? It'll be fine, I tell her. *Get a wax, a mani pedi. Be ready for anything. I dare you...*

If I can persuade him to do what I want, she'll never be able to trust him again. And then I'll have them both right where I want them.

TWENTY-EIGHT

Alice, being Alice, can't leave me alone in the run-up. Pestering me, wanting to meet for coffee, texting me at 3 am. It's like she's got nothing better to do.

"You need to stop this, Alice. You're massively overthinking it."

"Am I though? What if I'm wrong?"

"What if you are?"

"This is my marriage, it's not a game!"

People in the pub turn around at her raised voice. It's still too early for drunks.

"He won't turn down this girl."

I haven't answered any of his messages. I haven't seen him or spoken to him since I learned about the baby. Sometimes saying nothing is more effective than doing something. And when she's not messaging and calling, he is.

"I'm worried he'll know it's a trap."

I want to laugh. "Babe, men only think with one thing…"

She can't wriggle out of this plan now. If she won't acknowledge what she did to me all those years ago, then I need to make her. And this is the only way. Sometimes people need to be taught a lesson.

"Remind me of the plan again."

"Alice. This is not my first rodeo."

"I know, I know. It's foolproof."

"Have you thought about what you'll do when he does what you think he will?"

She shakes her head.

"It's gonna make you mad, you know. It makes me mad even thinking about it." I drive the wedge in further, levering them apart.

"I don't know. Kill him. I'll kill him."

"Well, let me know if you need an alibi."

She laughs at that. Thinks I'm joking. I am. I'd never give her an alibi again. Not now.

"Seriously though, what's the endgame here? Are you just going to take him back?"

"No!"

She hasn't questioned why I'm helping her. Just assumes I will.

"What's the plan then?"

"We signed a pre-nup." Now we're getting to the meat, the heart of everything. I knew from the start that Alice would only agree to this if there was something significant in it for her. And proving her husband is cheating is embarrassing; it's not worth everyone knowing that she wasn't enough for him. But here, here is a motive. And that's something I can work with.

"Did you?"

"Yeah. Jake's got a trust fund. But I can't access it. It's water-tight, even if we divorce."

"Has he?" He kept that one quiet.

"But I had a clause put in, to say that if he cheated then I get fifty per cent of that trust fund. Of course at the time it was unimaginable that he would cheat on me. but now..."

"...now you can catch him. And prove it... you're so devious! I love it."

"Exactly. If there's evidence – if there's a witness or something to swear he's been cheating on me, with her, what's a court going to do?"

The old Alice is right in front of me. She never went anywhere. She's been masking this whole time. I'm impressed and annoyed. She made me her puppet before, the difference this time is that she's also mine.

"Clever girl! You're going to be rich."

I chink my glass to hers.

"Okay, so, your friend – she'll meet him at the bar he goes to after work?"

"Yeah, and then persuade him to come up to her hotel room."

"Yes exactly."

"What if he doesn't go for it?"

"Isn't that a good thing? He's faithful to you."

"Okay, but the whole point of this is that he hasn't been. And who's to say he will be in the future."

"But there's not a lot I can do if he doesn't go for it."

"Well, all we need is for the court to believe he cheated on me. That doesn't mean we need him to actually cheat on me. And then I get the money – and a divorce."

I didn't realise Alice was so far gone, to suggest this. Even for her it's pretty bad.

"Okay..."

"Can you ask your friend to maybe mess up the bed a bit, leave some condom wrappers out? Anything, just make it look like he slept with her."

I pause. This is not what I expected. I thought I'd have to twist Alice's arm.

"Are you sure you want her to do that, Alice?"

"Oh, Evie, I don't know. I'm just so tired of all this shit. I'm so bored!"

"Okay, okay. I'm here. We'll work it out. Let's just stick to the original plan yeah, for the honey trap? And once she's in the room..."

"You'll text me, yeah? With proof."

"Wait – what about if you burst in and catch them in the act?"

"*If* he goes for it..."

She was certain he would, and now uncertain. Her mental processes are giving me whiplash.

"He'll go for it." I feel like it's better to reassure her of his cheating than let her continue down her set-up plan. That has disaster written all over it.

"What's she going to wear? If it's too slutty, he won't go for her." *Little do you know*, I think.

I look at her, eyebrows raised. "When it comes to men who cheat, nothing is too slutty."

"If it's too obvious, he'll suspect a trap though."

"Look, my friend is perfect for this."

"Can I see what she looks like?"

I show her a picture of a model I found on Instagram. Wholesome, great skin, luscious glossy curls, not too tall, not too short. And none of those marker pen eyebrows either.

"Okay. She's fine."

"We good then?"

I want to get going, but Alice doesn't look like she's done yet. What's next, wanting a script for the evening?

"Are you sure this is the right thing to do?"

Has she not listened to a word I said? And then I remember this is how she plays things, makes herself the victim in every-thing. It's okay, I can play along.

"Alice, sweetheart, we can stop it all now, just say the word."

"No... no, I don't want to stop. You're right. Let's just do it. At least I'll know then."

What's that quote... something about wanting the truth and not being able to handle it?

"Good girl. Look, I've got to get going, early start in the morning – heading over to the client's office."

"Good thing you've got that meeting in London next week, huh? It's perfect timing for our plan."

"Yes, isn't it." She's so stupid. Sometimes I wonder how someone who managed to get away with so much is now just a frustrated housewife.

"I'll call you, yeah?"

"Sure, babes."

She walks out with me and before we part ways, she surprises me with a hug. Leaning in close, that scent of roses overwhelms me.

"Thanks, Evie – for everything."

Her eyes meet mine – and there is it again – that look. She hasn't forgotten any of it, at all.

TWENTY-NINE

"Look, Evie. Back then I thought you were gone, I thought you were never coming back."

It sounds like Jake is building up to a confession here, an excuse. He doesn't know what she's told me already, but it's good to get his side, match up the stories, find the gaps. They're both lying. And now they've lied to the wrong girl.

"I didn't expect you to be a monk if I wasn't around, it's okay."

"No... but you don't understand. It was all her, you have to believe me. If I'd known the truth, I would never have done it. She wore me down. I was only hanging around her house all the time because I wanted to know where you were. I wrote you letters, she told me she'd get them to you."

Part of me believes this. The Jake I knew back then was wholly good. He would have pined like a Labrador puppy. Unfortunately, he would have also walked straight into Alice's trap. I know he wasn't innocent here either – but she drove this. It's all on her.

"Well, I never got them."

"She gave them back to me, marked *Not known at this address, return to sender*."

"Why did you do it, though? With her? I thought you loved me."

"It was a mistake. It was meant to be one time. I needed a distraction, Evie, I needed to forget about you. And then..."

"And then what?"

"And then she got pregnant. It was an accident, but I couldn't just ditch her."

It's always women who "get pregnant" – like they do it by themselves, with no help from anyone else. He could have simply not slept with her. But I know I'm only fooling myself here. And mistakes get made, accidents happen. Terrible things are only a heartbeat away from all of us.

"How do you even know it was yours? Did you get a test?"

It's clear from his expression that this occurred to him, but he just shakes his head. "In the end it didn't matter – she lost it. And by then it was too late. Plans had been made."

"What plans? I thought it was just the one time." I can imagine him, finding her, like Ollie found me, crying into the toilet. The shameful trip to the hospital. The blood tests. But unlike me, the relief that they would have felt – no longer tied to each other. Except... it seems that's not the case.

"Oh, Evie, we just fell into the relationship. I didn't plan it. And I couldn't just dump her, you should have seen her, she was in bits."

I know this is where I need to sympathise. And I tried to when Alice told me herself. But I feel like, how bad can it really have been? She didn't want a baby, it wasn't planned, not like the babies I lost. I bet she doesn't think of her baby, how old it would be now, miss all those firsts and lasts. I want to feel badly for him too, I do.

But I can't. I can only fake it.

"I'm sure it was very tough on you both."

"It was so scary. I really didn't know what to do to help her. And she refused to talk about it after. Just lay on her bed in silence. All I could do was be with her."

"So... why did you stay together though? After that?" I'm pushing this hard, I need to hear all of this, I need to set my trap well, with the best bait.

"I don't know! It was easier, being with her, than not. I was scared of the alternative and besides, her dad had bought us a flat, got it all ready."

"Sounds awful."

"Shut up. I was terrified of that dude, he was one creepy shit."

"Did you see the shotgun he used to keep in the sitting room?"

"Oh yeah... the first time I picked Alice up for a date, he was waiting by the front door with it, all *you mess with my daughter you mess with me*. I just about shat myself and then he was all like *jokes, jokes* and clapping me on the back."

I wonder if he's forgotten what else he knew about Uncle John. He's not mentioned it now. But I guess it's tricky to bring up. I haven't talked about it either.

"Still doesn't change the fact though – you slept with my best friend, knocked her up and moved in with her. It's like I never existed. You have no idea what I went through, what I had to do to survive."

I flash back to my memories of that time – the smell of urine and fear. A voice asking for cigarettes. Distant laughter. Pills in paper cups.

"Tell me then, I'm here for you now, even if it is too late. What happened? Where did you go?"

It's just words though. Last time I thought he was on my side, but Alice blew my life clean apart and it seems like he just danced on the ashes.

"I don't know if now is the time to tell you. It's painful."

It's not. It's nothing to me now. After everything that's happened this year, I'm numb. There's a cold clean space inside me where my heart should be.

"Tell me, please? I'll do anything for you, you know that."

Amazing isn't it, what a few months of screwing someone else's husband gets you. Undying loyalty and devotion. Isn't that in the marriage vows?

"Where do you want me to start?"

My head hangs low, my hair shielding my eyes. If he saw my expression right now, he'd be confused. He's never seen me cry and he's not going to start now. I have to hide my smile, I love it when a plan comes together.

He needs to see me as the victim I am. He needs to want to rescue me. He needs to feel in control. And then it's simple.

"Wherever you want. I mean, like what happened to you? Where did you go? Not to Boston, I know that bit. But before – after – after everything."

"They took me away one Sunday morning. My mum woke me up before it was even light. I don't remember much. A big car, a creamy sunrise flushing all the world pink and peach, open countryside, gates. And then, like Sleeping Beauty, the prick of a needle sent me to sleep."

"What are you talking about?"

"They sent me to reform school. Oh, they could dress it up with a fancy name, talking about rehabilitation, but it was still a prison, I was still stuck there for three years, with no escape, no help, nothing. Do you know what that does to someone? Can you imagine having no privacy, nothing to call your own, to work to someone else's schedule every minute of every day?"

"Sounds like married life."

"Glad you think it's so funny."

"I'm sorry. I am. It sounds awful. I don't get it though. Why were you sent away?"

"Maybe you should ask your wife, Jake? Ask her what she did."

"She told me about some trouble at school – some girls being bullied or something. I don't understand."

"Remember Rosie?"

"No... oh shit, yeah! That girl that jumped out of a window or something."

"Yeah, that girl. Did Alice ever mention anything? That she was there when Rosie died?"

"What? I don't know what to say. But... and then you left. I don't understand."

"It's fine, Jake. Nothing can change the past."

"So... then you just went to university, like nothing happened?"

"Pretty much."

"But... didn't you need any..." He spreads his hands apart, as if to clutch the answer from thin air, as if to clutch at what would fix me.

"Any what?"

"I don't know – help? Support?"

"I applied to university like any other teenager, followed all the processes despite everyone telling me it was pointless. So when I got a place at my first choice, it seemed unreal, but it also seemed like a way out, of everything.

"Mama picked me up, I had one suitcase, we stayed one night in a Travelodge – no more fancy treats. I didn't find out why until later though."

"I bet you were fit at uni." And he smiles at me, leans back on his arm, pushes my hair off my face.

I'm still a fantasy for him, but there's only so long I can maintain that for. I need some commitment here. I've put all my money on him. I need a return on my investment and I need it soon.

"Have I ever not been fit?" I cosy up to him, nestle in close, stand between his legs as he sits back on the bed.

He just raises an eyebrow and smirks at me. A normal woman would be worried about a man who cared so little for her pain that it made him want to sleep with her. He pulls me on top of him, pushes his tongue into my mouth, grinds into me.

"Oh, like that is it?" I pull away and smile. He thinks he has me exactly where he wants me. I move my hips, watch his face, I think about the other people who've slept and cried and screwed on this same hotel mattress. I wonder whether anyone has died on it.

"Where've you gone?"

"I'm here." Sometimes I despise myself, and then I blame him for it. "I'm right here with you."

He winds a strand of my hair around his finger, tucks it behind my ear like the romantic lead in a movie. He used to say I was his rocket, I let him climb on board, strap himself in, take him far away from here.

"What are you thinking about?" He runs one hand down my face as he undoes his flies with the other.

"Nothing, I'm not thinking about anything but you and me."

He thinks I'm thinking about sex. I'm not. I'm thinking about death – his, mine, hers.

THIRTY

"What do you mean, she's not there? She has to be."

I tap the pen against my desk. What's the point of having a therapist if you can't actually get any therapy when you need it? All that bullshit about reaching out, asking for help whenever I need it. Well, I'm doing it, Dr Lucinda, and you're not here.

"This is ridiculous. I'd like to speak to the practice manager please."

Their hold music is atrocious. ABBA? Really? I look at my mobile to check I haven't actually called IKEA. Except I know I haven't. A tinny voice is coming out of the speaker.

"Sorry, what? There's no one there by that name? That's crap – you need to check again. I paid a lot for that appointment."

I mean okay yes it has been several months. And I'm in a different country. But still, she's my therapist. Even if we only had one session.

"Wait, no I'm sorry, don't hang up, I apologise, I'm just... I'm having a crisis... yes, a crisis. No, I don't want to talk to anyone else. Just Dr Lucinda Thornberry. Oh, don't put me on hold again."

I bite the pen so hard it cracks in my mouth, I spit the plastic shards out onto the floor. More ABBA.

"No, I've just told your colleague. I don't want anyone else. No... oh! Don't bother."

It's never satisfying hanging up on a mobile. Terminating the call by touch is nowhere near as good as slamming the receiver down into the base, letting the person on the other end know exactly how inadequate they are.

I end up hurling it across the floor. That too is a poor substitute. I clank together ice and a tumbler, glug in a risky measure of whisky and sit on the sofa.

This little room is starting to annoy me. At first, I liked the anonymity. It was kind of sexy. But now I can see all the scuffs and marks on the units, the dust on the skirting boards. It's all cheap and nasty. It's all fake.

If I half close my eyes, the room fades and blurs, just vague shapes and outlines. *Jake is quicksand*, I think. *I've been sucked in before – what's to stop it happening again?*

Why do you think that is, Evie?

It's like Dr Lucinda is here. Even though I know she's not.

I'm tired of it. Why is everything such hard work? It was so simple. To start with.

What was so simple?

The plan.

What plan?

This is ridiculous. I pour myself more whisky. The burn shakes me up, wakes me up.

Oh there was no plan. Silly me. No plan.

Everyone lies to their therapists, right? Especially their imaginary ones.

So, what's the matter then?

This is all your fault, Dr Lucinda. You planted the seed. You made me drag the bodies out of the lake. Wash away the silt. I'd

*tried so hard to weigh them down. Compartmentalise, isn't that
what it's called? But it didn't work.*

Can't you put them back in?

No. I came back here for a reason. I mustn't lose sight of that.

And what reason was that?

I don't remember her asking such stupid questions before.

To find out why.

Why what?

*Just everything. And to take it all away. Just like Alice did.
To me.*

What's stopping you?

*It's just so much worse than I thought. And now like I say,
the compartments aren't working anymore. I'm confused.*

Why?

*I need to talk to Jake again. He needs to decide, once and for
all, who he wants. I'm not waiting anymore.*

Is that wise?

Are you making me question myself?

Isn't that my job?

*You're imaginary. This version of you anyway. Your job is to
do whatever I say.*

I pour more whisky. The room is one blur of light.

Well, what should I say then?

Tell me to go for it. Burn it all down. Take everything.

Do it then.

And like that, the best therapy session I never had is over.
We are our own wise counsel, our own best friends. If I don't
love myself, set my own boundaries, how can I expect anyone
else to respect them?

"Come over. Now."

"It's not that easy."

"Make it easy."

"Evie..."

"Oh, for goodness' sake, just tell her you're taking the dog for a walk."

"I'll see what I can do."

He presses the buzzer fifteen minutes later.

"What the hell, Jake!"

"Can you mind your language?"

"You're the one bringing a small child over."

"Look, it was the only way I could escape."

"Fine."

"I need to talk to you anyway."

"Oh yeah?"

I let them in, the child gets plonked in front of the telly with a sharing bag of Doritos.

"Want a drink?"

"Probably shouldn't." His eyes skitter over to the sofa.

"Never stopped you before."

And there it is, I see the crook of his mouth. Dammit. He feels it too.

I think about being in his arms, in the dark. The peace I felt twenty years ago. The peace I feel just being with him. No matter how much I want to be angry. This is the right thing to do.

"Sit down." I push him into the chair behind him. "I need a drink even if you don't."

But I bring out cups of tea.

"See, I can be normal."

After all, someday soon, if all goes to plan, I'll be a mother. In a house. With a husband. Time to get these domestic goddess skills brushed up.

"Okay, go. What's up?"

"Look at this."

He passes me his phone.

"I don't understand."

I do understand.

"Alice sent me this."

"Why?"

"Who the hell knows. I don't think she meant to."

"Are you sure it's her?"

"Well, who else would it be?"

"How long do you think it's been going on?"

"You think it's not just a one off?"

"Look at the facts. Your wife is sleeping with someone else. And she's taken a photo of them together. And she's sent it to you. We just don't know if it's accidental or on purpose."

"Does my wife ever do anything by accident?"

"She's your wife, you know her best."

He looks at me like I'm the dickhead here. "You don't seem too bothered."

"That's the odd thing. I don't think I am."

"Why not?"

"Do you even need to ask?"

It's making me hot just watching him eat up everything I'm telling him. Doesn't matter whether it's true or not; he believes it, so it is the truth to him.

When I was little, I had one of those horrible knitted dresses that were really fashionable in the eighties. All itchy angora and smocked across the chest. I must have been about four. Somehow, I got it caught on something.

Don't pull that thread! Mama made me jump when she caught me. *It'll all unravel.*

"Look, I think you need to go home and talk to her."

"I don't want to talk to her?"

"Okay. Want another cuppa?"

He's so distracted he says yes.

When I come back in, he's tucking the kid in on the sofa with a blanket over him.

"He's really cute when he's asleep."

"They all are."

And he is angelic looking, all blonde curls, flushed pink cheeks, thumb in his cherry lips. A perfect Botticelli. Just like his mama was.

"Look, Jake. We need to talk. I need to tell you something."

He's busy adjusting the blanket, not looking at me.

"She's planning to divorce you."

He turns around then.

"Not to sound too Shakespearean – she's plotting against you."

He's still, his face a careful blank.

And then I tell him everything. The infidelity clause, the money, the honey trap, all of it. Well, almost all of it.

"That bitch! She's no saint."

He stands up, sits down again.

"I've wanted to tell you for so long. You can make a decision now. You've got the upper hand."

"Damn straight I do!"

Now he's pacing around, fists clenched, shaking his head.

"Please don't punch the wall again. I had a hard time explaining that away."

"I just can't get over it. She's sick. It's so messed up. And I married her."

"Jake, sit down for a second."

He slumps into a chair, drops his head into his hands. "What about our kids?"

"She's planning to go for sole custody, she told me."

"She is not taking my kids away from me! Call your friend now, the honey trap – call it off!"

"Are you sure?"

"Yes. I've got a much better idea."

He wants to meet her in the hotel room, confront her – have it out.

"Well, you could do that or..."

And then I tell him my idea. Because it's much better than his. I just don't tell him my part of the plan. A woman has to have some secrets, after all.

By the time he leaves it's getting dark. He scoops the sleeping toddler back into the buggy.

"Won't she wonder where you've been?"

"She's not called me. She's probably just glad of some peace with this one out."

I'd never be like that. Fobbing my kids off for hours on someone else.

He kisses me goodbye, cups my face in his hands. Tender and sweet, the Jake I remember. Closing the door behind him, I clear away the cups and crumbs.

It was Callum who told me about it, how to send texts and make it look like they'd come from someone else. And after that it was easy. I took a picture of Callum when he'd stayed over one time – purely platonic of course. There's only one bed in this apartment. Alice and I look similar enough if I don't show my face – and people see what they want to see, don't they?

If you get a text from your wife, with a picture of someone who looks like your wife in it, then you're going to assume it is actually your wife. Who's to say it isn't?

Jake is so focused on making Alice pay, he's forgotten that he's guilty too. And he needs to realise that. It's time to test that loyalty he promised me. Let's see how much he really loves me.

THIRTY-ONE

There's a thief in this bar. Trying to take the chair next to me.

"It's taken."

"Oh... sorry."

"No worries."

He's hot, the thief. I bet he steals lots of things.

I'm waiting in the hotel bar that Alice picked for us. Assuring me it was round the corner from Jake's office and he often drank there.

"I wouldn't keep you waiting." The thief is back. Familiar gleam in his eye. "Not if you were mine."

Still trying to take things that aren't his.

"Too bad for you I'm not yours."

"Not yet."

He's in a sharp suit, lines like razors. Clean-shaven but five o'clock shadow, cropped salt-and-pepper hair, big watch, wedding ring. Tall, wiry, containing his power. This is a man in control.

"I guess not."

"Can I buy you a drink?"

I shake my head even as I can't stop myself from smiling at him.

He smiles back, a proper one, lines fanning out from his eyes.

"Beg."

"On my knees?"

How much does he want this? How much does he want me? He's here alone. A married man in a bar by himself, it's a red rag, especially this man, this bar.

"If you please."

And he does, get down on his knees, on that hardwood floor. His eyes trail up from my heels, to the slit in my skirt, to my lips and to meet my gaze. When he swallows, I know he's just making me think I have control.

"Please can I buy you a drink?" He holds his hands in front of him, supplicant even as his mouth quirks up. Somewhere, in a hidden speaker, a guitar wails plaintively, goosebumps crack a whip over me.

"Get up. Kneeling is for later."

"Promises, promises. And she says she's taken. Lucky guy, whoever he is."

"I never said I was taken."

"There's hope yet then."

I look at his left hand, but he doesn't say anything, doesn't move an inch. He's still got his ring on. I can't wait until he's wearing mine.

"I'll have an Old Fashioned, thanks."

He's passed my test and now I'm passing his.

While the barman makes my drink and pours him a whisky, we introduce ourselves.

"I'm Jake – Jake McDonald." His hand is firm in my grasp, solid, his fingers brushing my wrist.

"Evie."

"Just Evie?"

"Yep. Just Evie."

I do have another name, but the only people who called me it are dead now.

He takes my drink and leads me to a booth, the high leather seating rising above our heads, cocooning us away from the world.

The lights are dim, the alcohol makes me hum and blur. The scent of his cologne, the crisp weave of his shirt, the golden hair on his forearms. I allow myself to enjoy these few moments. We never had the chance to do this before. I never got to see him like this, all grown up.

We're sitting so close but not touching, the pretence is making my skin crawl off my bones to get to him. But I can't touch him. Not here. Not now. It's too soon. It's not part of the plan.

"Where does she think you are tonight?"

"She knows exactly where I am. I told her I was going out for drinks in the hotel bar."

"Clever." Or experienced, he's done this before. Alice said he has. Before me.

He runs his finger across the back of my hand and my whole body trembles. This time is so different. We are elsewhere, we are an us outside of my hotel room. The pretence is cracking.

"What's wrong?"

My face must register my unease, the good wolf and bad wolf, fighting inside me for control. I need to feed one, make it stronger.

"Nothing. It's fine. I'll be right back. Need to powder my nose."

He winks at me as I leave. I'm already out of control.

I lock myself in a plush bathroom cubicle. All marble and mahogany, as if it's still the eighties. *Evie*, I say to myself *Get a grip. Get this one over the line. It's a done deal. What are you waiting for?*

But my lizard brain, my subconscious, is reading signs in the ether, prickles of electricity. *Warning, Danger, Run for your life. Don't get your heart broken again.*

It's self-protection, not fear. That's not something I allow myself to feel anymore, I don't have that luxury. I need to follow the plan, it's foolproof. Not Alice's plan. *My plan.* I haven't done what she tells me to do for a very long time now.

My phone vibrates in my pocket, impatient.

How's it going?

My friend says it's all good. She'll message when she's got him in place.

By the time we're riding the lift up to his room, I'm back in the game. I am satin skin and baby fine, I am glossy promises and peachy flesh, I am bursting to be bitten and he knows it.

In the hotel room, it feels like the last time. When it's meant to be the first time. Is this what it's like being a proper grown up? It's all my nightmares all at once, chasing the light away, obliterating everything into the dust.

"Stop, stop."

I pull away, pull back, the edge is so close, the abyss so deep. This time I might jump across, make it to the other side. His wrists are in my hands, I'm in so deep, I'm drowning again, this wasn't supposed to happen.

"What?"

We are a cocked pistol. One more touch and that bullet won't ever go back in the gun.

"I need a minute. I'm sorry."

I need to remind myself who I am, what I'm doing, which plan to follow when. The bathroom is bright and safe, a toilet, a bath, a shower, a sink. The world is the same, the world is different. I can't do this not now. There's fractures and cracking at the edges.

What's happening?

Give her five minutes

And just like that I can face myself in the mirror again. Ashy blonde hair, blue eyes, olive skin. I see myself like he does, broken into pieces. Legs, breasts, bum, heart. Red tears run down my face, a blink and they're gone. Time to get this show on the road.

He's still on the bed, dishevelled, confused, unreadable.

"All okay?"

"Yeah, I just needed to check something."

And then I crawl back up the bed, into his arms, pull my dress up, push his jeans down, watch the muscle in his jaw twitch, the tension trembling between us. But the pin is out of the grenade now and the explosion is walking down the corridor in Ugg boots and a Boden coat. Footsteps stop outside the door.

I lower myself onto him, feel the rush of air against my neck as he exhales. I hold him tight and then move against him. I put my lips to his ear, whisper his name. He makes a noise, inarticulate sounds of desire.

And then the door opens.

Three.

Two.

One.

Boom.

THIRTY-TWO

He doesn't notice her at first, fixated on that finish line.

"Jake."

Her whisper is a shout in the silence. He freezes beneath me. I look him in the eye. He knows what's coming.

"Get off him." Still that low, quiet voice. But the calm is brittle. "How could you?"

He's getting dressed, I pull the sheet around me, tumble my hair over one shoulder. She taps her foot and it's a giveaway.

He looks from her to me and back again. "Why are you here, Alice?"

"It's our wedding anniversary, darling husband of mine. Surprise!"

And she undoes her coat. Alice has gone off plan too. But I was expecting this.

"Isn't this what you wanted? Just not with me?"

Her lingerie is expensive. But it can't mask the difference between us, the loose skin, the stretch marks. All the weight loss and toning in the world can't cover up motherhood's ravages. Funny that I'm tight and she's loose. But I'm loose and she's tight too.

"No, Alice." He shakes his head.

"Aren't you even going to introduce us?"

"Why are you doing this?"

"You don't love me anymore. I just needed proof."

"That's... not true."

"Jake, give me some credit. I literally caught you with your pants down."

He gulps. But I know he'll be working out how to get out of this.

"It's always been Evie, hasn't it?"

"No."

"Shut up. Don't lie to me."

"I don't know what to tell you."

"How about the truth? This wasn't the first time, was it?"

"No."

"Did you plan this? All this time?"

"No – God. I..."

He looks at me, waiting for me to dig him out of this trap.

"What's she got that I don't? Actually, don't answer that. I don't care. You were pathetic when we were teenagers, moping around after she'd gone – and you're no different now. What do I have to do this time to get you to notice me?"

"Screw you, Alice! Don't make out like you're the perfect wife here. I know you've been playing away too."

"What? I gave up everything – EVERYTHING – for you. My job, my body, my life. I wash, cook and clean. Anything you wanted, I did. From the start. But still, no one compares to your precious Evie-Lynn."

The name causes us to all freeze.

"No one calls me that anymore."

"Oh, it speaks."

Alice always did fight dirty. She shakes her head, even though I can see her mouth flickering up into a smile. "Was it all fake? Did you ever want to be my friend again? Or was it all just about him?"

"No. It was real to me." But then many things are real to me. "I missed you."

"I missed you too."

It's complicated, our relationship, Facebook doesn't have that option for no reason. Love or hate, they're both about someone else. Someone haunting your thoughts and driving your behaviour, driving you crazy. About obsession.

"My best frenemy."

"Always."

"So why... why him?"

"He was mine first. You took him."

She doesn't deny it. "You took my things too."

"Like what?"

"You know what."

"You're crazy."

"It wasn't fair."

"It's not like I had any choice in the matter."

Alice huffs to herself. I'm telling the truth though. I do sometimes.

We make an awkward triptych. Me in the bed, a *pietà* in sheets, Alice on one side, my avenging angel, Jake on the other, hunched under the weight of being caught red-handed. When judgement day came, this isn't what he thought it would look like.

Alice crosses her arms. "I'm done here. Don't bother coming home. Just stay here with her – or don't, whatever. I don't care."

"Alice—" Jake starts.

"You still haven't even said you're sorry. I mean, what kind of shit are you? Don't you care about me at all?"

"Of course I do. You're the mother of my children."

"It's always about you, isn't it?"

It's true. Jake has nothing nice to say about his wife. To her face or behind her back.

"Look, it was a mistake, okay? All of this."

"Excuse me? I'm not here for you to weigh up the pros and cons of your mistress versus me, Jake. Don't call me, don't talk to me, just fuck off – and when you get there, fuck off some more."

The door slams behind her.

Jake gets up and goes into the bathroom without another word.

When I hear the shower go on, I know it's time to start the next part of the plan.

The next time I open my eyes, the room is dim with the hopeful half-light of dawn. I am wrapped in a binding sheet, twisted around my legs, and yet I am also cold and damp. My eyes are sticky and filmed, crusted with who knows what, I don't look at the other side of the bed.

Stumbling to the bathroom, on the legs of a newborn colt, my mouth is fusty and chemical. Somewhere, there's the smell of iron and copper, so thick I could bite it. I don't put the light on, just leave the door open and turn the shower up as hot as I can stand it, let the water and the grey light wash everything away. When I get out, the dregs of the water in the bath look pink but I blame the dawn. Dressing, it's easy to ignore the dark spots on the carpet. Still, I don't look at the other side of the bed, Jake's side. Try not to think about what happened last night.

I pick up my things. There's not much. I wasn't planning to stay over. Last night's dress and last night's shoes go back on, dirty underwear and tights I push to the bottom of my bag. There are other things to put back in there, but like the bed, I just don't look at them. I wash my hands again after soaping them thoroughly. I rinse and rinse, until the water runs clear. I make an attempt to tidy the room, skirting the bed, just piling throw pillows at the foot of it, pushing the club chairs straight, dumping my used towels in the bathroom.

My phone is going nuts in my bag, humming and pulsing, but I ignore it. Pulling on my coat, I step out of the room, hook the *Do Not Disturb* sign over the door and walk down the silent corridor.

It's still early when I get on the train at London Bridge. Rivers of commuters push past me as I swim against the tide and settle in an empty train to Gatwick. A woman walks past me, and I smell roses. I blink and she's gone. Somewhere there's a snatch of music, a guitar and a wail. As we pick up speed, I dig out my headphones, press shuffle. As Carly Simon tells me nobody does it better, I send a single message.

Mission accomplished.

THIRTY-THREE

Ollie always claimed I was impossible to buy presents for. I never wanted anything he got me. *Diamonds, bags, shoes, cars, houses, holidays – none of it is good enough for you.* He never knew how to give me what I really needed. He'd only managed it once – and that was with a lot of help.

What next?

Where are you?

Call me!

My phone lights up like the Eiffel Tower. I wrap it in a towel and put it in a cupboard. I'm back from London now, I've been back for a few days. Did everything I planned to, stuck to my guns, followed the rules. I mean, Alice might have had a different plan – but I did what she wanted. Only, she forgot to ask me what I wanted. Why I was so up for it.

She wants me to go round to her house, to have a coffee, to "regroup", and work on the next step of her plan. Spot the ex-lawyer. More like she wants to have it out. I'm keeping her hanging though. Called in sick to work again. Maybe they're getting worried, maybe they're not. I don't know, don't care.

I've been taking lots of hot baths, relaxing. Looking after myself – having a little smoke here and there too, courtesy of Callum. Taking my mind off things. Off what comes next. I need to stay calm, to think about the long term, tempting as it is to get carried away. I always had a vivid imagination. *Breathe in, breathe out. I can do this, I can.* It's only another day or so – really, just a few hours.

I count to ten. Take deep breaths. *I can do this. I am almost there, so close to the prize – only a few more steps.* First, I know I need to call her. Then I need to tell her what happened after she left that night. I practise in front of the mirror.

Oh, Alice... I might have jumped the gun.

Alice, I'm so sorry. I didn't mean for it to happen.

Oh, Alice, it's such a shame... but you said it yourself. You'd kill him if you found out he'd cheated.

One thing I know, one thing I've learned, there are so many versions of me. I get to choose, every day, who I want to be. But when you strip it away, it leaves a void. And nothing, no matter how hard I try, fills that up. But I think maybe I know a way and I think Alice does too. She just doesn't realise it yet. She is the question and the answer. All those years ago, she took every-thing that mattered from me – even my future. And now it's my turn to take it back.

I go to the cupboard. Unwrap my phone. Damn notifica-tions. I'm blocking them all. There's only one person I want to talk to right now.

Hey, Alice, call me. We need to catch up asap.

I can't right now, I'm with the kids. What's the hurry?

Just that little work situation I was telling you about

Even saying that much is risky. Leave no trace, that was the deal. No evidence. If someone reads my phone, her phone, his – it should all be ambiguous. Innocent. Clean. It's not like I haven't done this before.

Okay well I'll call you tonight yeah? When the kids are asleep.

Sure. Sounds good

It's important to set the scene. To be relaxed. We're not amateurs. I take another hot bath. I deign to answer some work emails. Even take a client call. Rupert messages me constantly as soon as I come online.

What's happened? Where are you? You can't keep leaving us in the lurch. I've involved HR. I'm sorry but you left me no choice. The client complained. Evie! If you don't reply I'm going to send a courier for your laptop and phone. That's company property.

I turn my status to do not disturb and play online poker to kill time. What are they going to do – Rupert's already made his mind up.

That evening, when the phone rings, the whole room is in darkness except for the glow of the laptop. I'm on the bed surrounded by takeaway packaging.

"Hey."

"Shit – the kids – shit, sorry." There's a clattering noise and the smash and tinkle of glass.

"You okay?"

"Yeah, just trying to tidy quickly. Jake's still hiding away somewhere, not had the guts to come home and face me yet, so muggins here has to do everything."

"Have you heard from him since...?"

"Nope, not a dicky bird."

"How are you feeling about it all?" Alice has trouble with her emotions, but we both like to pretend otherwise. Plus, I need to know where I stand. I need her to believe I still want the money.

"It's fine. I just want to get on with it. But if he's not here..." She speaks fast, spitting the words out.

"Are you sure that's what you want?" I know I'm pushing her here, but I need to make all this work for me.

"Are you kidding? Of course it's what I want."

"No regrets?"

"No. I never really loved him."

And then I see why she's so calm. She wants me to know I'll always be her sloppy seconds.

"What do you mean?"

"Oh, you know – he was just a teenage crush that snowballed. I never really wanted him. Just curious to see what you saw."

She can be a real bitch when she wants to be.

"But, Alice... you got pregnant. He stood by you."

"Why are you defending him? Oh wait, don't tell me, you were *in love*. Please, spare me. I only bothered making friends with you again to get his money. I knew you'd know how to con him."

"I'm almost impressed. You haven't changed a bit. But the difference is, no one cares about your sob stories anymore."

"Wanna bet? I did it once, I can do it again – still can't believe he fell for that though. It's the oldest trick in the book."

"Yeah... wait, what?"

"That old pregnancy trick. I didn't want him to lose interest."

"You were never pregnant as a teenager?"

"No. Course not. I'm not that stupid." Her smugness sickens me. She's like her father in more ways than her looks.

"But what made you so sure he'd stick around?" I can't let on that I've already guessed all this. That a baby is so inconsequential to her either way that she'd lie about one for her own ends.

"Don't you remember where we lived, who his parents were? I knew Daddy would make him stay."

"You're really something you know, Alice?" The anger is a wave of fire in my veins. It makes everything I need to do from now on so much easier though. And it's one thing that I guessed she'd lied about losing the baby, it's another to hear the truth directly from her.

"I know." I can hear her smile down the phone. This is the Alice I remember. The one no one else sees. She's only for me. The hair rises on my arms, the back of my neck.

"Did Jake know?"

"No."

"Okay."

"People like you don't understand, Evie. A life like mine takes time to build. Early investment is crucial. You need good foundations too. And it's hard work. You can't just stop. None of this comes easy. Big house, kids, being someone's wife. I've made it. I feel sorry for single people, for the childless. Never to experience that sense of fulfilment."

"Is that how you feel about me?"

"Oh, Evie – I can't possibly explain how I feel about you. It's like asking me to describe the importance of breathing."

"But you managed without me for twenty odd years."

"I did, yes. But I missed you."

She didn't miss me. She missed what I did for her.

"But, Alice, if you go through with this, you'll be alone too."

"Oh, I won't be. Not for long anyway."

That's when I realise, she's already set her sights on a new target.

"You'll still get your money, Evie, if that's what you're worried about. I can overlook the fact you were screwing him. He's better off out of all our lives – even yours. I mean, he's such a coward – taking off like this, leaving all my messages on unread. What if one of the kids was seriously ill? He doesn't give a crap about us. I really don't care if I never see him again."

"Funny you should say that... I hope the maid that found our room wasn't too upset, too shaken up."

"Wait, what? Evie. What have you done? What have you done to my husband?"

"Nothing that you didn't want done to him, really."

There's a long silence, punctuated by her breathing. It's so deep that I even wonder if she's fallen asleep, or maybe passed out. Perhaps she's self-medicating too.

"Is... is he dead?" She gulps. "Did he cry?" Her voice is a whisper. "Or did he scream? Did he ask for me?" It's interesting that she accepts what happened straight away.

"I don't know." And that's the truth. "I wasn't there. Not at the very end."

"How did you do it? No... don't tell me. I don't want to know."

There's another long silence punctuated by the click and spit of a lighter. I feel her inhale. I feel her exhale. I put her on handsfree, look at my phone, we've been on the phone for thirty minutes already. We need to be careful. She knows this.

"It's what you wanted. And this way it's easier for you. There's no suspicion."

"What about you?"

She's not asking because she cares. She's asking because she's hoping she can keep all the money.

"Don't worry. I'm safe too. I want my share of that cash."

"You're stone cold, you know that."

"Takes one to know one."

She doesn't answer back. She knows I'm right. Mama knew too, the only other person who did. *Baby, be careful,* her voice was slurred, *she's not right, that one.* She saw what I couldn't back then. A girl running from her safety net, throwing herself into the flames. Anything to be seen. Lighting up the night.

"It was you back then, Alice. I know that now. With the lighter."

"What are you talking about?"

"The shed. You burned down Uncle John's shed."

There's a quiet chuckle. "How did you know?"

"Are you kidding? You wanted me to know. You couldn't stop playing with your lighter whilst we watched the firefighters."

She doesn't say anything though.

"Everyone thought it was me."

"Sorry about that." She's not though. Another inhale. Another exhale. I'm not sure who's breathing in and who's breathing out. "Okay. I'm ready now. Tell me what you did."

I think back to the last time I did what she asked and told her what I'd done.

"You don't need to know. If you know the details, then you're complicit. Don't you remember that?"

"Where's his body?"

"Somewhere safe."

"What am I supposed to tell people? This is too soon. We were supposed to do it together."

"Alice. Are you jealous?"

"You're forgetting I need a body to register his death." Her tone is chilly, the bond between us fraying as she thinks ahead. And she's right. If he's a missing person, we'll have to wait seven years for his money. I can't wait that long.

"Chill, babes, I'll get it sorted."

"Who do you think you're talking to? I'm not some

boyfriend of yours. I can't believe I trusted you." Her anger makes me laugh. To think I gave her any power over me, back then.

"What's so funny? You're the one that's going to lose out here, not me. You're the one on the hook for murder. Look where that got you last time?"

"Oh... I'm definitely not going to lose out. Don't you worry."

"Where's his body? Bring it to me. We need to get this sorted. You've screwed up the whole plan. I should have done this myself."

"You never liked getting your hands dirty."

"Shut up, Evie."

"Look, it's fine – the plan will work, it'll look like a simple accident. Mixing sleeping pills and alcohol never works, everyone knows that."

"Or they'll think it's suicide, with no note and then they'll investigate it!"

"Seriously, Alice, you need to take a chill pill."

This is fun. I don't have enough fun. I should have more fun. Why have I only just figured this out?

"I can't talk to you when you're like this."

"So don't."

But she doesn't hang up. She can't. She needs this.

"Just fix it, okay? We don't have long to do this. I don't know what you were thinking."

"Maybe I wasn't thinking? I was angry. Or maybe I was bored?"

"I'm done. Call me when you're prepared to be a grown up about this."

And she hangs up.

THIRTY-FOUR

THEN

After the miscarriage, after Ollie cheated with Cassie and moved out, everyone seemed so eager to tell me about well-being and self-care. Stressing that I needed to look after myself. But beyond mindfulness and adult colouring books, no one seemed to have any idea how I might go about doing this. My mind was a nuclear wasteland, arctic and wiped clean inside. The sort of things you might do after a bad day at work, or a row with a friend, were like offering a plaster to a fresh amputee. So, I tried something else.

I went to Vegas. Ollie was there, on a trip for his birthday. He still thought he was a player, that he had game. But all the reality was a balding, white, middle-aged, upper middle-class man-boy, thinking a signet ring was enough still.

I knew he had visions of tucking hundred-dollar bills under garter belts and spraying Cristal everywhere. If he could, he'd re-enact the coke and hookers scene from *The Wolf of Wall Street*. Like that hadn't been done a million times before. Like Cassie would be okay with that.

I knew no one would miss him, not really. Not his father, he got fed up with bailing him out years ago. He still talks to me though – we had a nice lunch last time he was in Boston on business. Not his mother, she's never coming back from France, not with – what is it – her third husband? And anyways, she spends all her time off her face on diazepam.

His sister didn't even talk to me anymore, let alone him. Not after that incident with the babysitter. She still thinks that was *my* fault. That I should have been able to control her brother. She was a prize cow anyway. As if her own husband didn't have eyes for anything in a skirt, the younger the better. I saw him with the babysitter myself. But it's much easier to blame a woman, than a man.

Ollie was staying in The Bellagio – he watched *Ocean's Eleven* religiously. It was easy enough to find out his room number. I've always been good at getting information out of people, information they don't think they want to give me.

Walking down identical, endless corridors, motion sensor lights illuminated my path, doors on either side, until I reached his – and let myself in with the swipe card. It's easy being someone's ex-wife. Easy to slip a ring back on and fake a message saying he should leave a key for you.

His room looked luxe, but it was the cheapest suite available. If anyone looked closely they'd see that. It was a mess, unsurprisingly. Chairs at odd angles, jackets and shirts slung around. Magazines and papers on the floor. I had no doubt that the bathroom was disgusting, unflushed toilet, seat up, spooling paper, damp towels everywhere, spatters of toothpaste and flecks of stubble; the vague aroma of aftershave not masking the underlying smell.

There was white powder residue all over the coffee table. Ollie always did love coke.

All his friends had already gone back to their rooms. Or at least, back to have slightly numb sex with a random hook-up, or browse PornHub and cry.

He didn't notice when I first slipped into the room. But

when he did, he was pleased to see me. Which tells me how drunk he was.

"Hey... Love you sugar." He was so far gone, he didn't even wonder why I was there. "I miss you."

I couldn't say the same.

Ollie wasn't there for the aftermath of my final miscarriage, the appointment with the hospital, before they would discharge me. He'd gone to take another call from work.

He didn't hear what they said. About the infection – probably caused by an STD which led to the bleeding, the risks, the damage, the scarring – the long-term impact. Because I'd unknowingly been carrying this disease, it was extremely unlikely I'd ever be a mother unless we used a surrogate or adopted.

It wasn't enough to ruin my present, Ollie had to ruin my future chance of happiness. Since we'd been married, I'd only ever been with him. So God knows how long he'd been sleeping around for and when he'd given it to me. Perhaps I might have handled things differently, if the outcome of everything I learned that day hadn't been so life-changing.

Back in Vegas, I waved a little baggie at him. Even slumped on the sofa, half asleep, he knew what I'd brought. *Sit, doggie, good boy. Have a treat.*

I'd barely chopped out the lines before he was hoovering them up.

Be right back, I whispered to him. But I wasn't coming back. I was never coming back. My face would be the last thing he saw, my voice the last voice he heard. By the time the door closed behind me, he was already convulsing, tumbling off the sofa.

I walked back towards the lifts, pulled my hood back up, avoided the cameras, like I did on the way up. I left him to be found in the morning, the sunlight picking out all his wrinkles and pores, the grey hairs and slack, saggy flesh. Just another overdose in Vegas.

I disposed of the empty baggy and my latex gloves – he didn't notice those, in his haste – in the trash can in the lobby bathroom, along with my brown mid-length wig, baseball cap, contact lenses... I took a deep breath, inhaled the scent of artificial lily and rose.

Although there were no clocks and no windows, I knew what the time was – gone 3am – although surrounded by Blackjack tables and retirees from Wisconsin and Milwaukee in leisure wear, it could be 3pm. It was strange to have the freedom to be anyone, to be anonymous. No one was expecting anything of me.

Ollie wasn't the first person I killed. He wouldn't be last, I was sure of it. And where I should feel fear, or guilt, I only felt relief, that a weight was lifted off me, like part of me was returning. After all these years of performing the part of Ollie's wife, of trying to hide myself. To be smaller, less than – even though he told me he loved that I was different, he didn't, not really. He only loved me as myself, when he wanted it. As if I should switch my personality off and on for him.

I was so tired, so exhausted. I didn't want to eat, or drink, or consume my emotions in any form. Instead, I went back to my hotel room, folded myself into the clean, plush sheets on my bed, the thick pillows and blankets. I put on my eye mask and counted backwards in my head, guiding myself into sleep, the pure, weightless sleep of a child.

THIRTY-FIVE

NOW

When the end comes, it's in the season of the witch, the moon rides full and high and all around me are the ashes of her life, my life, our lives. Only one of us gets to be reborn this time. For so long I believed I was only as much as the sum of my parts, but now I see that I am capable of so much more. Tonight, enough pretending to be friends, to have girls' nights out; instead, we will face each other, open and honest, spilling our truth out like blood.

Except, she doesn't know the truth. She only thinks she does. I give it a day or two after our phone call. This time she's not chasing me, not after our argument. And then I send her a single text, telling her to get ready, I'll be over tonight, we can sort it all out – what I did, the body, finalise payment.

Driving through the early March dusk, the colour of the night incoming is a midnight blue plush velvet around me, liquid shining in the night and the rain. The wipers tick back and forth, my heartbeat, the hands of a clock. Jake's right there with me, crammed in the back, hidden from view. Underneath me, the wheels snort up the white lines of the road. The lights on the way, every single one, are green for go.

. . .

When I get there, Alice's house is ablaze. She seems to have switched on every lamp and every light in each room, making it a fiery beacon. Are they bringing me home or harbingers of doom? It seems like, all this, all of everything all these years has come to this moment, to what happens this evening. I can't wait to see her face when she learns that I was the one playing a long game.

I shut the car door. Leave Jake for later. Ring her bell. Roll the dice. Take the red pill. Step inside the rabbit hole again.

"What's that saying? If these walls could talk?"

Alice just looks at me, her face a blank canvas on which I could paint her carelessness in streaks of red blush. But I don't.

"Come in, Evie. Do you want a glass of wine?"

I never know which Alice I'm going to get. At least before, I had certainty, she was one thing to everyone else, another to me. Apparently tonight we're playing Real Housewives of Surrey?

"Sure."

Her kitchen is white. Her apples are green. Her roses are red. Is she going to stuff me into her oven and eat me?

"Cheers."

She's asked me over to request I move her husband's corpse to a place that will enable her to claim not only his trust fund, but also his life insurance. And we're toasting like we're at Friday night work drinks. Seems like the only certainty tonight is uncertainty.

"How are you, Evie?"

"I'm... fine."

"You don't sound very sure."

"No, I'm great, I'm good – I'm wonderful. I just wasn't expecting, you know – this..." I gesture at the marble floor, the Smeg fridge, the six-burner range oven, the door to the wine cellar recessed into the floor. Oddly, this is the first time I've properly been inside her house. We always meet in coffee shops, or bars.

And obviously Jake never has me over. Even though I knew Alice curated a yummy mummy look, a domestic goddess way of living, it still surprises me to see she has all the accoutrements to back her up, the wealth and luxury that I crave. It's so extreme, I almost see her morphing into Aunty Meredith in front of me, with her frilly apron tight around her waist, holding a martini ready for Uncle John when he's back from work.

"So anyway—" I begin.

"I thought you liked making small talk, Evie. Isn't that what you get paid to do?"

"Ouch. Okay... what have you done with the kids tonight?"

"They're with Jake's mum."

"Wow. I forgot about her."

"Yeah, well – she's my mother-in-law."

"Guess she won't be for much longer though."

"Just because someone's dead, doesn't mean their mother stops being your mother-in-law."

"If you say so."

Dunno why she cares though. Jake's mother was always frumpy and frosty. House full of doilies and chintz, cut glass decanters for their port, was always offering his dad a snifter of something. Not that I went over very often. She made it clear she didn't approve of me.

This whole setup tonight could be awkward. It's like Alice is waiting for something, for me to do what, I don't know. But I'm not bothered, what's the worst that could happen?

There's kids' artwork on the fridge. A handwritten poem's Blu-tacked above the dresser:

I did a bad thing.
I picked an apple and I ate it.
I did a bad thing, I did a bad thing.

But you did too. And now it's your turn. To pay.

"Wow," I say. "Kids come out with some crap."

"Sure do."

But looking closely, I see the poem is dated – *AR July 1988*.

"Why did you really come back from Boston, Evie? What do you want?"

Why everyone is obsessed with asking me that, I don't know.

"I could ask you the same thing, Alice."

"I haven't come back from anywhere. I've been here the whole time, living my life."

"Just as you planned. So… we *are* going to talk about it?"

"I don't know what you mean."

"Yes, you do, Alice."

"Look, it was a terrible accident, okay? We all did stupid things when we were young."

"We didn't all kill people."

"I didn't kill her. You know that."

I raise my eyebrows, fold my arms. "Well, I didn't either. We agreed that she fell. That's what you said I should tell the teachers."

"Evie… come on, you can stop pretending now. It's me. I've kept your secret all this time. Why would I change my story now? And it was *my* boyfriend she stole. I know you did it for me."

"That's not what happened! You stepped towards her, you whispered in her ear, she stepped back and she fell. And then you blamed me."

"Is that really what you believe? That I pushed her? How could I have pushed her? You were right next to her. You're remembering this all wrong. And besides, why would I want to blame you? What reason would I have for doing that?"

"I don't know, you tell me, Alice."

"You never could see the truth, even when it was staring you in the face. Did you think you were better than me? I know you pretend not to know, but you do, sister of mine."

"I'm not your sister. Don't call me that."

She's crazier than I've ever seen her, tonight. Gulping back the red wine, bloodily staining her mouth.

"Truth hurts."

"What?"

"He was mine. I was his one and only, his daddy's girl. But then you came along and nothing was ever the same."

"What?"

"You're just upset because you tried to make out that he was the one in the wrong, but you were. You offered it to him on a plate. What kind of teenage girl tries to seduce her friend's dad? And now you try to say that it was his fault because he rejected you and you can't cope. And that I killed Rosie. No wonder he never told you the truth."

"You're crazy, Alice. You were so blind to it all, he could tell you the sky was green and the grass blue and you'd believe him. But this" – and I gesture at us – "this mess – this is his fault."

"Shut up." Her knuckles are white around the stem of the wine glass.

"He did though. He created me. And he created you. All of this."

She slams her glass down on the counter, cracking and shattering it.

"I never wanted you here, ever, from the very start. It was always about you, everyone obsessed about poor little Evie with no daddy. I tried everything – the apple tree, but you only broke your arm. The pool, but you didn't drown. The burning shed, but you didn't get the message."

She sweeps the shards of broken glass away with her foot, blood seeping onto the floor. I stare at her, open-mouthed. And yet a part of me is relieved. Finally, we are having this out.

Finally, the truth of her feelings. Even if it blindsides me with the cruelty, she's right, I always suspected on some level that she hated me. I just never knew why.

I wonder if she would be so envious, if she knew everything her daddy had done. Even with the truth staring her in the face, she won't believe it. It's a step too far, even for her. She might want to feel special, but not like that, no one wants to feel special the way Uncle John told me I was.

"And I finally, finally got rid of you, Evie. Finally had my family and my life to myself. But you came back. I hated you then and I hate you now, and somehow I just can't get rid of you."

"I don't know what you're talking about, Alice. Can you even hear yourself? How long have you been holding on to this for?"

And in flash I see the truth of it, the truth that even Alice herself is blind to.

"Alice – you don't hate me. You love me. You need me. There's a part of you that knows, deep down, we could have had everything. We could have survived, and for it all to be okay and to be fair. But you can't let it rest, you have to be the winner."

"I didn't... I don't."

"Everything you do is about me, everything you do is for me. I left you and went away and even now twenty years later your life is revolving around me. You're obsessed with me."

I pity Alice, for being unable to identify her emotions. Because although I'm the same, it hasn't always been that way. Once, I was innocent too. And then I met Alice, and Uncle John.

"You're talking nonsense. You're nothing, you're no one."

"Why are we here then? Why are we having this conversation?"

"We're not. You're crazy. I don't love you. I despise you. You are nothing. I took everything from you and you still won't see it. I took Jake, I took your chance to have a baby, I took your life. And what are you, Evie, you're disposable."

The ground shifts underneath me, just a tremor, a rumble, a threat. But I stand firm.

"You might have taken it, Alice. But that means it never belonged to you. What if I want it back?"

"You can never have it. You couldn't even keep your own father when he was right in front of your face."

"What? Stop with this now, it's awful."

"You're blind, Evie – your daddy never left. He was right there all along. Don't you ever wonder why everyone thought we were sisters? Look in the mirror."

And she traipses out to the hall, feet sinking into the plush carpet, crosses into the sitting room, preens in front of the gilt framed mirror above the fireplace.

I watch her. And I wonder.

"Your hair is different, of course – but that's just your cut and colour. But look, dearest sister of mine, dearest *baby sister*."

And that smile, a saturnine slice of satisfaction, is one I know so well, and is so familiar to me. It's the smile I used to see when I walked into the shed, when I sat on his lap. But when I look in the mirror, I see it too, only this time, on my face.

"No. No!"

"Don't you wonder why you alone know me, Evie, why you can see the truth of me? Takes one to know one, isn't that what you said? We're two sides of the same coin. The housewife and the whore."

This time I didn't answer her. This time I turn and run back to the safety of the car.

I can't be her sister, I can't.

Somehow the thought of being related to her is so much

worse than the thought of being related to her father. It makes what I have to do next even more certain.

And it explains so much. Why we lived next door for so long. Why we spent all that time together.

I fling open the car door and retch bile onto Alice's neatly paved driveway.

Disgusting girl, the voice comes from nowhere. *Disgusting and dirty.*

It's all in my head, I tell myself, it's not real, I'm not there anymore. Some places make you and some places break you, and some places do both.

Clean up that mess you've made. The words are a dirty yellow colour. The colour of grout, tiles, industrial grade paint. That day they sent me away, the car on the street. The memories are purple with bruising. I will not look back, I will not remember. And besides, I am grateful. Without that place, I would not be here today. It taught me to take what is mine.

I get out of the car. Jake's not going anywhere. I go back up that path, I have news for my darling sister.

"You do like an encore don't you, Evie."

I just sweep past her, through the open door. "Hell yeah."

"Let's just get this done. I should never have agreed to this."

Alice isn't the only one who can flip a mood. Maybe it's in my genes.

"Yeah, but how about we have a little bit of fun first?"

"No. How about you stop acting like a spoilt teenager?"

"Learned from the best."

"You're crazy."

"I refer you to my earlier point."

"Where. Is. Jake?"

"In the car. Where do you want him? Oh no wait, you don't want him, I forgot, silly me."

Alice just looks at me.

"Don't frown, you'll get wrinkles."

"Stop trying to be your mother. It didn't suit her, and it doesn't suit you."

"Just tryna help. I mean, you're gonna need all you can get, being single now."

She taps her fingers.

"Okay, okay. But come on, one more glass of wine first. One for the road. It's not every day you commit murder."

She stalks to the fridge. Extracts the wine bottle.

"Come come, Alice, you can do better than that."

I push past her, reach for the bottle of Dom Perignon. Because of course she has DP yellow label just chilling in her fridge.

"What? We're celebrating, right! You're going to have access to that big old trust fund of his. Isn't that right? And I get half of it. Aren't you pleased?"

She's looking at me the way a cat looks at its owner waving a treat. *C'mere, pussy, c'mere for a little catnip.*

"Cheers."

She necks her glass, of course she does.

"Whoa, that's not very ladylike now is it, what would your mum say?" Auntie Meredith was always fixated on us being ladylike. I mean, I failed there obviously, but Alice was her masterpiece, her perfect progeny.

"Well, she's not around anymore is she, so we'll never know."

"What happened to dear old auntie Meredith anyway?"

"What do you think? Dad died and she had a heart attack and died of grief."

"Well, you sure do seem cut up about that."

"It was years ago, I'm all cried out. Why are we talking about this?"

"Dunno. Family catch-up?"

"You never cared before."

"Still don't."

"Evie, just spit it out, whatever you're trying to say. I want to get the paperwork sorted before the kids get back tomorrow. I don't have time for your little dramas."

Evie's such a drama queen, she's making it all up, that's what Alice told everyone. That I was lying, that she wasn't involved, that it was all me me me.

"How did Uncle John die?"

"Why do you even care?"

"Well he's my daddy now, isn't he? I have a right to know."

"You're such a freak."

"Here we go, this is the Alice I remember. What is it that Mama used to tell us – anger is a mask for fear.

I chug champers direct from the bottle and the foam spurts from my nose and mouth.

"Are you done now?"

"Tell me what happened to Uncle John. Tell me how he died. Did it hurt? I think it did."

"He died in hospital. He had cancer."

"And that's what he died of, yes?"

"Yes."

"How can you be sure?"

"Because I have his death certificate."

"Huh. Okay."

"Stop screwing with me. Unless you're actually able to spread cancer telepathically, you had nothing to do with it, so just stop."

"Just that... well, I was in the country at the time. Did you know?" Of course, I still don't know, for sure, that I killed him. But I definitely contributed and it's nothing less that he deserved. I won't tell her that though. About the visit and what I did. It's not worth it, not tonight.

"Shut up."

She rams on her shoes, pulls open the front door, marches out to the car. "Unlock it now. I want this over and done with."

"Babe, it's like 9 pm. Are you literally trying to put on a show for your neighbours?" The street is all lit up, every window a view into our fishbowl.

"Good point."

She turns back and walks into the hallway, padded coat off, heels chucked aside.

"Alice, have another drunk... I mean, drink."

She throws herself onto the sofa in the sitting room. The fight appears to have gone out of her. But also, this is when she's dangerous. But I don't care.

"You didn't really kill him, did you? My daddy?"

"Don't you mean our daddy?"

"Yeah – your daddy too. And you didn't even know." The smash of the wine glass shocks me. "It wasn't enough that you took him from me when you were here, you took him from me when you weren't."

"I never took anything that wasn't mine to take. And he came freely."

"Bitch."

"At least I didn't lie about being pregnant. Leave my best friend to rot! Steal her life and everything she loved!"

Suddenly, she's standing over me with a slice of glass in one hand. She was always quick.

"Alice!"

And the blood drains from her face, not mine. She looks like she's seen a ghost.

"Surprise!" I say. And turn to look at the doorway. At a dead man walking. My man. Walking to me. Not dead. "Say hello to your husband, Alice."

THIRTY-SIX

Alice has one hand to her chest and one to her mouth.

"You really believed me? That I'd do that? That I'd kill him?"

"You've done it before."

"No, Alice. You said it yourself, Rosie fell... *you* pretended I'd killed her." Even though we know the truth. Jake slides in next to me on the sofa, flesh and blood, takes my hand in his. Alice shakes her head at me, paces the room, muttering and glancing at us.

"Sit down, Alice."

"Shut up."

But she does sit down, on the sofa opposite, puts her head in her hands, gets up again. Starts to speak, stops. Starts again.

"I need a drink." And she stomps off to the kitchen.

"Baby..." Jake kisses me.

"Is everything ready?"

"Yep, we're good to go."

I can hear Alice now, discovering what we've done.

"Are you having a laugh?" She comes back clutching a tumbler, full of what I presume is vodka.

"I thought we could sit down together, have a meal – like old times."

"You're out of your mind. There is no way we're doing anything like that." And her gaze falls back on Jake. "And as for you. You sick shit. I bet this was all your idea. What's the plan now? She's crazy, you're making a big mistake."

"Oh, cry me a river, you were hardly the widow in mourning. All you wanted was money."

"And now I suppose you have a solution to that, do you?"

"I like to think so, yes. Where everything is resolved for all of us. Why don't we go through to the kitchen?"

She huffs as we usher her in and pull out a chair for her – at her own table no less.

"It's not your house yet, bitch."

I don't think she knows who she's more betrayed by. Me or Jake. She must realise that now he's still alive, there's going to be less money to go around. I'm surprised she hasn't worked out a resolution. Instead, she's started stuffing her face.

The table is covered in plates of meze. I have no idea how Jake managed this undetected. But I don't care. In the car he said he'd take care of it and he did.

It was easy to fool Alice, I never did anything. Only sent her some pictures after our call – just so she was clear what had happened, so she didn't doubt me, what I was capable of. It was all his idea. He's been staying at mine since the evening she discovered us. We made a bit of a mess in the hotel room. Enjoyed ourselves. But it was fun to make the most of it, knowing that pretty soon, to get a night away we'd need to pay for babysitters to allow a night in the pub even.

So now, everything is spot on, going according to the plan. But I've got a few tricks up my sleeve, a few surprises. I need to keep Jake on his toes, if I'm going to keep a man like him. Like I did with Ollie.

Eyes on the prize, Evie, eyes on the prize. And it's Mama's drawl and mantra that comes to me now. Perhaps we're not so different after all, doing what we need to to get by, to get what we want and what we deserve. Except I'm not sure she ever did. But I will.

We sit around the table. Jake at the head, a woman on each side. He pours us wine, to his left and to his right. Both of us buttery blonde. We'd make a great movie, the camera panning out and away from this last supper. But who is Jesus and who is Judas and who is the devil, the snake in the grass? After all, Alice offered me the apple, all those years ago. If I hadn't taken it, none of us would be here now.

"Come on, what's the plan, Jake? Because if I file for divorce – and I'm going to – I'm going to take you for every single penny you've got. And alimony too."

Jake spoons hummus onto his plate and then some plump green olives. I pick up my wine and take a sip.

"I was thinking we could come to some sort of... arrangement?"

"And why would I do that?"

I can see her trying to puzzle it out, thinking she's always been one step ahead, trying to figure out all the possible next moves. Her hands are shaking. She's pale.

"You're a smart girl. Can't you work it out?"

Jake might sound harsh here, but Alice does, in fact, have a higher than average IQ. Something she liked to go on about when we were little. How she was taken to some special doctors and asked to play with dolls and draw patterns and things. How they whispered about her and Uncle John told her she was special, so special – until I came along.

Jake tops her up with a fresh bottle, but I cover my glass.

I watch expressions cross her face, clouds across a blue sky, one after another – doubt, suspicion, anger and frustration. "This is not a game, guys, these are people's lives. Jake and I have kids together, stop messing about. I don't understand—"

"What we're suggesting... people do this all the time. It's the modern way of doing things," Jake says.

"I am not having an open marriage. Not with her. Are you joking?"

She's still drinking. Good. *Drink up, baby girl, take your medicine.*

When Alice drains that glass, she stumbles to the bathroom.

"When will it kick in?" Jake asks me. I'm not the only impatient one it seems.

"Shh! She'll hear you."

"Like I give a crap."

He's excited. Dilated pupils, fast breathing. I wonder if we can sneak away, just for five minutes. I put my hand on his thigh.

"Evie! Focus!" But his smile tells me it's a rain check, not a rejection.

"What are you two muttering about? Shit... I'm drunk. Why are you looking like that?"

She walks back in, tries to sit down but only knocks her chair over. Good thing the kids are with Jake's mother.

She stumbles and sways and grabs her granite worktop. "What have you done to me?"

"You did this all by yourself."

Beads of sweat are forming at her hairline now. I've never seen her sweat before, lose control.

She moves her hand and a crystal vase tumbles to the floor. Red petals and broken crystal scatter between us. As she slumps down, crushing them below her, the rich scent fills the air.

With almost comedic timing, the song on the Sonos speakers changes and Stevie Nicks crackles into being. Alice is mumbling and clutching her chest, wheezing and coughing.

"You couldn't just be a friend, Alice. You had everything. Why did you have to take what I had too?"

"Babe—" but I shake Jake off.

"I didn't ask for Uncle John's attention. No one wants that, no one asks for it. He was sick. Really sick."

Jake's waving his phone at me now, I know it's time to make the call. I wave him into the hallway, nod consent at him, but I can't stop talking to Alice now she's able to listen. Not interrupt me.

"Did you make me like this, or did he? If we unpicked it all, would it still have happened? Or would we be best friends, our children growing up together, holidaying together. Would Rosie have died? Ollie? Would our father have made it another few days, weeks even? We'll never know now, because of what you did. Or what you didn't do, leaving me to take the blame for something you asked me to do."

Jake is coming back into the kitchen now, still on the phone, talking to the paramedics.

"We don't know, she just collapsed... yes, she's breathing... no, unresponsive."

He tells me to keep talking to her, that the paramedics will be here soon, everything will work out fine. So, I keep whispering my story.

"I blame you, I do. I blame all of you. Uncle John and Auntie Meredith and Mama. But you most of all. You had a choice. You didn't have to tell me to do it, and you didn't have to see me as the enemy. We could have protected each other, we could have been free and we could have had so much more."

Blue lights are flickering across the hallway now. The ambulance is here. Jake opens the door and paramedics rush in.

"I love you, Alice," I whisper into her ear, watching her mouth turn blue. "I always did."

The paramedics are pushing me aside, attaching wires and probes pushing and thumping and pulling at her.

"The trouble is," I murmur to myself now, wrapped in Jake's arms, tears running down my face, "I love myself more."

EPILOGUE

ONE YEAR LATER

"Auntie Evie, watch me!"

Five-year-old Alex is halfway up the tree, but I don't tell him to be careful, he knows what he's doing. He's a good little climber, lots of promise.

I rearrange myself on the picnic blanket, adjust my top. I'm not loving breastfeeding if I'm perfectly honest, and don't get me started on the state of my body – so much for snapping back.

But it's worth it. For her, our baby girl. She might be part Jake, but she's already showing signs that she's all mine. She's a miracle. All the doctors said so. She wasn't planned, so the positive test was a big surprise. They can't explain it. Except to say maybe some of the issues before were with Ollie, not only me. That I must have healed. I don't care. I have my rainbow baby, my angel girl. And I don't miss work for a second. I quit before they could fire me, so I can spend every minute, of every day, with my family. After all, they say being a mother is the most important job in the world.

"Babe, can you fill up my water bottle? I've run out."

All three of Alice's boys are in the tree now, Thomas is rapidly catching up to Alex, Sebastian's chunky little preschooler body not far behind. We had a treehouse built in the summer and now we can't get them out of the damned thing.

They seem to be coping well with everything – but then I know better than anyone how resilient kids are, how they grow and change and develop. But we're still keeping a close eye on them. They see a grief therapist and the doctor checks in regularly. A year on and they don't ask for Alice anymore, they know she's not coming back. That Aunty Evie loves them and their daddy. And they love me. I give them everything she wouldn't.

"Here you go." Jake winks at me as he lies down on the rug, passes me my drink, the early spring sunshine warming us all. "Do you want me to take her for a bit?"

"Yes, please!" But he has to prise her plump arms off my neck, she snuffles and snuggles into me, soft and pink and precious.

"I could eat you up," he mumbles into her squidgy tummy and blows a raspberry. She burbles in pleasure. She does love her daddy too.

The garden falls silent as they doze next to me, the boys plotting in the tree. And I am left to my thoughts.

Jake took the boys to visit Alice's grave this morning. Sebastian was so young when she died, he doesn't even remember her. But he still took his bunny to see her, knowing she has meaning somehow. Thomas drew her a picture, *it's Mummy in heaven* – and I didn't have the heart to disabuse him of the notion that his mother was anything other than a saint.

Alex didn't take anything, the look on his face confused. He remembers her better than the others, but he grieves differently.

Any other woman would count herself lucky – a handsome, wealthy widower, a beautiful house, a ready-made family and a newborn. They say that the secret to a good marriage is not to have any secrets, but that's not true. You can have secrets, you just need to trust each other to keep them. And we do – *his, hers, mine*. It's mutually assured destruction.

Jake has never spoken about that day since. Never asked me what really happened with Rosie. Because he trusts me. And as he said, it doesn't matter now. So the truth will go to my grave, like it did with Alice. I wasn't lying when I said she did it... only, it was my hands that did the pushing. Because it was her mouth that did the whispering – *Push her, Evie, push her*. We didn't think she'd actually fall. We only wanted to give her a little scare. At least, that's what Alice told me after.

As for Ollie. Well, even Jake doesn't know about that. Doesn't even suspect I had a hand in it. How could I have? A cocaine overdose? Happens all the time if you're not careful.

Jake tells me he loves me because I'm a survivor. He knows everything about Uncle John, because he remembers, he is my witness. I told him what happened in the hospital was an accident. Uncle John knocked his oxygen mask off and it was too late. I wasn't there – or, at least, not in time. And he was dying, he was an old man. What's a few days, hours even, between friends, between father and daughter?

I asked Jake once if he ever missed her. Just to be clear, I'm not doubting myself. But I wanted to be sure he knows the value of what he's got. And he didn't even take a second to think before saying no.

"Auntie Evie! Alex is at it again." It's Thomas, always keeping a watchful eye, even now, aged six. Sebastian is oblivious.

Alex is an interesting child. I guess if you were being unkind, you'd call him peculiar. A certain lack of understanding about others, lack of thought. *Callous and unemotional*, the psychiatrist calls it. *With help, you can learn to support him.*

"Alex, come down here."

He knows he's not in trouble though. He's safe here. I give Jake a nudge.

"Can you go and sort out the treehouse, Jake?"

They thought it was the cats at first – Jake told me it started long before Alice died.

"Alex, darling, we've talked about this. It's okay to experiment. But not in the treehouse, not where Thom might see it," I call up to him.

I remember Alice being the same when we were younger. She liked to play with bugs too. Trapping them in buckets to see how their wings worked. One time I caught her with an ear pressed to a jam jar containing a cabbage white butterfly. *I'm listening to her heart, she* said. But I could see the frantic beat of its wings. Alex has moved on to bigger prey though – mice and rats.

The specialist says there's not much known about the condition, that there isn't much they can do unless his experiments get more extreme. He didn't need to say what he meant. He may grow out of it though. *Many children do, I haven't met a toddler that isn't sociopathic, frankly,* he said. So it's possible he won't ever turn into his grandfather or his mother... or me.

"You're so good with him." Jake puts an arm around me, keeps Lily propped between his legs as she plays with her own toes. Alex sits next to me and holds out a flower for his half-sister. Just a daisy.

"That's lovely, darling, so kind of you."

"Can I hold her?"

The way he looks at her, strokes her little cheek, makes me want to show the doctors who presume so much. I believe that Alice did love me, just in her own unique way.

I know I need to watch Lily like a hawk though. Alice was almost the same age as Alex is when she tried to drown me in the pool. When we told the boys their mother had died, Alex didn't cry. He just wanted to know how – why she'd died.

The doctors hadn't been able to explain it either – a heart attack out of nowhere. And she was so young, no health troubles. They did a post-mortem of course. But it proved inconclusive.

Jake played the grieving husband well, desperate for answers. But the police didn't get involved. There was no case.

I told you it would be fine, Jake. I have my sources. Callum told me where to look for what we needed.

Are you sure – I mean, we could end up with anything.

But I knew Callum would keep us straight. I did him a favour a very long time ago. He's never forgotten it. And I wasn't wrong – I'm never wrong.

Shhhh, it'll work, okay? There will be no signs.

Alex is singing to Lily, telling her she's his only sunshine, making him happy when skies are grey. Sebastian and Thom come over too, cuddle into Jake, asking for stories. Soon enough neither of them will remember Alice at all. I'll be the only mother they ever know.

We must look a pretty picture, in the garden on a blanket, to an observer. A fly keeps buzzing past me, annoying me. Without a second thought, I grab it in my hand. I don't want it going near Lily or the boys.

"Wow!" Alex and Thom are looking at me in awe. Sebastian is distracted by a ladybird.

"Your Auntie Evie always did have ninja reflexes. You need to watch out!"

And Jake then reaches over and tickles the pair of them, reducing them to squirming giggles and shrieks.

He's right though. It's the mistake Alice and Uncle John and Ollie made. They didn't watch out. And now I have what I want.

There's no saying what I won't do, to keep it.

A LETTER FROM THE AUTHOR

Dear reader,

Huge thanks for reading *Best Friends*. I hope you were hooked on Evie and Alice's rollercoaster ride! If you want to join other readers in hearing all about my new releases and bonus content, you can sign up for my newsletter.

www.stormpublishing.co/rebecca-de-winter

If you enjoyed this book and could spare a few moments to leave a review that would be hugely appreciated. Even a short review can make all the difference in encouraging a reader to discover my books for the first time. Thank you so much!

I've always loved psychological thrillers, especially about the secrets people keep. But I wanted to read one when the female characters were the bad guys, instead of always looking over their shoulders, waiting to be killed. So I wrote this book!

Thanks again for being part of this amazing journey with me and I hope you'll stay in touch – I have so many more stories and ideas to entertain you with!

Rebecca de Winter

ACKNOWLEDGMENTS

I'm so excited to finally be able to write these acknowledgments, something that I never thought I'd get to do! Apologies for the length, but this book has taken the best part of six years to write – so there's a lot of people to thank.

First up the "co-parents" of this book baby – Alison Bonomi from LBA and Kathryn Taussig from Storm Publishing. This book would be nothing without your excellent pastoral care!

Alison – I still can't believe you picked my weird little novel opening as a runner up in the *Daily Mail*/PRH First Novel Competition 2018, and I'm so very grateful for all your hand-holding, tear mopping, support, ideas, editing – and under-standing what I was trying to do from the start!

Kathryn – I don't know where to begin – from our DMs on Twitter and chats last October, to offering me a deal on Goth Xmas, to somehow making sense of my word-vomit and psycho-pathic Surrey Mummies plot. I'm sorry for all the swearing, drug-taking, violence and sex.

I also need to thank the whole team behind the scenes at Storm, I know well enough, it takes a village - or an army even - to bring a book to life, so thank you for everything!

Next up, all the amazing writers I know – online and IRL. The writing community on Twitter is incredible. In particular, I'd like to thank CB Creative, Retreat West, Blue Pencil, Ellip-sisZine, BIFFY50 and also Judith Kingston, Gaynor Jones, Kathryn Whitfield, Nikki Smith, Laura Pearson, Lia Lewis,

Stephie Chapman, Barbara Byar, Laure Van Rensburg, Eleanor Wasserberg, Aimee Horton, Emma Kernahan, Bella Harcourt, Rachael Smart, Anna Vaught, Nicola Monaghan, Genevieve Stansfield, Sally Brooks, Kit de Waal, and Ed Solomons.

I'd also like to thank the bands and musicians who have kept me company on my playlists whilst I wrote this book, in particular, Crystal Castles, Chvrches, Wolf Alice, Lana Del Rey and Florence & The Machine.

I've had a fair few day jobs since starting this novel in 2017, so thank you to all my colleagues across Employability, BT, Deloitte, and Indeed, who weren't (too) alarmed by my obsession with psychopaths and have been so excited and supportive of my writing. In particular, thank you to Afonso, Becky, Emily, Mark T, Nay, Rach, and Sammi, and also Audrey, Trashleigh, and Vitsou – couldn't have done it without you!

Thank you also to all my local mum friends for being so excited about all this and asking me for updates on the school run! In particular, thank you to Team Flake – Amy, Helen, Karen, Rhian and Sarah – for all the handholding from the very start.

I also need to thank my family – my mum and my sister, who are definitely the more talented writers, for their love and support, and my Welsh in-laws who have provided so much childcare/writing time over the years.

Finally, the biggest of thank yous to my baby dragons, Thor & Uther, and their Daddy. Boyos, I love you to the moon and back. You both try so hard in everything you do and you constantly inspire me to keep going and follow *my* dreams. Also thank you for all the poo jokes, brainstorming titles, the cuddles, the demands for snacks and also, writing your own books too. Sadly, you can't read this book until you're older – because there's far too much swearing in it...

CRW, I love you "c". Thank you for everything and our

lives together. Without you, I probably wouldn't even be here, let alone this book. Here's to so many more years – and books – together.

Made in United States
North Haven, CT
20 September 2023